"Don't

Moonlight glinted on the steel of her blade.
I'll make your wife a widow."

"That's not a problem. I don't have a wife." He
lowered himself onto his bedroll in a slow, non-
provoking movement. One knife nick was enough.
"Okay if I light a candle? I'd like to find my clothes."

"Those Yankees gone?"

"Yes."

"You're sure? Because if they're waiting out
there..."

"The soldiers are gone, ma'am. Otherwise, I'd be
risking both our lives after that tale I just told."

She hesitated, then gave a soft grunt of
agreement. "Fine. Get your clothes. But no quick
moves."

His things were stacked in neat, easily
accessible piles. It always paid to be prepared.
Naked was not the way he wanted to greet visitors,
especially half-crazed, knife-wielding women. He
pulled on his trousers, then thumbed a match to life
and touched it to the candle. Soft light filled the tent
and—

Gripes. Bright hair didn't begin to describe it.
Whatever he'd expected, it wasn't this untamed,
flaming wildness. Below the blazing red halo, pale
green eyes met his. She had a pert, defiant nose and
luscious pink lips just made for devouring. His gut
clenched as though he'd been sucker-punched. This
woman was dangerous—in more ways than one.

Other Books by Donna Dalton

The Rebel Wife

by

Donna Dalton

I hope you enjoy
Jack and Lou's story!

Donna Dalton

This is a work of fiction. Names, characters, places, and incidents are either the product of the author's imagination or are used fictitiously, and any resemblance to actual persons living or dead, business establishments, events, or locales, is entirely coincidental.

The Rebel Wife

COPYRIGHT © 2012 by Donna Dalton

All rights reserved. No part of this book may be used or reproduced in any manner whatsoever without written permission of the author or The Wild Rose Press, Inc. except in the case of brief quotations embodied in critical articles or reviews.
Contact Information: info@thewildrosepress.com

Cover Art by *Arial Burnz*

The Wild Rose Press, Inc.
PO Box 708
Adams Basin, NY 14410-0708
Visit us at www.thewildrosepress.com

Publishing History
First American Rose Edition, 2012
Print ISBN 978-1-61217-520-1
Digital ISBN 978-1-61217-521-8

Published in the United States of America

Dedication

This story is dedicated to my loving husband,
who patiently puts up with field trips, neglect,
and blackened meals,
even though Cajun wasn't on the menu.
~
I want to thank my critique partners
Mary Ann Clark, Wendy Rome,
Alleyne Dickens, and Pam Roller
for helping me bring life to this wonderful story.
And for all the support I receive from
the members of the Virginia Romance Writers.
Thank you all.

Chapter One

Southern Maryland
1864

"We can't stay heah, Miz Lou. It's too dangerous."

Louisa Carleton lifted her head. A dribble of sweat tracked between her shoulder blades. Until their task was done, every step would involve some shade of danger.

Jeb hovered closer, the white of his eyes bright in his ebony face. He shifted the knapsack on his shoulder, then tossed a glance down the dark roadway. "We gotta go."

Labored gasps drew her attention back to the man lying at her feet. A pang stabbed her heart. This could be Lance, bleeding into the dirt, with no one to help or comfort him. "We can't just leave him, Jeb."

"It ain't safe. Too many soldiers hereabouts." Jeb looked frantically back and forth into the thick woods on either side of the road. "The others might be lookin' for him."

"But he's bleeding, and..." She pressed down on his chest. Blood oozed through the rough wool of his uniform, warm beneath her fingers. She leaned forward and applied more pressure with the weight of her body. The soldier moaned softly, his eyes flickering open, then closing again. The circle of blood widened, darkening the blue uniform. A Yankee uniform. Yet he was still a casualty of this miserable War just like the hundreds she'd tended at the Richmond hospital and like many of them, dying.

"There be trouble if 'n we're found with him," Jeb added. "You know how soldiers be nowadays. They shoot first and ask questions later."

"What if this were Lance lying here? I'd want someone to help him."

"But it ain't Master Lance. We only puttin' ourselves in danger by stayin'. What good we do your brother if we dead?"

The woods lining the road were dark and still, the deadness broken only by the whir of the night insects. What little air stirred carried the scent of smoke. A campfire. Most likely built by soldiers. Was she putting their mission at risk?

Fingers clamped around her wrist, cold and clammy and limp with the fading of life. A garbled whisper rose over the croak of a bullfrog. "Elsa..."

She leaned closer to the fallen man. "What? I couldn't hear you."

"Tell her. Tell my Elsa—" A harsh cough seized his words, and his body convulsed with the effort.

She patted his hand, her heart torn between staying to help the man or leaving to keep Jeb and her safe. "You rest now. No need to strain."

"She's new here...Immigrant. If I d-die..."

"Shhh. Don't talk like that. You're gonna be fine."

"Please. Write her for me. Tell her..." He sucked in several ragged breaths, the air gurgling in his throat and rattling his ribs. His eyes rolled back until only the whites showed.

An image surfaced of another man, his chest pierced by the prongs of a pitchfork. Blood and hisses leached through the holes. After what seemed an eternity, his body had heaved with a violent shudder, and then death had claimed him.

No. Not this time. Peebles bit into her knees as she applied more pressure to the wound. "Hold on, soldier." She looked up at Jeb. "Go. Find someone to help."

Jeb shook his head. "It's no good."

"You must go. He needs a doctor; someone who can—"

"He be dead, Miz Lou. Nuthin' we can do for him now."

The rise and fall beneath her fingers had stilled. The soldier's grip on her wrist slackened and dropped. Heaviness settled over her like an undertaker's blanket. Another senseless death. She'd seen far too many of them since the War started. Would her brother be added to the growing pile?

"You there! What're you doing to that soldier?"

She jerked her head around at the harsh command. The moon slipped from behind a cloud to reveal the man's rifle, the blue of his uniform, his angry, purposeful approach.

Jeb snagged her elbow. "Come on, Miz Lou."

"But..."

"You did your best. We gotta go now."

Her throat thickened with regret. If only they'd stumbled upon the wounded soldier earlier. Perhaps she could have done more to stop the bleeding— saved him from an agonizing death.

"Hurry, Miz Lou."

She swiped blood from her hands onto the soldier's sleeve, gave his shoulder a parting squeeze, then shot to her feet and darted across the road. Like Jeb said, there was nothing more to do, except make sure they didn't end up like the poor soldier, spilling their blood into the dirt.

Footfalls pounded behind them.

"Halt! Stop where you are."

Not while there's breath in my body, Bluebelly.

She fled with Jeb into the undergrowth. A shallow ditch hugged the edge of the roadway and might as well have been a thirty-foot ravine for all the ease she crossed it. Her foot slipped in the loose earth, and she stumbled. If not for Jeb's hand on her elbow, she'd have fallen flat on her face.

"They kilt Riley! After them!"

Heart hammering, she yanked bunched skirts to her knees and clambered out of the ditch, pushing through the snarl of vines trying to spoil her escape. They couldn't risk being caught. Not now. Not when they were so close.

A gun barked, and a bullet ripped through the leaves. More angry voices and gunfire rang out. Others had joined the chase.

She hunched over and ran, not daring to look back and slow her pace. Jeb's hand stayed curled around her elbow, comforting, but unnecessary. She was more at home in the woods than a spinster in her musty parlor. That stumble in the ditch had been a freak misstep. It wouldn't happen again.

They crested a shallow rise and plunged over the other side. "Over heah," Jeb urged, tugging her toward a thick tangle of brush.

She crouched beside him, slowing her breaths and becoming a silent shadow in a forest of darkness. The sound of pursuit drew closer. She ducked her head to hide her face, a trick she'd learned years ago to avoid being spotted and tagged *it* by her brother.

Footfalls rushed past and faded. She lifted her head. Nothing moved. Just blobs of firefly light winking in the night. She waited a few more seconds to make sure the bluebellies were good and gone, then turned to Jeb. "They think we killed that soldier."

"Hush now." He gave her arm a reassuring pat. "I won't let 'em hurt you."

"You won't...no, Jeb. Promise you won't put yourself in danger for my sake."

"Can't do that."

"Jeb—"

"I gave my word to Master Lance. Gotta watch over you." He straightened and swung his knapsack over a shoulder. "'Sides, looks like we're safe now. Let's go, before—"

The crack of a branch pierced his words. Then came a shouted warning, "They're over here!"

Jeb shoved her arm. "Run! I's right behind you."

She gulped her last bit of moisture and raced for the safety of the dense woods ahead. Jeb's footfalls thudded behind her as they weaved through the maze of trees and brush. Just a ways more and they'd disappear into—

A shot exploded, then came a pained grunt. She turned to see Jeb stumble and plunge headfirst to the ground. A dark stain blossomed on the back of his shirt.

"Jeb!" She skidded to a stop and dropped to his side.

With effort, he lifted his head. "Keep goin'. I'll be..." His words trailed away on a pained breath.

"I won't leave you."

"You have to. Won't do no good...if both taken."

No. No. No. She sucked down a sob and tugged on his arm. "Get up, Jeb. Please."

"Can't." He gave a strangled cough. "Go. Save yourself. Save him."

The crackle of brush grew louder. The bluebellies were closing in. Hide. They had to hide. She nudged his shoulder. "Roll over," she whispered. "Bury into those vines."

He grunted an agreement, and with trembling hands, she helped him into the cover of greenery. Not a great hideaway, but it would have to do.

"Stay quiet and still as you can," she whispered.

He didn't answer. His body had gone limp as soggy bread. She prayed it was from losing consciousness and not from losing his grip on life.

Movement flicked in the nearby pockets of moonlight. The Yankees were getting close. Too close. She had to protect Jeb, had to lead the soldiers away from his hiding spot.

She whirled and fled deeper into the woods. Branches lashed her as she ran, scraping her face, throat, and arms. She defended her bare skin as best she could and pushed onward, her footfalls thankfully deadened by a thick carpet of pine needles.

Behind her, the noise of pursuit swelled—the crack of flattening brush, the jingle of spurs, a horse's snort.

"Don't let her get away!"

At the shouted command, she increased her pace. Shadows wavered around her, masquerading as bluebellies and startling her at every turn. Another sob threatened in her throat. How many times had she and Lance raced through the Virginia woods, laughing and playing tag? If only this were a game like back then, and not a life and death struggle.

A thought took root. She'd once out-witted her brother with a daring cutback. Perhaps such a trick would work now. Her pursuers were gaining ground, their muttered oaths and the crash of brush getting louder. It was risky, but she had nothing to lose by trying.

She darted into a thick stand of trees and crossed ahead of the patrol. A low-hanging limb snagged her hair, pulling so hard she barely stifled a yelp. She slid to a halt and with tears burning in her eyes, yanked free.

"After her!"

The gruff command was much closer than

anticipated and spurred her forward. Tree trunks blurred into fuzzy columns as she flew through the forest. Her lungs burned with the sharp tang of pine and the effort to escape. As she spun to make a cutback, her boot heel caught a protruding root. She reached out, grasping at...

The woods tilted.

The pathway disappeared, and she crashed in a heap of skirts and bruises. Robbed of breath, she braced on her hands and knees and panted like a winded dog.

"This way, men."

Oh Lord, they've gotten close. She inched under a bush as hooves thumped nearer. Fear climbed in her throat, almost strangling her. She bit down on the inside of her lip to keep from crying out and eased a hand to her left boot. Her fingers closed around the familiar and reassuring steel of a knife hilt. She'd hoped it wouldn't come to this, but she couldn't let the Yankees take her.

Footsteps and shouting surrounded her, echoing as the soldiers called back and forth. No matter which way she turned, she expected any minute to see a blue uniform break through the cover.

Dear God, please...please...

Leaves rattled nearby. She froze, trying to listen above the pulse booming in her ears. Something rustled again, stopped for an instant, then skedaddled off in the opposite direction.

"There she goes!" The fool Yankees plunged blindly after the noise, their pursuit taking them away from her hiding spot.

She relaxed her grip on the knife and blew out a relieved breath. *Thank you Mr. Fox, or Bobcat, or whatever you are.*

As the sound of the chase faded, she tucked the knife back into her boot and rolled upright. Her hands were scraped, and leaves and dank earth clung to her torn gown. Several dark stains streaked her skirt where she hadn't cleaned all the soldier's blood from her hands. Nanny Belle would have a fit if she saw her charge right now. Though it wouldn't be the first time she'd looked like a hoyden.

She brushed off stinging palms and peered into the darkness. Which way back to Jeb? The dark and the maze of trees had her all turned around. His pain-wracked face swam before her, and her vision grew misty. He would be fine. He *had* to. No one else would die because of...

No. She swept at her burning eyes with the back of her hand. Such thoughts would not defeat her. Lance, and now Jeb, depended on her being strong. She'd let people down before. She wasn't about to allow it to happen again.

Using the moon as a guide, she headed in what she prayed was the right direction. She'd find Jeb, get his wound dressed, and return to their task. This was a minor setback. Nothing more.

Cool night air played across her sweat-soaked skin. A shudder coursed through her, and she tugged her cloak tighter, reassured by the heavy thud against her ankles. She'd sewn all her hard-earned money into the hem. With any luck, the Yankee guards at Point Lookout Prison would be as corrupt as the Confederates in Richmond.

A distant clamor echoed in the woods. The soldiers were circling back. It wouldn't be long before they picked up her trail. She had to find cover. Fast.

She hiked up her skirt and raced forward. A patch of white loomed ahead. She pushed through the brush and into a small clearing.

A tent. Just the cover she needed.

****

"Don't move. Lay still."

The deep, soothing voice grew silent. Hands pressed on his arms, holding him down. Something draped over his body, heavy and smothering...

"Don't move, son."

No. Can't breathe...

Jackson Porter jerked awake. Cold sweat coated his skin. Heaviness sat on his chest, making breathing a torture. He sucked in several deep slugs of air, working to chase the last remnants of the nightmare to the darkness.

Dream. It was only a dream.

Yet it seemed so real. As if he'd been transported back in time, back to the river bank where he'd been hauled from the mangled remains of a submerged carriage. He'd survived. His parents had not. His muscles twitched with the memory.

"Don't move."

Not the mellow voice from the dream. This one was harsh, though a bit delicate, almost feminine. He froze as instructed but sneaked a glance to the side. Just enough moonlight seeped through the tent walls that despite his sleepy haze, he could distinguish a petite silhouette hovering over him. A woman. He blinked and rolled up on one elbow. "What the—"

"I said don't move!" She shoved a knife under his chin.

"Take it easy." He kept his tone even and steady, though his pulse thumped like an Indian war drum. "I'll keep still."

"See that you do."

Well now, wasn't that interesting. They were deep in Union territory, but that was damn sure a Southern twang. He resisted the urge to dive at her. He was fairly certain he could take her. The shadow was a dainty thing. But better to fully knock the sleep from his head before attempting any risky moves. His trespasser appeared to be comfortable with that knife.

He slowly eased back, away from the blade, and

laced his hands behind his head, feigning a calm he was far from feeling. "What are you doing in my tent?"

Hooves thudded outside, stalling her answer. *Wonderful.* Just what he needed—more company.

"You, inside the tent." The voice was gruff, authoritative, and definitely not Southern. "Show yourself."

The woman snapped her head around. She stared at the closed tent flap, then turned back, the knife steady in her hand as she poked a warning against his throat. "If you value your life," she whispered, "you won't give me up to them."

His gut seized in a nasty twist. What the hell had he gotten caught up in?

"Inside the tent. This is your last warning. Show yourself now, or we'll come in and drag you out."

He tested his muscles, flexing from head to toe. All responded without hesitation. Purged of his dream, his body and mind were his once again. He couldn't have needed them more.

With a jerk of his hand, he snagged the woman's wrist and forced the knife away from his neck. She tried to wrench free, hissing cat-like as he tightened his grip.

"I'm going out to talk with them," he whispered harshly.

"No—"

"From the sound of their horses, there's at least three of them and only one of you. Not good odds." He gave her no chance to reply as he shoved her hand away and rolled to his knees. Cool air hit his sweat-dampened skin, trailing gooseflesh down his bare spine, hips, and thighs. In the future, maybe he should reconsider sleeping naked.

He secured the blanket around his waist and with a quick swipe, found his eye patch. He slipped it on and ducked through the tent flap.

Pale moonlight illuminated the four riders dressed in unmistakable Union blue. One of them had dismounted and was poking around. Jack clamped his teeth around a curse. There could be any number of reasons why his Southern intruder didn't want to be seen by Yankee soldiers—none of them good. And that didn't bode well for *him* either.

"What can I do for you, Lieutenant?"

The officer nudged his horse closer, the barrel of his pistol aimed at Jack's chest. "What's your name, mister, and what're you doing camped here?"

He put on his best smile. "Name's Jackson Porter. I'm a journalist for *The New York Herald*, heading to Point Lookout Prison on assignment. I'd shake your hand, but..." He tightened his hold on the blanket. "I've papers, if you want to see them."

The Lieutenant peered at him, then lowered his weapon. "One-eyed Jack. I've heard of you. The papers won't be necessary."

He fought the urge to adjust the eye patch. Helluva thing when a man was known for a mangled eye. It'd cost him more than his sight, and if he had it to do over again...

No. That was past stupidity. He needed to focus on the matter at hand, before he found himself not needing his good eye either. "What brings you out so late, Lieutenant?"

The officer leaned over and spat a stream of tobacco juice to the ground. "We're trailing a woman."

"A woman?" He made an effort to sound shocked.

"She fled from us just north of here. We didn't get a good look at her face, but she's a scrawny thing with bright colored hair."

"Blonde?"

"Not sure. But she definitely wasn't dark."

"Why are you after her?"

11

Leather creaked as the lieutenant straightened in his saddle. "A courier was found knifed to death on the roadside. His dispatch sack is missing."

"And you think this woman is responsible?"

"She was seen kneeling over him, hands covered in his blood. We captured her Negro, but he's in no shape to talk. Took a bullet in the back. Once he's patched up..." The officer gave a meaningful pause. "Perhaps, he can be *persuaded* to answer a few questions about his mistress."

"So, she wasn't traveling alone?" *Gripes. How many more people might show up tonight?*

"We only saw the two of them, but better to be safe than sorry."

"Sir." The nosey soldier had made his way to the tent and now had his pistol drawn. "I think there's someone in there."

The lieutenant again leveled his weapon on Jack. "You're not alone?"

He fisted the blanket. Now what? Did he risk a noose for concealing a suspected murderess? Or protect her, and risk getting murdered himself? And yet, guilty or not, he knew what the soldiers would do if they got their hands on her. War brought out the worst in men. In Pennsylvania, he'd been powerless to stop an assault on a woman accused of aiding the Rebels. She'd been beaten and raped, despite her denial of the charges. If the soldiers suspected his petite intruder of wrong-doing, she likely faced an equally brutal torture. He couldn't allow that.

Damnation. Think fast, Porter. "No." A long shot, but it might work. "I'm not alone. I...uh...brought my new bride along with me."

The officer looked skeptical. "New bride, eh?"

"She'd come out and greet you, but..." He let the blanket hang open. "We weren't exactly dressed for company, if you take my drift." The lie pricked at his conscience. He'd dedicated his life to the black and white truth. And here he was, shading his words in gray. She damn well better appreciate his sacrifice.

There was a bit of snickering and expressive throat-clearing. One man coughed.

"Odd place for a honeymoon," the lieutenant said, still scowling.

"As I told you, I'm on assignment. *The Herald's* got deadlines, you know, and if I don't meet 'em, I don't get paid. Mrs. Porter..." He raised his voice to be sure she heard. "Well, my wife made it clear what she'd do if I left her behind."

The soldiers chuckled good-naturedly, heads bobbing in agreement at the unreasonableness of females in general. The lieutenant considered it a moment, then holstered his pistol. He nodded to the meddlesome soldier, who grinning, shot a glance at the tent before moving back to his horse.

"So, I thank you for checking on us, Lieutenant."

"Not very comfortable accommodations for a new bride," the officer replied. "Even if she insisted."

"We're quite satisfied."

"I'm sure the Major can find more adequate accommodations for you. You're welcome to ride back with us to our field headquarters."

"Thank you, but no."

"Not very far. I'm certain the lady—"

"Thank you, sir," he repeated firmly and gave the man a pointed grin. "We're content here. With our privacy."

"Er...well then, I reckon we'll be on our way. Be sure to watch out for that fugitive. If she killed our courier, she'll be armed and dangerous."

Yes indeedy, she was armed, and he had a nick on his throat to prove it. "I'll be sure to do that. Thank you, Lieutenant. Good night."

The officer reined his horse toward the woods. The others followed. A few seconds later, all four riders disappeared into the darkness. He rolled down his shoulders. One crisis averted—one to go. He ducked into the tent and found the woman crouched in the back, weapon at the ready.

"Don't come any closer." Moonlight glinted on the steel of her blade. "Or I'll make your wife a widow."

"That's not a problem. I don't have a wife." He lowered himself onto his bedroll in a slow, non-provoking movement. One knife nick was enough. "Okay if I light a candle? I'd like to find my clothes."

"Those Yankees gone?"

"Yes."

"You're sure? Because if they're waiting out there..."

"The soldiers are gone, ma'am. Otherwise, I'd be risking both our lives after that tale I just told."

She hesitated, then gave a soft grunt of agreement. "Fine. Get your clothes. But no quick moves."

His things were stacked in neat, easily accessible piles. It always paid to be prepared. Naked was not the way he wanted to greet visitors, especially half-crazed, knife-wielding women. He pulled on his trousers, then thumbed a match to life and touched it to the candle. Soft light filled the tent and—

Gripes. Bright hair didn't begin to describe it. Whatever he'd expected, it wasn't this untamed, flaming wildness. Below the blazing red halo, pale green eyes met his. She had a pert, defiant nose and luscious pink lips just made for devouring. His gut clenched as though he'd been sucker-punched. This woman was dangerous—in more ways than one.

"Reckon I should thank you for not turning me in."

Her full lower lip bloomed into a slight pout. He wanted to reach out and touch it. "Always happy to help a lady," he said instead.

Any man in his right mind would be wary of *this* lady. Strangely, he wasn't. She might be desperate, but instinct told him she wasn't a cold-blooded killer. In spite of her ease with that pig-sticker, her eyes were way too soft. As for her knife...

"Now that we've settled that ugly business with the soldiers, I imagine you'll want to be on your way."

Several seconds passed. She merely looked at him, knife lowered but still steady in her grip.

What was she waiting for? "You *are* planning to leave?"

"Not just yet."

"Why the hell not?"

She started and thrust the blade toward his face.

"Whoa, lady. Take it easy." He shoved up his hands in surrender. "I didn't mean to startle you. Just wondered, since that patrol is gone, if you'd want to be on your way."

"And I said I'm not ready to go yet. For all I know, the bluebellies are just off in the woods. They're not going to give up that easy."

Damn this was turning into a long, unpleasant night. Eye on the knife, he inched away. "So, how long *do* you plan to stay? It'll be dawn in a few hours. You're much better off leaving under the cover of darkness."

A moment passed. Then another. "I didn't kill that soldier."

There was something different in her tone, softer, slightly vulnerable. He decided to press his advantage. "And yet, here you are, using my tent to hide from a Union patrol and holding me at knifepoint." He dabbed at the gash on his neck.

A rosy glow stained her cheeks. He kept his gaze fastened on her flushed face, refusing to apologize for any discomfort she might feel. She'd intruded on his sleep, threatened him, and now had the gall to defy him.

"I'm sorry for hurting you," she said. "But I couldn't take any chances. There's too much at stake."

"You mean your accomplice."

"Accomplice?" She frowned, then dipped her head in understanding. Pale eyes glistened with moisture. "Jeb. Yes, there's him..." She swallowed and averted her gaze. "But there's more than that."

Must be a hell of a lot more for her to behave in such a desperate manner. Even if she didn't kill the courier, there was no predicting what she might do now. "May I ask a favor, Miss..? Ummm...I don't even know your name."

"Does my name matter?"

"Since we're going to be spending time in each other's company, it might be nice to know. And I presume you heard mine is Porter. Jack Porter."

She furrowed her brow as though considering a response.

"Or you don't have to tell me if you don't want." Always wise to give a cornered rattlesnake an out.

She relaxed and gave a half shrug. "No harm in your knowing, I s'pose. It's Louisa. Louisa Carleton."

"Nice to meet you, Louisa Carleton." He donned the same smile he'd used earlier on the lieutenant, the one reserved for politicians, government officials, and newspaper editors. Anyone he needed to get on his side. "Now as to that favor I mentioned...since we're on such friendly terms. Is there any way I can entice you to put down that knife?"

Her shoulders and head came up. "I won't give up my weapon."

"Nobody asked you to. Just tuck it away somewhere."

She wagged her head. "I don't know..."

16

"There's no need to hold me hostage. I got rid of those men. If I'd intended to hand you over or try to escape, I certainly had the opportunity."

"Well..." She lowered the blade a notch, yet she continued to eye him with distrust. "Yes, well, I suppose that makes sense. But I know how to use this, so don't try anything funny. And don't go thinking you can *entice* me to do anything."

She put a hard edge on the word, turning her pretty mouth down in an ugly twist. Her clothes bordered on threadbare, besides being torn and filthy. Streaks on the dress looked suspiciously like dried blood. If he had to guess, he'd say someone had done a serious wrong by this girl to make her so wary and unpredictable. There was more to her situation than the Yankees, he'd bet his next paycheck.

"Why are you hiding if you didn't do anything wrong?"

She held her ground. No telltale shifting or blinking. "It's just like that Yankee officer told you. I was seen with that soldier, but I swear, I was only trying to help him. Not that those bluebellies would believe me. They'd hold me for as long as they pleased, asking questions, and..." She swallowed again. "I can't afford the delay."

"Where are you in such a hurry to go?"

"I need to get to Point Lookout Prison."

The prison? No wedding band adorned her left hand, though that didn't mean anything. Many women donated their jewelry to the War effort. Still, he could think of only one obvious reason why a woman would take this kind of risk.

"A sweetheart or husband?"

Pools of sadness shimmered in her eyes. "I just need to get there. And I'm running out of time."

A million questions filled his journalist's mind, not the least of which, what would it feel like to have a woman care so much. Not that he wanted or needed one, even if she was beautiful and intriguing and could handle a four-inch blade.

No. Miss Carleton's man could have her and all the aggravation that most likely came with her. And that would be plenty—he was sure of it.

Hot wax trickled onto his fingers. As he adjusted his grip, candlelight flashed on the steel of her blade, a potent reminder of the threat he faced. *No more questions, Porter. It's time to get rid of this crazy lady.*

"If you're in that much of a hurry..." He nodded suggestively at the tent flap.

Hardness replaced the sadness on her face. "My plans have changed a bit."

"Oh?"

"With the soldiers looking for me, I need another way to get to Point Lookout."

"You have something in mind?"

"Sure do."

"And, pray tell, what is that?"

Her almond-shaped eyes gleamed like a cat with a fresh kill. "Apparently we're married, so I'll travel with you, Mr. Porter."

Chapter Two

The newspaperman's jaw sagged. "Are you addled?"

Addled. Stupid. Dim-witted. The names stung. Just like they had most of her life. Anger rose in her, and she forced a calming breath. Now wasn't the time to be showing temper. "Don't call me names. Please."

His lips puckered for a brief moment. "Forgive me. I didn't mean to imply..." He flicked his gaze to her knife as though deciding if he was about to get gutted for his insult. "Your suggestion of traveling together...well, it's just not a good idea."

"I disagree." She lowered the blade to her lap. Just enough to put him at ease, but not so far she couldn't protect herself. "I can pose as your new bride."

"My bride?"

"Yes, like you told those soldiers."

He shook his head, sending dark locks skidding over a deeply furrowed brow. "That was a ruse to get rid of them."

"A very *clever* ruse." Already her mind raced toward the possibilities. If he was heading to Point Lookout, Jackson Porter could very well be the answer to her prayers. She wasn't as *addled* as he might think. "What's this assignment you have for *The Herald*? Will you have access to the prisoners?"

"My assignment has no bearing on this."

"It has every—"

"I'm sorry, but I can't be part of...whatever

trouble you're in." His tone, though hard-edged, was polite.

Candlelight played over his firm lips and mulish, jutting chin. Convincing this man of anything was going to be harder than catching a mud-slicked pig.

"Why are you being so unreasonable?" She shifted to a more comfortable position. It appeared she was in for a long battle. "We're both heading in the same direction."

"Me, unreasonable?" He gave a harsh snort. "You crawl into my tent in the middle of the night, threaten me with a knife while I'm half-dressed, and make ridiculous demands. And *I'm* unreasonable? Gripes, woman."

"Don't call me ridiculous."

"Not you, in particular. I mean this farcical idea of yours."

"Give me one good reason why my idea is...what'd you call it?"

"Farcical."

"I suppose that means you don't think it'll work. Why?"

He scowled at the top of her head. "In large part, that."

"That what?"

He made a gesture. He had long fingers, clean nails, no calluses that she could see. But then a man wouldn't get rough hands working a pencil all day.

"That fiery mane of yours."

"What's wrong with my hair?"

"The soldiers are looking for a woman." He scoured her from head to toe. "A scrawny woman with brightly colored hair."

A slight? She couldn't be sure. "Many women have brightly colored hair."

One eyebrow drifted upward. "Not like that, they don't." He looked her over again, slower this time. The corner of his mouth curled into a faint smile. "Though I must say, you're not as scrawny as I thought based on their description."

Heat crept up her neck and into her cheeks. She wanted to look away, but even with a single good eye, he held her captive. She'd felt it before, that intimate male inspection, and it usually led to no good. Perhaps she should rethink her plan. Experience warned she could be making a pact with the Devil.

She forced in a steadying breath. As much as she hated being dependent on anyone, especially this uppity, pig-headed Yankee, she needed his help. Nanny Belle's favorite lecture rose in her mind.

You kin catch mo' flies with honey, Miz Lou.

Lordy, for all the honeyed words she'd choked up lately, she ought to be coated sticky-sweet by now. "Perhaps," she said, with that good-natured voice she always used with the Lawrences, "we can come to some sort of agreement."

"No."

"But—"

"With all due respect, Miss Carleton, why would I want to make a deal with a wanted woman?"

"An innocent woman."

He hesitated, thinking about that. She worked on looking innocent.

"Regardless of your innocence or guilt, if I'm caught hiding you, my assignment, hell, my life, could be at risk." He shook his head. "I'm not willing to take that chance."

Well, if honey wouldn't work... "What if I paid you? How much would make it worth the risk?"

His grunt this time was downright rude. "You don't look like you have more than a nickel to your name."

That came as a slap. For most of her life, she'd worn the Lawrences' cast-offs and never minded. An overseer's daughter had to make do, after all. The clothes, like everything else Fannie and Beth had, were the finest their daddy's wealth could buy, and the girls tired of them long before the gowns showed any real wear. She'd felt almost pretty in the dresses.

She wrapped both hands around the knife hilt to keep from smoothing out the wrinkles in her gown. She was merely rumpled from travel, was all. Never thought of herself as second-hand. Until now. In front of this man.

She held her head high, refusing to give him the satisfaction of knowing he'd hit his mark. "I can assure you, Mr. Porter; I have money."

"Not enough to persuade me to take you near the prison, I'd wager."

"You'd lose that bet."

He scrubbed a hand over his chin, thinking. He seemed to do a lot of that.

"You're taking a big risk telling me this, aren't you? You don't know me. I could kill you while you sleep. Take your money."

Yes, she was taking a big risk. But given a choice between him and the Union patrol, the newspaperman seemed the lesser of two evils. Besides this probably wasn't the last risk she'd face before her task was done. "You wouldn't do that," she said, not sure which of them she was aiming to convince.

"And you know this because..?"

"You ain't—" She bit off the words with a click of her teeth. She'd worked hard to refine her speech, watching, listening, and mimicking the Lawrences, so she'd be accepted at the big house, so Papa would be proud of her. But low-bred talk often found a way out of her mouth, especially during times of great fluster and distraction. This man, with his questions and his mule-headed stubbornness, had her all

22

fiddle-fuddled.

She licked her lips and tried again. "I know this because you didn't turn me over to that patrol. Unexpected gallantry from a Yankee."

He rummaged in the pile of clothing beside him. "It wasn't gallantry; I assure you. I just didn't want to explain what you were doing in my tent and make trouble for myself." He shrugged into a shirt, sleek muscles flexing as he moved.

The breath caught in her throat. He'd mentioned being half dressed. It hadn't registered until now. Another time, another man, darted through her mind. Her mouth went dry. She yanked her gaze back to his face. "E-Even so—"

"Thanks, but no thanks, Miss Carleton."

"But—"

"No buts. I decline your proposal of matrimony." His gaze trailed over her again, lingering on her breasts an instant too long for politeness. "Intriguing as the notion might be."

Apprehension rifled fast and hot through her belly. That bare skin and flash of heat in his gaze uprooted memories she thought she'd buried. Her control slid away. The tent walls closed in. Her nostrils filled with candle smoke, damp earth, and the sharp scent of male sweat.

She needed fresh air. *Now.*

She made a frantic dash for the tent flap, batting at the stiff canvas to clear her path. Outside, cool air bathed her face, and she drew in breath after breath in an effort to recover her wits.

Slowly, the songs of night insects surrounded her. Stars winked in the broad, black sky. Her pulse slowed. Her breathing evened out. It'd been a long time since thoughts of Bart Lawrence had troubled her. Mainly because she'd managed real well to stay clear of anything, or anyone, who raised those old ghosts. Why here? Why now? Well now, that was a silly question, wasn't it? If she were smart, she'd put miles between her and Mr. Fancy-Talking, Half-Dressed Porter.

Around her, the clearing glowed in the pale moonlight, giving her the first good look at the lay of the land. Just the other side of the fire pit, hoof prints roughed up the ground. Beyond that, trampled grass stretched to the darkened edge of the forest.

Yankee tracks.

She couldn't rush headlong back into the woods. The patrol might still be lurking about, doubling back, trying to catch her slipping through. Her best bet would be to remain near the tent. Ease back inside to hide if need be. Then, come daylight, she'd resume pleading her case to the mule-headed newspaperman. Perhaps after a good night's sleep, he'd be a little more agreeable.

A head poked through tent flap. "Miss Carleton, are you ill? Do you need any help?"

She squared herself. She lied better standing up straight. "No, I'm fine."

"You're sure? You seemed to be a little... spooked."

"I wasn't spooked. I just needed some air. It's been a long day, and wrangling with you...well, I'd had enough." *For tonight at least.*

"Glad to hear you've given up on that idea."

"The farcical one, you mean?"

He smiled. She gave a little grunt. Let him think what he wanted. In the morning, he'd sing a different tune.

"So you'll be heading out?"

"In a bit. I s'pect those soldiers aren't too far off yet. Thought I'd lay low a while."

"Stick to the woods and off the roadway," he added, like she was too dumb to know that on her own. "Less chance for the patrol to come up on you unawares."

"Thank you, Mr. Porter."

"And you might want this." He tossed her the knife. "You dropped it during your rather hasty exit."

She thought of Nanny Belle and fastened on her sweetest smile. "Thank you again," she managed through her teeth. "Good night."

"Good night, Miss Carleton. And good luck with your endeavor." He nodded and ducked back inside.

Endeavor. Farcical. Lordy, he loved those big, fancy words. A book man. Just like Papa and Lance. While she...

She swallowed her shame in a hard gulp. Fancy words and book-learning wouldn't get her brother free. Grit and determination would. Those she had a'plenty.

She squatted next to the campfire. Several of the rocks ringing the pit had been knocked aside. Probably by one of those big-footed Yankees. She rolled the rocks back into place. Using a fallen pine bough as a broom, she swept at the ashes that'd scattered outside the circle. Papa had liked things neat and tidy. She had preferred to spend her days cooling by the river. The clutter certainly wasn't going anywhere, and if cleaned, it always found its way back. But Papa had always said, *a place for everything and everything in its place.* Papa also said *look before you leap.*

Tears she'd held in check while wrangling with the newspaperman spilled over. She'd ignored that warning, hadn't she. Had landed herself and everyone she loved smack in the middle of a briar patch.

A muffled thud sounded in the woods, then came the faint hoot of an owl. She jerked upright at the familiar signal, one she'd heard hundreds of times at Spivey Point.

"Jeb," she whispered into the darkness.

The woods remained silent. She walked to the edge of the clearing. "Jeb," she called out again. Nothing. She slumped over, remembering. The Yankees had Jeb. That hoot had come from a real owl. Jeb wouldn't be waiting behind some big oak before they snuck off to the river to do a little night fishing. If his bullet wound got the better of him, he wouldn't be waiting for her anywhere but in God's house.

****

She drifted up from the blackness. Warmth radiated from the solid form resting next to her. She snuggled closer. Nice. Very nice.

The hardness groaned and shifted.

As the fog of sleep faded, realization dawned. She opened her eyes. A bare back lay inches from her nose. A little ways higher, black locks curled just below the nape of a tanned neck.

Her pulse skipped. How had she ended up beside him? Last night, she curled up next to the fire pit, but the sound of crackling brush had woken her and sent her scurrying inside the tent. She'd lain at the entrance, as far from him as she could get. Somehow, she'd managed to—

The smooth muscles bunched. A second later, cool air churned around her as the newspaperman bolted upright.

"What the..!"

She rolled away and scooted for the tent flap. Best to put a little distance between them until she sized up his mood.

He rounded on her, his good eye glaring, the other covered by the patch he'd slipped on quicker than a fox darting into a hen house. "You! I thought you'd left."

Still ill-tempered, it appeared. She stopped at the entrance and thrust up her chin. She'd never backed down from a fight and wasn't about to start. "You thought wrong."

"I told you last night I wasn't interested in your offer."

"And I can't take no for an answer."

"Sure you can. It's easy." He jerked a nod at the tent flap. "Just back out and head south."

"Believe me, Mr. Porter, I'd rather be anywhere than here with you. But I don't have a choice. I need to get to Point Lookout. And right now, you're my only option."

"There are always other options."

"None that will get me there as quick as traveling with you."

"Why are you in such an all-fire hurry to get to that prison?"

Mule. She couldn't risk telling him her reasons. He might have earned a small scrap of trust by concealing her from the Yankees, but not *that* much. Perhaps this required a different approach. If that brief flash of heat in his gaze last night was any indication, he wasn't immune to a woman's charms.

"I understand your reluctance." She mimicked Fannie Lawrence's sugary, simpering tone. All those years of playing handmaid to a spoiled, rich girl might finally be worthwhile. She batted her eyelashes. "I'd be an awful burden on you, not to mention I'm wanted by the Yankees."

"Precisely."

She dug her fingernails into her palms, using the pain to keep from cursing, and forced a smile. "Couldn't you just open up that lil' ole heart of yours and help a desperate, defenseless woman without knowing the why-fors?"

"You might be desperate, Miss Carleton. But you're far from defenseless." His gaze drifted to her neck. "Even with your dress undone."

Her dress un...

Heat scorched her cheeks. She'd loosened her collar during the night to cool her skin. Now *too much* charm was on display.

She reached up and fumbled with the loops. *Tarnation.* Why couldn't she fasten buttons like any normal woman? Even Belle with her stubby fingers had no trouble.

"Need a hand?"

"No, I don't." A button slipped from her grasp, and she muttered a curse under her breath.

"Take your time," he urged, his cheery tone like fingernails on slate. "Rushing will only make it more difficult."

"I know how to fasten buttons, thank you." She shot him a glare, then returned to her task. One loop slid on. Then another. And another, until she had all three buttons refastened. *Hallelujah.* One chore done. She eyed the newspaperman. One thornier one left.

"Good." He flashed that same breath-robbing smile he used the night before. "Now, you're ready to leave."

"Please..." In any other circumstance, she'd be mortified by pleading. "I understand how risky traveling with me is. But I promise, once we reach the prison, you can wipe your hands of me."

"I doubt getting shed of you will be that easy."

She sensed an undercurrent as though he meant more than what he said. He raked back his hair, missing one unruly lock that stuck out over his ear. Something made her want to touch it, something else told her to stay away. Perhaps he was right, and this was a bad idea. She could get into real trouble pretending to be his loving wife.

A chirping chorus sifted through the tent walls now glowing with a faint rosy blush. Dawn. A new day, and she was still miles from her destination. Trouble or not, she had to make use of the handsome newspaperman.

"And just how will you explain the absence of a new bride?" She gave him a pointed look. "That patrol is sure to spread your joyful news to the other soldiers."

"I'll tell them the truth. That you held me at knife point and forced me to lie."

Clearly a good night's sleep had done little to curb his orneriness. Was he a late riser like the Lawrence brood? He certainly acted like them with his educated talk and puffed-up airs. "Perhaps we should discuss this after you shake the sleep from your head." She began backing out of the tent. "I'll just wait outside."

To her dismay, he followed her. "I'm fully awake. And there's nothing more to discuss."

"You don't understand..."

"Oh, but I do understand. Perfectly." He shrugged into his shirt, making short work of the buttons, unlike her feeble efforts. "And the answer is still no."

"But—"

"You're wasting your breath, Miss Carleton." He pulled on his boots, then crouched beside the fire pit and began adding small twigs to the ashes. "I'll cook us some breakfast, then we part ways."

"I don't have time to waste on breakfast."

He glanced at the woods. "Well, then..."

Lordy, he was far more pig-headed than she had imagined. Talking him into anything was going to require a good helping of patience. Not her strong suit.

A low nicker sounded in a nearby thicket.

Well, well. Porter had a horse. She crossed to the edge of the clearing and parted the bushes. A long-legged bay gelding jerked up his head and blew a noseful of air at her. Had she known such a fine-looking animal was available for the taking, she might've reconsidered her plan to hide in the tent. She smiled, pleased by her find. It wasn't too late to correct *that* mistake. She freed the tether and led him out of the thicket.

Porter rose to his feet. "What are you doing?"

She pulled the bay to a stop beside the tent where a saddle sat canted on one end. "I'm using one of my other options."

"That's my horse."

"Not anymore." She bent and scooped up the saddle, a light-weight McClellan. Odd that he owned a cavalry model and not some fancy leather and brass contraption like all the other uppity, rich folks.

"Are you planning to steal my horse?"

She slung the saddle and pad across the bay's sleek back. "Borrow. I'll leave him near the prison for you when I'm done."

He closed the distance between them, and she inched a hand toward the knife tucked at her boot. She didn't want to hurt him, but she couldn't allow him to interfere. She'd already lost too much precious time running from the bluebellies.

He merely shouldered against a nearby pine. "I doubt Maryland law will see any distinction between stealing and borrowing."

Keeping a wary eye on him, she pulled the cinch under the bay's belly and slipped the leather end into the buckle. "Will you have me arrested, then?"

"I might."

Ornery fingers slipped, and she almost dropped the cinch strap. *Drat.* Of all times to fumble.

He cleared his throat, and she stiffened, waiting for his jeering remark. None came. A Christmas gift in July. She wrestled the buckle fastened, then snatched the bridle off the ground. The gelding took the bit good-naturedly, and she soon had him bridled and ready to ride.

"Do what you must, Porter." She tucked up her

skirts and footed the stirrup. "I'm taking your horse."

The bay pranced backward. She sprang upward and eased into the saddle. Once seated, she clucked softly and nudged the horse with her heels. Muscles bunched beneath her. She squeezed her knees to secure her seat, then reined the animal away from the camp. The horse spun around and leapt forward.

A piercing whistle rang out.

The bay skidded to a halt, haunches plowing under him.

Unprepared, she slammed into his neck like a rag doll. She grabbed for anything she could get her hands on. Before she could secure a firm hold, the horse scrambled to right itself. She snagged his neck and swung under him, dangling like a possum from a limb. A second later, her hands slipped, and she crashed to the ground. Sharp pricks stabbed through the thin material of her gown and into her skin. She moaned and closed her eyes, willing the burn away and the earth to stop spinning.

As her breathing evened out, fear gave way to fury. She'd fallen from a horse. Something she rarely allowed to happen. All because of—

Footfalls sounded beside her, then shiny black boots came into view. "You knew," she spat. "The whole time, you knew I wouldn't make it out of camp on your horse."

"I did."

"You polecat. That was a rotten trick."

"Only got what you deserved."

Frustration and rage pounded in her head until she thought her skull might explode. She needed to get to Lance and Jeb. And this arrogant, black-hearted Yankee stood in her way.

Not for long. She thrust her legs to the side and caught his ankles in a scissor-kick.

He went down with a grunt.

She kicked free of him and scrambled away. But he reacted quicker than expected. He lunged forward, grabbed her arms, and rolled until he rested atop her.

Images surfaced of other hands holding her down. Panic galloped inside her. Her blood ran cold. *Trapped. Again.* She began thrashing from side to side, trying to get free.

The hands restraining her tightened. "Whoa, Miss Carleton. Settle down."

"No. Don't." She couldn't contain a whimper.

His weight pressed down on her, containing her efforts. "Stop fighting," he said in a low, soothing voice. "I won't hurt you."

"Let me go. Please."

"Easy now. I'll let you go as soon as you calm down."

She tempered her struggling. A few seconds passed, then a few more. The body atop her remained in command, but unmoving. The stampede in her chest slowed. She stilled all efforts to escape and just lay there, waiting.

"You see. Nothing is going to happen to you."

He spoke the truth. For once. She sucked in several deep breaths and worked to recover her raveled wits. Her racing pulse quieted. Sounds came to life around her, the twitter of birds, the gurgle of the nearby creek, and the gentle breaths of the man above her.

Porter shifted slightly, his lean body pressing along her length. A sliver of heat formed in her belly and slid lower. Though slight, it was a pleasant sensation. How could she feel such things after what Bart had done?

"Why'd you do that?" he asked softly.

Fight him or respond in an unseemly manner? She had no answer for the latter and didn't want to discuss the other. "D-Do what?"

"Take me down."

She covered her relief with a scowl. "Hmmph. Got what you deserved for trying to kill me."

"You seemed to know what you were doing with a horse. Besides, Socks was barely moving when I called to him."

"He could've trampled me."

"He wouldn't have done that. He was trained by a cavalry officer."

That explained the saddle, but not Porter's continued closeness. She shoved at his chest, letting anger override her fear. "Get off me, you oaf."

"Hmmm...it's usually One-eyed Jack or Cyclops."

"I can oblige you, if you'd like. I'm sure I could come up with a few new ones."

"I'm sure you could." His mesmerizing gaze held her captive before drifting to her mouth.

Was he going to kiss her? She should move, push him away, do something. But God help her, she couldn't summon the strength or the will.

A warm, moist muzzle prodded her cheek, jolting her from her stupor. What was she doing? Being near this wit-robbing man was far too dangerous.

"Looks like Socks wants to apologize," Porter said, his voice strangely hoarse.

She pressed harder against the wide span of male chest. "I said, *get off.*"

He gave her one last lingering look, then heaved himself upright. He stood over her, hand extended.

Ignoring his offer, she rolled to her feet and brushed at the dirt and embedded thorns, giving herself needed time to regain her composure. To add insult to injury, her empty stomach decided to rumble its need for food. Embarrassment burned in her cheeks. When she finally looked up, an infuriating, amused glint lit his gaze.

"Are you always so impetuous?"

Another of his high-falutin words. Did he think he was better than she? "I'm not im-imp—"

"Impetuous," he supplied.

"I know what it is."

"Good. Then perhaps you'll think before you rush into doing something foolish again."

The only foolish thing she'd done was to trust an arrogant Yankee. She thrust up her chin, daring him to mock her. "You're right. Traveling together would be a bad idea, a *very* bad idea."

"Well, at least we agree on one thing."

She glanced at the brightening sky. Day was wasting. She treated Porter to one last barbed glare, then strode around Socks and headed for the woods.

"Wait," he called out. "At least have breakfast."

"No thank you," she tossed over her shoulder. "I've had enough of your hospitality." If she never saw the no-good, overbearingly handsome newspaperman again, it would be too soon.

Chapter Three

Jack stowed the last of his gear beneath the overhang and rocked back on his heels. He lifted his hat and swiped at the sweat trickling down his forehead. God, it was hot. Oppressively so, even with dusk approaching.

The image of Miss Carleton stomping away earlier that morning plagued him. How was she handling the heat? There seemed to be plenty of creeks around for her to slake her thirst. Would she unbutton her gown—let the air cool her sun-warmed flesh?

His loins stirred at the memory of how soft she'd felt lying beneath him after he'd finally tamed her into submission. Gently rounded breasts had pressed into his chest. Long, supple legs stretched along his...

Lovely. Absolutely—

He jerked upright and nearly butted his head on the outcrop. What the hell was wrong with him? Wanting a woman, especially *that* woman, was the last thing he needed. She was a powder keg just waiting to explode. He was better off not thinking about, or desiring, the volatile, knife-wielding Rebel.

He pushed away from the ledge and eyed the dark clouds gathering on the horizon. If the suffocating closeness and those thunderheads were any indication, they were in for a hell of a storm. Good thing he'd found the deep overhang. It would definitely offer more protection than a flimsy tent.

Had Miss Carleton wisely sought shelter as

well? She'd trailed him for most of the day. He detected her movements an hour after breaking camp. She followed closely but not enough to expose herself. She had plenty of pluck, he'd give her that. But would it see her through the approaching tempest?

He forced thoughts of the intriguing woman from his head. Socks needed tending, and supper needed cooking before the squall hit. Miss Powderkeg had made her bed by stomping away from him. She could damn well sleep in it.

An hour later, the storm struck. Jagged streaks of lightning lit the dark, rolling sky, followed by the sharp cracks of thunder. Outside the overhang, rain drummed a deafening beat on the parched earth. A cool mist drifted on the swirling air, dampening his face and evaporating with a hiss in the fire.

He pressed further back against the wall in an effort to stay dry. A tiny brown fur-ball scurried into the nearby shadows. Wasn't even a fit night for the forest creatures. And Miss Carleton was out there somewhere, most likely cold, wet, and miserable. Not to mention hungry. She'd haughtily refused his offer of breakfast, even when he knew from the rumble of her empty belly she needed it.

Guilt pelted him. He knew firsthand the difficulties of being dependent on the land for sustenance. A lady, no matter her background or temperament, didn't deserve to be put through such torture.

Cursing at his foolhardiness, he yanked on his hat and darted into the sheeting rain. He trotted slowly, seeking firm footholds on the wet pine needles as he hurried toward the last location he'd detected her. A gust blew the rain sideways. He paused to swipe water from his face, little good it did, and to regain his bearings.

Lightning flashed overhead accompanied by the

boom of thunder and cracking wood. The hairs on the back of his neck stood on end. His ears rang. His skin tingled.

A second later, a huge limb crashed to the ground a scant ten feet in front of him. Startled, he jumped and crouched low. The acrid scent of scorched wood filled his nostrils. He blew out a ragged breath. *Damn, that was close.*

A faint scream filtered through the buzz in his ears.

He planted a hand on his hat and raced toward the sound. A flash lit the edge of a ravine. He skidded to a stop and leaned over, angling his head to get a better view. Another burst illuminated the figure clinging to a protruding root, her hair and muddied gown plastered to her body.

"Miss Carleton," he yelled over the pounding din.

The shadowy form shifted, head lifting.

He reached for her. "Grab my hand."

She hesitated, her fear radiating up the gully in waves. Angry water churned around her, threatening to sweep her away.

"Hurry!" he shouted.

Her fingers found his in the darkness, and he hauled her to the top. She swayed against him, and he slipped a steadying arm around her waist. Using the lightning bursts, he guided her back to the overhang where he ducked inside and pulled her with him. She curled against the back wall, arms crossed over her chest, shivering.

His own skin pimpling from the dampness, he shrugged out of his wet jacket and began stoking the fire with tinder he'd collected earlier. The flames erupted into a warming blaze.

Across from him, Miss Carleton stared out into the darkness, shoulders sagging, her customary fiery gaze doused by weariness. He poured coffee into a tin cup and held it out to her. "Here, drink this."

Pale eyes shifted in his direction. "Why?"

"To warm your insides."

She shook her head. "Not, the coffee. Why'd you come after me?"

Why indeed? Something told him he'd regret his rash sprint into the woods. He gave a half-hearted shrug. "I'm impetuous?"

"Uh-uh. You think on things far too much for that." She narrowed her gaze. "Have you changed your mind about helping me?"

Brains to go along with all that beauty. "No."

"If it's money you want..."

"I don't need your money." He swallowed the lie with a gulp of the coffee she clearly didn't want. A bit of extra pocket money would come in handy until his next paycheck arrived. But she didn't need to know that.

Thunder rumbled in the distance. The storm had passed, leaving only a gentle shower and cool breeze in its wake. Miss Carleton shivered and rubbed her upper arms as though trying to generate some warmth.

He fished in his haversack and hauled out a wool blanket. "Here. This'll help warm you."

She stared at the blanket a moment before taking it from him. "Thank you." Weary eyes met his. "And thank you for rescuing me from that flood. I seem to be doing a lot of that lately."

"What? Needing rescue?"

"Thanking you."

"Eats at you, does it?"

She fell silent, head bowed, fingers absently plucking at the folds of the blanket.

Perhaps that was a bit uncharitable. From what he could tell, she'd been through hell trying to get to Point Lookout. He tugged the blanket from her hands. "It works better if you put it around you." He flicked the blanket over her shoulders and tucked the ends under her chin.

Her soft musky scent teased his senses, and his loins stirred. Though his own choice, it'd been months since he'd had a woman. And this one called to him like a siren to a drowning sailor. He leaned closer, heeding the summons.

Green eyes flashed with heat and a good dose of panic. Her mouth thinned, no doubt preparing to deliver a tongue lashing for his familiarity. He rocked back, away from temptation. Only a fool would set lips to a powder keg, especially one primed by fear and anger.

"How'd you know where to find me?"

He leaned against the rocky wall, using the roughness to stub the fire in his groin. "I sensed you from the moment I broke camp. Knew you were following me."

"I wasn't hiding from you. Figured since we were going in the same direction anyway, I'd stick close. If the Yankees showed up, I'd be hidden, and—"

"And the patrol's attention would be focused on me."

She gave a half smile. "Exactly."

"You're bound and determined to get to Point Lookout, aren't you?"

"I have to." Her smile faded. "As soon as I can."

"Why the rush?"

She remained silent, the muscles beneath her milky skin twitching as if she clenched her teeth. Gripes, she was one stubborn female. She reminded him of the high-strung filly his grandfather had purchased years ago, a head-tossing, long-legged bundle of trouble. Yet, with a lot of patience and soft words, the stable master had finally persuaded the willful thoroughbred to trust him.

Calling on his own waning patience, he gave her a steady look. "Have you given up then?"

"Given up?"

"On trying to convince me to help you."

"Makes no sense beating a dead mule."

"I'm very much alive, Miss Carleton." He had an uncomfortable bulge in his trousers to prove it.

She regarded him through wary eyes. "What do you want from me?"

"Only an explanation." There had to be a powerful reason for her desperate and dangerous undertaking. The journalist in him hungered for her story—among other things. "Perhaps I might be compelled to help you."

She peered beyond him into the darkness. After a few seconds, she blew out a soft sigh. "I'm going after my brother."

"A Reb soldier?"

She pulled her bottom lip between her teeth and nodded.

Such pretty teeth. Pearly white and perfectly formed. He busied himself with adding another log to the fire and ignored the one smoldering in his loins. "How long has he been at Point Lookout?"

"I'm not sure. He was captured at Rappahannock Station in early November. I only found out last month where he was being held."

He pulled reports of the skirmish from his memory. "Jubal Early's division was overrun by Meade there. Over fourteen hundred Confederates were captured."

"That was Lance's regiment."

"I know prison isn't the most enjoyable place to be, but why the urgency to see him?"

Tears glistened in her eyes. She blinked and averted her gaze. "Lance is different than most. He's..." She swallowed, her throat muscles quivering with the effort. "He's a thinker, like you. Not at all the type to fight in this War, much less suffer the torture of being in prison. He never should've enlisted."

"Then why did he?"

She pulled the blanket tighter around her. "He had to."

"He was conscripted?" He moved the coffee pot closer to the flames. "If I recall correctly, Confederate law allows for substitution or exemption. Surely if you had the means and your brother didn't want to fight..."

"Let's just say, I'm here to right his mistake."

"So you intend to buy him special treatment. Even care for him yourself. If the Yankees will allow it."

"I'll see to Lance, but not inside the prison."

If not inside, then... "Gripes, you want to help him escape."

Louisa stiffened at his outraged tone. *Gripes, indeed.* He sounded as though she aimed to murder the Yankee President. She lifted her chin in defiance. "Yes, I plan to get him out of prison."

"How?"

"My methods are none of your concern."

"How, Miss Carleton?" He folded his arms over his chest, his expression that of a stern guardian unwilling to put up with any sass from his charge.

She returned his glare. Even in the backwoods, with his linen shirt and tailored vest dark with rainwater, he looked the perfect, polished gentleman. *Very well, Mr. High-and-mighty, choke on this.* "Bribery."

"Bribery," he repeated in his customary, mocking tone.

She ignored the dig. "I s'pect the Yankee guards at Point Lookout are little different from the ones in Richmond. Many a bluebelly disappeared from Libby prison during the night with rumors of pay-offs whispered the next morning."

He uncrossed his arms and leaned closer. "If by

41

some strange stroke of fortune you manage to get your brother out of prison, how will you get him home? He'll be weak and possibly ill after months of imprisonment. It's no picnic inside those prisons."

The air went out of her, and she slumped against the rock wall. Jeb was supposed to help her get Lance home. He'd insisted on accompanying her to Maryland despite the danger. And look where his loyalty had gotten him. A bullet and possibly a prison cell.

She closed her eyes against the ache of despair. "I'll do whatever I have to." *For Lance and for Jeb.*

"I have no doubt you will."

Another man had befriended her with softly spoken words. Would this one turn out the same? Earn her trust, then shatter it without a second thought? She squared herself and pushed back into the rocks, gaining strength from their hardness. Only fools let themselves get burned twice.

"Well then, Mr. Porter. Was my story *compelling* enough for you to accept my offer?"

"Jack."

"What?"

"If we're to act as husband and wife, you'll have to start calling me by my first name."

Hope warred with caution. "You'll help me then?"

"Your notion of corruption at the Union prison intrigues me. It could be an interesting angle for my article."

"Thank you, Mr...er...Jack. You don't know what this means."

"Don't thank me yet. You haven't heard my conditions."

His bedroll loomed in the corner of her vision. Panic slithered into her belly. He'd mentioned acting as husband and wife. Would he insist on the intimacies that came with it?

She groped in the dirt, fingers finding and closing around a large rock. Not if she had any say. "What are your conditions?"

"This will be a business arrangement only." He prodded the fire, and sparks shot skyward. "Until we part ways, you'll defer to me on every aspect of our journey. No arguments. No lone undertakings. And most definitely, no knife wielding."

Those conditions she could handle. "And what about you? Do you promise not to hand me over to the bluebellies at the first opportunity?"

"I assure you, I won't."

Could she trust him? He *had* rescued her from the storm and brought her to warm by the fire. Had even tenderly wrapped her with a blanket. But he was still a stranger—a very smooth-talking stranger.

She loosened her grip on the rock. Regardless of her doubts, accepting his help seemed to be her only option in getting to Point Lookout without precious delays. She poked a hand through the gap in the blanket. "We have a deal then. A business deal," she emphasized.

He clasped her fingers in his warm grasp. "It appears we do." He released her and reached for the soot-blackened coffee pot warming by the fire. "What shall I call you?"

"Is there a problem with my name?"

"Miss Carleton obviously won't work, and Mrs. Porter seems a bit too formal. Louisa..." His mouth flattened into a thoughtful line. "If the soldiers manage to get any information out of your Negro—"

"He's not my Negro," she interrupted. "He's my friend. If those bluebellies do anything to hurt him..." Beneath the blanket, her fingers found the hilt of her knife. She pulled the blade out of its sheath. Then pushed it back in. Out and in. Out and in. No one would hurt Jeb. She would see to that.

"I doubt they'll torture a black man, especially one who may have been forced into servitude."

She sheathed the blade with one last shove. "He wasn't forced. He offered to help."

"Fine. In any case, we don't want to slip up regarding your name and cause anyone to become suspicious." He studied her, cocking his head from side to side, humming softly as he thought.

She shifted under his scrutiny.

"What about Kitty?"

"Kitty? That makes no sense."

"Certainly it does. For those amazing, green cat-eyes of yours."

"Oh..." Her chest tightened, thick with sudden self-awareness. No one had ever called her eyes amazing. "It's silly."

"It's perfect. I'll have no trouble remembering it."

"Most people..." She paused, wondering if she was getting too comfortable. Talking to this man came so easy. She needed to keep up her guard. "People usually call me Red."

"Nope, too obvious. And from what I've seen in the short time I've known you, I suspect you wouldn't like that name." He poured coffee into the tin cup and handed it to her. "I prefer Kitty. That will be ours."

Chapter Four

Porter reined Socks around a large limb lying in the road. "You mentioned corruption at the Richmond prison. What do you know about it?"

She swayed with the horse's motion, wishing she could swap places with the bedroll and tent secured behind the saddle. Riding sideways in the newspaperman's lap was much too intimate and conjured up too many painful memories. Yet, if it got her to Lance, she would deal with the torture.

"Mostly what I heard in rumors." She braced herself on the pommel. "Just this past January, one hundred Yankee officers escaped from Libby prison during the night."

"One hundred." He gave a soft whistle. "That's a sizeable amount for one night. How'd it happen?"

"They tunneled under the prison."

"Tunnels are a usual method. A man's got nothing but time to burrow out of his cell."

"They didn't dig out of their cells. The tunnel entrance was clear across the prison. They had to sneak through a hospital room and down a stairway to get there. Surely *someone* would've noticed three months of such goings-on."

"It does sound suspicious."

"The tunnel ended in the yard of a nearby, unguarded warehouse. That smacks of outside help."

"Or inside. Were the guards questioned?" He shifted his weight in the saddle, reaching to brush a horsefly off Socks' neck.

Firm thighs bunched and relaxed beneath her

backside. For a second, she forgot what they were talking about. "Uh...yes. The guards on duty that night were arrested, but no proof of bribery or wrong-doing was found. They were released and returned to duty."

"Hmmm. Something that significant, I'm surprised I hadn't heard about it before. I generally have a pretty good nose for such things." He swept the fly off her shoulder. "How'd you hear the story?"

"Little bit of gossip, like I said." The horsefly buzzed around her head, no less bothersome than Porter's questions. How much did she really want to tell him?

"It's been my experience that you need to be at the right place at the right time to hear decent gossip," he went on smoothly. Likely the voice he used for his fancy newspaper interviews. "What took you to Libby? You know somebody being held there?"

She flapped at the fly, which had lighted on her ear. The back of her hand smacked into Porter's face. He howled and grabbed his nose. The reins dropped to trail in the muddy road. Socks, as well-schooled as he claimed, slowed to a halt.

"Sorry. Didn't mean to..." She wiggled around to see if she'd actually hurt him. There didn't appear to be any blood.

"For God's sake, can't you keep still?" He rubbed his nose. The horse snorted in what sounded like agreement. "You're squirming worse than a worm in hot ashes."

His comment tickled at her. She chuckled. "That sure is a funny way of putting it."

"My grandfather used to say that when I was little."

She got a quick image of him as a small boy, dressed all clean and proper, seated at his desk, nose buried in a book, one foot swinging back and forth as he lapped up word after word. Certainly not squirming like a worm in hot ashes.

"I've never heard that before. It's an odd saying."

"No odder than the man himself."

She never knew any of her grandparents. They'd all died before she was born. "Did you spend much time with your granddaddy?"

"Entirely too much." With no warning, he bent forward, pushing her against the horse's neck. Porter's face filled her vision, his nose inches from hers. His breath smelled of the bitter coffee he'd drunk earlier at the campsite.

Her mouth went dry. "What are you—"

"Just a minute...need to get..." He stretched. His arm slid across her back and pressed damp muslin along her shoulder blade. She was sweating more than she'd realized in the hot, unmoving air.

He straightened and gathered the retrieved reins. "Damn, what a mess." He wiped the leather across his knee, leaving a dark smudge on his britches.

"I'm sorry," she muttered. "I'll try to be still."

His faint grunt could've meant either it mattered or it didn't. He nudged Socks forward.

For a long while, they rode in silence. Sunlight poked through the treetops, dappling the surroundings with bright, golden spots. The horizon shimmered with heat. She swiped a trickle of sweat from her brow. Looked like they were in for a roasting. A pang of longing stabbed her. She and Lance and Jeb would've sneaked off to the river on a day like this.

"You were going to tell me about your family," she said. Maybe talking about his folks would take her mind off her own.

"Was I?"

"You said you spent time with your granddaddy."

"Yep." The arms around her tensed.

"Do you see him much anymore?"

"Certainly are full of questions this morning."

"Just trying to be friendly. I was thinking maybe—"

Socks stumbled, tossing the words from her mouth. She jerked forward, then back and collided into Porter's rock-solid chest. She let out a squeak of surprise.

Strong arms folded around her in a steadying embrace, and her body hummed with warmth that had nothing to do with the heat of the day. Lordy, but she reacted to this man so easily—a temptation she couldn't afford. Even if her body didn't remember the pain, the guilt of Bart Lawrence, she certainly did.

Hands on his chest, she shoved upright, putting some space between them. Not that there was any place to move, trapped together on horseback like they were.

His shirtfront was dark with sweat, his face flushed and tight. "I heard you cry out. Did you hurt yourself?"

"No. I'm fine." She slid her hands to her lap and folded them into a tight ball. "That stumble just caught me off-guard is all."

"Yes, well...according to the directions I obtained in Saint Mary's City, there should be a farmhouse up ahead. We, um..." He cleared his throat. "We can stop and rest. Give us a chance to eat something."

And give me a chance to rein in this body of mine.

"While we're there," he added. "We ought to see about getting you another dress. That one won't do."

Good. He was thinking about her wardrobe. That arm curled around her waist didn't mean a thing except to keep her from falling in the mud.

"You're right." She fingered the torn, stained muslin. Might as well be flying a banner—*Here's your fugitive, Yankees. Come and get her.* "This gown is little more than a rag. Unfortunately Jeb has the knapsack with my spare clothing."

"Jeb?"

"We were traveling together."

He reached out to push aside a low hanging branch. "The man the Lieutenant mentioned."

"Yes. They shot him." She could picture Jeb where he dropped in the woods. Hear the strain in his voice as he urged her to go on, clear as if he were here with her right now. She swallowed around the thickness welling in her throat. Had the Yankees treated his wound? Did he suffer? She squashed the darker thought that tried to surface. Jeb was alive. To think otherwise would be to invite ill luck.

"I'm sure the soldiers are taking good care of him." Porter squeezed her waist in a quick gesture likely meant to be reassuring.

Heat rose soft and unexpected beneath her ribs, spreading outward. She drew in a much needed breath. Dealing with intimate closeness of Porter was turning out to be quite a difficult task, in more ways than one.

"How'd you come to be traveling with him?" he prodded.

She faced the road ahead, not wanting him to see the effect of his touch. Given his nosey nature, it might cause him to ask questions of a more personal breed. "Guess it must look mighty funny to you. Southern lady and a black man."

"It's been my experience that people have all types of reasons for doing what they do. I try not to make judgments until I know the facts."

"Judge not, lest ye be judged, huh?"

"Something like that." He dug a fresh white handkerchief out of his saddlebag and offered it to her.

She gave him a grateful smile and swiped the

sweat from her forehead. The day had grown too stifling for anything to move. Even the birds were still. "How far to that farmhouse?"

"Not much further. Another half mile or so." He accepted the handkerchief back, mopped his own brow, then swapped it for the canteen. "Would you like some water? It's a bit stale, but there might be a few swallows left."

"Yes, I would." She took the canteen. He sure was acting the gentleman. Scarcely resembled the mule she'd argued with yesterday. "Thank you."

"So, tell me about this Jeb."

She uncapped the canteen and took a long, soothing swig, buying some time before she replied. "You sure are interested in my business."

"You're an interesting lady."

"More like you're just plain nosey."

"It's my livelihood to be nosey, as you put it. Stories are my stock in trade. And you *are* interesting. Traveling under the cover of night, alluding Yankee patrols, sneaking into tents with strange men. You'd make a fine heroine in one of Wilkie Collins' novels."

Books again. The man was full up with them. Not being familiar with Wilkie Collins or his tales, she wasn't sure how to respond. When this was over, she'd ask Lance about Collins. She took another pull on the canteen.

"So, back to Jeb," he said. "You must trust him."

"He's a good friend." No harm in telling some of it, as long as she kept the particulars of Lance's troubles to herself. "He came along to help with my brother."

"You already knew him then?"

"He was a slave at Spivey Point Manor where my father was overseer."

"Jeb's a runaway?"

"Abandoned is more like it. The owners fled

north soon as the fighting drew close. Left us all to fend for ourselves."

"Never heard of Spivey Point. Who owns it?"

"Family named Lawrence. It's a large tobacco-growing estate east of Richmond. Sits up on a bend of land overlooking the James River." Or it once did. Was it still there with its wide porches and elegant columns? Or had the War come through and ruined the rose gardens and the grand old oak trees that ringed the house? Whatever had become of the place, it would never be her home again.

She cleared her throat of the lump that had sprouted of a sudden. "On a summer morning, before it gets real hot, you can sit out on the point and watch the barges piled with all sorts of goods and supplies, coming 'round the curve down from the terminal."

"Heading to the bay."

Heading to the bay and to places she'd only dreamed of seeing. Though she loved Spivey Point, she'd itched to explore beyond the estate. To touch and hear and taste new worlds, not just what she could see in a picture book.

She passed him the canteen but held onto the cap so he could take a drink. "There's just a little bit left. And you're right...water's not real fresh."

He tipped back his head and drained the contents. Sure did have a nice neck. All tanned and sleek. Except for that tiny scabbed-over nick. One she'd put there.

He lowered the canteen. "You live there long?"

So many prying questions. The nick on his neck pulsed. A moneylender calling in its dues. She prodded her stingy tongue. "All my life. Lance and I were born at Spivey Point. We're twins. We lived in a small cabin just up from the main house."

"You were comfortable there, I take it? Happy?"

There being no simple answer, she just nodded.

"And your father?" He gave her a questioning look. "As overseer, he managed the labor?"

"He was in charge of the slaves, if that's what you mean."

"Don't get prickly. I wasn't asking—"

"Sure you were. Or you were going to." She squared her shoulders as that old familiar resentment crept up her spine. "That's all you Northerners can see when you look at us. Haven't met a Yankee yet didn't think every one of us feeds on hate and mistreatment. You don't know there are respectable folks out there, trying to do right. Good overseers who stay on, working for ignorant masters, so they can guarantee decent care of those poor souls."

She fisted her hand around the metal canteen cap, squeezing until it bit into her palm. Nobody outside of Spivey Point would ever know of Papa's charity or the risks he'd taken.

"Your father sounds like a conscientious man. Can't imagine he thinks too fondly of his daughter running off on a foolish quest."

"My father's dead."

"I'm sorry. Was it recent?"

Some days, it seemed like years ago. Other days, when the grief snuck up on her, it felt like it'd just happened. "He died this past winter."

"And your mother?"

"Dead, too. For a long time." Tears burned in her eyes. She combed her fingers through Sock's mane, smoothing, straightening. Tidying.

Porter gave her another quick, unnerving squeeze. "I just keeping sticking my foot in my mouth, don't I? That leaves just you and your brother."

"Here." She thrust the canteen cap at him, almost striking him in the nose again.

"Kitty, I didn't mean to—"

"Oh look," she blurted, pointing to the white-washed structure taking shape through the greenery ahead. Thank heaven for small favors. "That must be the farmhouse."

He grunted in agreement and shifted around to stow away the canteen.

"I don't know about you," she added. "But I could use a break. Stretch my legs. Get the blood flowing again." Get away from all these pestering questions. And all that muscle and heat and that rich voice rumbling through her with every word. "That canteen needs refilling, too."

He grunted again, apparently having decided he'd eaten his own hoof enough for one day. Another gift from above. She settled her skirt. Nothing would be gained by telling him everything. What little he knew should be enough to get her to Lance.

She'd deal with the rest.

He guided Socks off the roadway and onto a narrow, rutted lane. The path opened up onto a large clearing occupied by a two-story, white clapboard farmhouse, several outbuildings, and a barn. Half-a-dozen chickens pecked at the sun-dried grass dotting the yard. Papa had often spoken of buying a parcel of land to farm. Had even mentioned building a big, white farmhouse. Her chest tightened. He'd never have the chance to realize his dream.

The squeal of hinges rang out, and a slender woman toting a rifle stepped through the doorway and onto the front porch. Narrowed eyes glared at them from a time-worn face. "That's far enough," she called out, leveling the gun barrel in their direction.

Jack reined Socks to a stop. "We mean you no harm, ma'am." He tipped his hat. "Name's Jackson Porter and this is my wife. We saw your place from the road and thought you might be able to help us."

"Help you with what?"

"Water, for one thing."

The woman jerked a nod at the side of the house. "Well's over there. What else?"

"Last night's storm spooked my wife's horse. He dumped her and took off with her belongings. We haven't seen hide nor hair of the beast since."

"No horses here. Yankees conscripted 'em all. Even took my plow mules."

He patted Socks' neck. "We can make do with this one. It's not much further to the garrison at Point Lookout."

The farmwoman frowned and stepped to the edge of the porch. A yellow tabby brushed past her skirt and darted down the stairs. "You don't look like a soldier. What business you got at Camp Hoffman?"

"I'm a journalist for *The New York Herald*. I've been assigned to write a piece on the treatment of Confederate prisoners being held there."

"The prisoners. Hmmph. Ought to be writing about how poorly the Yankees treat innocent folk outside the prison. Trampling their gardens. Raiding their livestock and larders."

He gave an understanding nod. "I'm sorry to hear about your troubles, ma'am, but as you can see, my wife's dress is ruined. We were wondering if you might have a spare one we might purchase."

Wary brown eyes focused on her. Louisa smoothed down a wrinkle, hoping the stains looked more like dirt from where the rifle-toting woman stood.

The farmwoman lowered her weapon. "Get yourself a cool drink from the well. I'll see what I can find for your missus."

As the woman disappeared through the doorway, Louisa slid from his grasp and slipped to the ground. She hurried toward the well, her skin tingling from his intimate hold. Yes, she definitely needed some water—a whole pail full to pour over her rebellious body.

Footfalls and the clop of hooves thudded behind her. Ignoring the newspaperman's approach, she grabbed the wooden pail and lowered it until a faint splash echoed up the well shaft. She began hoisting, a difficult task now that the bucket was heavy with water.

"Let me help you." Porter leaned over, spooning his chest along her back.

Flames licked at her spine. She twisted sideways to break the contact and lost her grip on the handle. The lever spun wildly and nipped her fingers. She yelped and cradled her throbbing hand to her stomach.

He reached for her. "Let me see what you've done."

Was he daft? Having him touch her was the last thing she needed. Her body was already smoldering. She shook her head. "There's no need. It's fine."

"Perhaps it is, but just to be sure..." He gently pried her hand free and examined each finger, his touch like hot coals on her skin.

After what seemed like hours, he finally halted his agonizing inspection and looked up. His dark gaze tunneled into her. "Nothing appears to be broken. Does it hurt?"

Only when I breathe. She shifted uneasily and looked away. "A little. It'll feel better in a few minutes."

Before she could pull out of his grasp, he lifted her hand and pressed a tender kiss to her palm. She gasped and tried to wrench free. "What are you doing?"

"Shhh." He tightened his grip, holding fast. "Our hostess is watching from the window. Play along. We don't want to arouse her suspicions."

She clinched her teeth together in frustration. This charade as husband and wife was proving more difficult than imagined. If she wasn't careful, she might find herself falling for Jackson Porter's enticing pull.

****

Jack eyed the stockade wall running parallel to the roadway. Fourteen-foot, at least. And well-guarded. Rifle-toting soldiers patrolled a narrow parapet built along the outer edge. A few gave them cursory glances; others remained focused on prison innards. All appeared to be Negroes. Bet that went over real well with the imprisoned Southern boys.

He reined Socks to a halt, then slipped an arm around the tantalizing female who'd tortured him for most of the day. She wiggled in his lap, fanning the fire he'd worked so hard to control. He ground his teeth around a curse. If their business partnership wasn't over soon, he might just be tempted to consummate this fake marriage.

He lowered her to the ground, then paused to let the blaze in his loins diminish before dismounting. He didn't want to unnerve her with evidence of his arousal. He needed her alert and attentive. One slip and she'd expose their ruse to the soldiers.

His lust corralled, he dismounted, snagged Socks' reins in one hand and Kitty's elbow with the other, and guided them toward the massive gate. At the base of the wall sat dozens of freshly lumbered pine boxes, waiting to be filled.

Muscles tensed beneath his fingers. She had to be thinking of finding her brother already buried in one of those coffins. His own thoughts ventured along those lines, given what she'd told him about the boy.

He gave her elbow an encouraging squeeze. "He's fine."

"He has to be," came her gravelly reply.

"How can he not? He's your twin brother. Surely you didn't get *all* the spit and vinegar."

She looked up at him, green eyes flashing with

challenge. "Is that your attempt at flattery?"

Ah, there was that she-cat he was coming to admire. He smiled. "I do my best."

"Hmmph. You should stick to writing."

"That bad, huh?"

She wrinkled her pert little nose. "'Bout as bad as the smell of this prison."

"Ouch. Writing it is then."

As they neared the gate, a guard stepped forward, blocking their path. "What business do you have at the prison?"

"Name's Jackson Porter." He poked a hand in his knapsack and withdrew his papers. "I'm here to see the Provost."

"Major Brady's headquarters are over there." The soldier pointed at a nearby building, then flicked a curious glance at Kitty.

Though the farmwoman's dress fit lengthwise, the faded blue-checked material sagged beneath her breasts and puckered at her tiny waist. She looked like a penniless street waif seeking a handout. He shrugged inwardly. Not much they could do about her appearance right now. At least she'd tamed her fiery mane into a respectable bun.

After securing Socks to the hitching post, he helped her up the short stairs and into the Provost's headquarters. A framed map of Maryland occupied one wall, a portrait of President Lincoln the other. An American flag and the swallow-tailed guidon of the 20th regiment stood in the far corner next to a wooden desk at which sat a soldier, his nose submerged in paperwork.

As the door clicked shut behind them, a faint, indrawn breath drew his attention. Kitty's face was pale and tense. Widened eyes flicked around the room and latched onto the open window on opposite wall.

He tensed. Gripes. Now was not the time for her

to fall apart. He placed a supportive hand on her elbow and whispered an encouraging, "Steady."

She blinked and gave a brief nod.

"Can I help you, sir?" The adjutant rose to his feet, a frown creasing his baby smooth face. Seemed the longer the War dragged on, the younger the soldiers got.

He moved closer and handed over his papers. "We're here to see Major Brady."

The soldier studied the documents, then looked up. "Very well, just one moment."

He disappeared into an adjacent chamber. A few minutes later, he returned and ushered them into the major's office. The faint odor of cigar smoke lingered in the air, an expensive brand like the one grandfather enjoyed with after-dinner brandy.

"Mr. Porter." Meticulously turned-out in a crisp uniform jacket and neatly pressed trousers, Major Allen Brady crossed toward them, hand extended. "What an honor it is to have you here. I've read nearly every one of your insightful articles chronicling the War."

He shook the officer's hand. "Thank you, sir. I do my best to report things as I see them." He inclined his head toward Kitty, grateful to see the color returning to her cheeks. "May I introduce my wife?"

The major gave a slight bow. "It's a pleasure to meet you, ma'am."

She dipped her head. "Thank you, Major. It's a pleasure to meet you as well."

"I wondered why I hadn't seen your by-line in *The Herald* recently." A smile lifted the officer's bushy mustache. "Now I see why."

Jack returned the major's smile and placed a possessive hand at the dip in Kitty's back. "We met last month in Virginia. I found myself hostage to her Southern beauty and charm."

She tensed beneath his fingertips, apparently

grasping his innuendo. She shifted and arched her back just enough to escape his touch.

"Ah, that explains the lovely accent." The shrewd officer regarded the ill-fitting dress, his smile fading.

Before Jack could offer an explanation, Kitty ran a hand down her skirt as though smoothing a wrinkle. "I do wish I could've been better attired for our meeting, Major. Unfortunately, we met with some difficulties, and my clothes were lost." She batted her lashes and heaved a disconsolate sigh. "I had to beg this dreary dress off a poor farmwoman."

Jack stuffed down a snort at her contrived grandeur. He needn't worry about Miss Carleton. She played her part well, too well, if the appreciative look on Brady's face was any indication.

"You poor dear," the officer said with a cluck. "Well, hopefully your stay at Point Lookout will ease the discomforts of your journey. I've ordered my adjutant to arrange quarters for you in one of the summer cottages. You can relax there away from the noise and odor of the prison."

"Summer cottages?" she asked.

"Before construction began on Camp Hoffman, Point Lookout was a civilian resort town. There's an old lighthouse at the southern tip you might want to explore while your husband tours the prison."

"I don't think—"

"How thoughtful of you, Major," Jack interrupted, pressing his fingers once more into her spine to get her attention. "I'm sure my wife will welcome a relaxing respite from our travels." He shrugged and forced a wry smile. "We barely said our 'I do's' before I had her on the road heading for the prison. Deadlines, you know."

Brady nodded. "Yes, indeed I do." He motioned to the pair of chairs facing his desk. "Please have a seat. We can chat while your quarters are being readied."

He assisted Kitty onto one of the wooden chairs, giving her a warning glare before settling himself on the seat beside her. Those pouting lips were oh-so-pretty, but dangerous as well. If the wrong words spilled out of them, their mission was dead.

As Brady took his seat behind the desk, Jack reached into his pocket and extracted a notepad and pencil. Time for a little investigative journalism. "We might as well take advantage of our time together, sir." He thumbed to a fresh page. "If you wouldn't mind answering a few questions?"

"Certainly. What would you like to discuss?"

"Let's start with the population. How many soldiers are you holding?"

"We have approximately ten thousand prisoners. But not all are soldiers. Some are civilians who sympathize with the South. Blockade runners mostly, caught on the Potomac and out in the Bay."

"That's a lot of prisoners to watch over. Any escapes?"

"Not since I took charge in April." The major puffed up his chest, full of his own self-importance. "I made certain of that."

"In what way?"

"First and foremost, I enforce all federal regulations to the letter. Body searches. Twice daily roll calls." He tossed a glance at the darkening window. "After sundown, all prisoners are confined to their quarters. Anyone caught outside is shot without question."

"I see." He wet his pencil nib with the tip of his tongue and struck a bold underscore beneath the notation *enforces regulations to the letter*. "Do you take any preventative measures outside of regulations?"

"Any I deem necessary."

"Can you elaborate?"

"I can. For example, any new captives found wearing federal blue are stripped of those uniforms. Too easy for them to blend in, if they do manage to escape."

"A wise precaution." Hell, with all those safety measures, Kitty might find getting her brother freed quite a difficult undertaking. The more he heard, the more he believed she was only chasing a fantasy. "Is alternate clothing provided for the prisoners should they need it?"

"We have a storehouse of donated items. Also, many prisoners write to their families and request clothes or money. Of course, all packages are inspected by this office before being distributed."

Warning bells clanged in his head. Packages inspected before being distributed? Even the most dedicated army officer might be tempted to steal from the helpless prisoners. Who would the Reb soldiers complain to? The idea definitely warranted further exploration.

"Clothes, I can understand," he tendered. "But why would they need to request money if they're imprisoned?"

Brady's gaze remained steady, no blinking, no tell-tale shifting. "Prisoners are allowed to purchase necessity items from the sutler's store against accounts set up in their names."

Damn. Either the man was a good actor, or he had nothing to hide.

"The sutler's carries a variety of stock," Brady continued. "Including female attire." He opened a drawer and withdrew a leaflet which he handed to Kitty. "I'm sure you could find a few things to tide you over, Mrs. Porter; though it won't be anything as fine as a well-bred Southern lady like yourself is accustomed to."

She stared at the paper, eyes wide, fingers clasped on the edges. A second passed, no more, then she gathered herself and treated the officer to a dazzling smile. "Thank you, Major." She folded the leaflet onto her lap. "I appreciate your thoughtfulness."

"Glad to help. I'll have my adjutant escort the two of you to the sutler's. Then you can join us for dinner in the officers' mess hall."

Jack stowed her strange reaction to the leaflet to the back of his mind for later reflection and returned to his questioning. "Speaking of feminine attire, do you have many female prisoners?"

"A few. Most were captured along with the units they fought with."

"And the others?"

"We have one female spy imprisoned, and another we're currently searching for."

"How do you know the other one's involved in espionage?"

"Won't know for sure until we capture and question her. However..." Brady tapped a packet of papers stacked on the corner of the desk. "This report says she was seen kneeling beside a dead courier just north of here with blood on her hands. Field orders were missing from his sack. That's mighty condemning evidence."

Kitty shifted in her chair, white-knuckled fingers clamped around the armrests. Her face had gone pale as the papers stacked on Brady's desk.

Damn. She was going to give them away. Jack cleared his throat in an effort to keep Brady's focus directed on him. "I believe we met the patrol looking for her. Do you have any information on this woman?"

"Only what we gathered from her Negro's feverish mumblings. He's being cared for at the prison hospital. Seems his mistress is from Virginia, and her name is Carleton, Miss Lou Carleton."

Chapter Five

Louisa pushed the fried summer squash into a neat pile with the tip of her fork. Jeb was here at the prison. And he was alive, feverish, but still alive. The garden peas formed a smaller hill. It'd make freeing him and Lance all the easier. She slid the crab cake to the edge of the plate. Provided the bluebellies didn't put two and two together and come up with her.

All around her, conversation hummed, low and threatening like the buzz in a busy hive. She sat in its center, an intruder in the nest, and any moment they'd spot her. Stomach roiling with unease, she forced a bite of crab between her lips and made herself swallow. It felt as though sawdust raked her throat. She grabbed for her wine.

The officer beside her on the bench shifted and reached for a basket of rolls. His thigh brushed her skirts. She tried to inch sideways but met the end of the bench. As honored guests, she and Porter were seated at the head of the table with Major Brady, and there was no place to go without landing on the floor.

She lifted her wineglass and hid her trembling lips as she peered over the rim at the blue uniforms lining the long, linen-draped table. Yankee officers. Two dozen of them at least. Another bead of perspiration trickled between her breasts, adding to the discomfort of her sweat-soaked chemise. Once again she'd trusted a man and now had herself truly trapped.

"You look oddly familiar, Mrs. Porter," said the officer beside her, a Captain Riggs, if she remembered correctly. He puckered his brow as he studied her. "Have you ever visited Southern Maryland before now?"

Her heart skipped a beat. Had he been part of the Yankee patrol chasing her and Jeb? She swallowed and lowered her glass. "No, Captain." She fought to keep the quiver from her voice and concentrated on speaking like a well-bred lady. "I've not had the pleasure."

He broke off a bit of bread and continued to look at her as he chewed. "Connecticut, maybe. That's where I'm from. Middletown actually. South of Hartford."

"N-no. I've never—" She dragged in a shaky breath. "—never been any further north than this."

"Strange." He brushed crumbs from his neat blond moustache. "You look..." His gaze drifted to her hair. He shook his head. "I'd swear I've seen you before."

Dratted hair. It always seemed to draw attention and comment, mostly of a non-pleasant sort. Once, in what seemed a lifetime ago, as she'd dressed Fannie's lank brown locks, the eldest Lawrence daughter had screwed up her face and declared Louisa's coloring more suited a pleasure house than a lady's parlor. There were times she wondered if maybe Fannie was right.

"Perhaps you mistake me for someone else."

"Where're y'all from then, darlin'," came a drawl from farther down the table. A lieutenant with a cocky grin and looking much too young for his rank leaned forward on an elbow. "Talk s'more so I can hear that lovely voice."

Y'all? Darlin' ? Her shock must've shown for Captain Riggs stepped in.

"Don't mind Calhoun, Mrs. Porter. He's from

Texas. Been complaining since he arrived here that the only folks he understands are the Reb prisoners. Oh, begging your pardon, ma'am."

She dismissed his apology with a shake of her head. "No offense taken. While I am a Southerner, I don't hold with slavery. Never have. However, I do feel forcing the issue with violence is wrong."

Calhoun snagged a chicken leg from a platter. "I disagree. Only way to get through to a slaver is with force." He ripped off a hunk of meat with his teeth, then chewed ill-manneredly while talking. "Give 'em back what they been dishin' out to the Nigras."

A knot of resentment coiled in her belly, for the moment muzzling her fear. She met Lieutenant Calhoun's smug gaze straight on. "Those are mighty Republican beliefs for a Texan." She deepened her own drawl. "When on earth did Texas take up the Union cause?"

Color rushed into the lieutenant's face. He dropped the mauled drumstick to his plate and opened his mouth to reply.

But she didn't give him a chance. He'd smeared Papa, Lance, and *her* with his comment. It was not to be borne. She heaved a sigh that would've rivaled any of Fannie's theatrics. "I do swear, one would think having a newspaper man for a husband, one would occasionally hear some news. Good or bad. Perhaps I should have married a soldier after all."

There was a moment of uncertain silence, then all down the line, laughter exploded. Calhoun, crimsoned-faced, pushed to his feet. He tossed her a furious glower, then slammed his napkin on the table and stormed toward the door.

His comrades threw taunts after him, several mimicking his Texas twang. Others toasted her witty humor and though the moment was clearly hers, she found little to enjoy. A chill scuttled down her spine. Curse her flap-happy tongue. Now she had a new, more personal enemy to watch out for.

She eyed the empty doorway. "Oh, dear...I didn't intend to upset the lieutenant."

"Don't you fret none, Mrs. Porter," Major Brady soothed. "Calhoun gets a bit hot-headed at times. He'll soon simmer down." He reached for the wine bottle. "Would you care for more wine?"

Perhaps a good slug of spirits would help settle her rattled nerves. "Yes, I would. Thank you, Major."

As the officer poured a generous dose into her glass, Porter gave her a pointed look across the table. "This is wonderful French wine, Major. *Very* potent. I'll bet the effects can sneak up on you real quick if you're not careful."

Brady chuckled. "Right you are. Very potent indeed. I only allow it to be served on special occasions."

Ignoring Porter's warning glare, she took a healthy sip. She'd have more wine if she wanted. He had no hold over her.

Frowning, Porter downed his wine and set the goblet on the table. "Where'd you come by such exclusive stock during wartime?"

"Ah, the rewards of capturing blockade runners. More?" At Jack's nod, Brady refreshed his drink. "A large crate was confiscated from a French schooner bound for Norfolk. I've no doubt some unhappy Virginia gentleman is settling for weak blackberry extract with his dinner right now."

No doubt. She shook her head, and her vision swam. She gripped the edge of the table to steady herself. Dratted wine was almost as potent as ol' Carson's corn liquor. Perhaps she should go easy with the spirit. Not that Porter was right. She just didn't need her tongue loosened any further. One furious Yankee was enough. She stabbed another bite of crab. Adding something solid to her stomach should help tame the wine's effects.

Porter's mouth turned up in a satisfied smile. She smiled back. Let him think what he would.

"You'll have to allow me access to this blockade runner, Major," Jack stated. "I'd love to discover his French source."

Brady motioned for the dark-skinned soldier standing behind him to remove his plate. It seemed, even in the Union Army, Negroes were given the lowliest jobs. "I don't think it'd be wise for you to question the prisoners, Mr. Porter."

She stilled her fork. How would they find Lance if they weren't allowed to talk to the prisoners? She clamped her teeth around the question hopping on her tongue. She'd already drawn enough attention with her remark to Calhoun.

Porter wiped his mouth, then set his napkin beside a plate nearly licked clean of crumbs. Man had a healthy appetite—for food *and* knowledge. He'd uncover the major's reason for denying them access to the prisoners. No doubt about that. She knew first-hand how the newspaperman worried at a bone until it was gnawed clean.

"Why shouldn't I speak with the prisoners, sir?"

"They're known to embellish the truth. I would hate for you to be misled by falsehoods."

"I've become pretty adept at seeing through falsehoods."

"Perhaps so, but..."

Jack cocked his head to the side, his gaze drifting over her before returning to the major. "I could make it worth your while."

Alarm shot through her at his words. It wasn't what he said, but how he said it. Slowly. Deliberately. As if he held a nugget the major couldn't resist.

Maybe *her*, for instance?

****

Shadows lined the pathway ahead, dark pockets

67

perfect for hiding an ambusher. Calhoun, perhaps? She shifted closer to the protective presence beside her, then tensed. Was she trading one threat for another?

Are we not friends, little Red? Have we not tendered cheer during times of distress? Protected one another from torment?

They had been slick words. Spoken with a friendly tongue and compelling her to go against all good sense. Porter also had the gift of gab. She'd seen him practice it on several occasions, first with the farmwoman and again with Major Brady. Would he use his smooth-talking talent, as Bart had, for ill? It would be wise to learn more about him and avoid such trickery.

"You shouldn't have embarrassed Lieutenant Calhoun like that," Jack admonished.

She glanced over her shoulder. Nothing moved in the darkness. She lowered her voice anyway. "What I should've done is stick a knife in the traitor's back. Texan, my—"

"Now, Kitty. We don't want to get on the bad side of these men."

"Do they have another side?"

He guided her around a large puddle. "We'll learn more if we show them we can be trusted."

Porter? Trustworthy? When words cloaked in sheep's wool rolled off his tongue? She gave a soft snort of derision.

"What was that for?"

"That what?"

"That enchanting expression of cynicism?"

"You were awful sociable with the Yankees, laughing, joking, toasting to their newborns." She toed a rock and kicked it into the underbrush. "Makes a body wonder where to place one's trust."

"Familiar with that old saying, 'you catch more flies with honey'?"

"Flies will light on garbage, too."

"True, and a good deal of what I say to them is just that. Rubbish. But it's how I uncover information. Get friendly with them. Earn their confidence." He reached up and pushed a low-hanging branch out of the way. It swished softly behind them when he released it. "Then they divulge secrets they wouldn't have otherwise yielded."

Time for a little uncovering of her own. She adopted a curiously polite tone. "How long have you been a newspaperman?"

"Since sixty-two, after my graduation from the University of Rochester."

"My, my, a college man. What'd you study?"

"A liberal selection of classes...philosophy, law, economics." His voice rose with enthusiasm. "I couldn't get enough of books and the knowledge they contained. Enrolled in every course the administrator allowed me to take."

Hmmph. People were more fascinating than dumb ol' books. "I imagine you had lots of friends."

"A few. Until the War started and Lincoln called for volunteers. Most of the students left to enlist."

"But you couldn't because of your eye?"

"That was one reason."

Muscles bunched beneath her fingertips. What was it about his eye? Just mention it, and he got pricklier than a hedgehog. "How'd you injure it?"

"Bar fight," he answered in a clipped tone.

She cut a glance at him. His jaw was clamped tight as a bear trap. Nothing more would be said on *that* subject. Still, she itched to ask more. When had it happened and where? What had the fight been about? He didn't seem to be the type to go around getting into bar brawls. Perhaps there was more to Jackson Porter than she thought—things that should make her wary.

A breeze swept down the path, and she clamped

a hand atop the pretty blue bonnet she'd bought along with a new dress at the sutler's. Porter said the color brought out the highlights in her eyes. Had he been play acting for the clerk's benefit, or...

A ribbon of gold flashed in the sky and then disappeared, a warning beacon from the nearby lighthouse. Was it a warning for her as well? Despite the warm evening, a shiver coursed through her.

"Are you taking chill?"

Lordy, even with one eye covered, he noticed everything. "No. I'm fine. It's been a long day, and I'm just played out."

"At least you'll sleep on a nice comfortable bed, courtesy of Major Brady."

Speaking of which... "I got the impression you knew the major before the War."

"What made you think that?"

"You seemed quite at ease with him. Like you were old friends."

"As I said before, it's how I acquire information."

She regarded him out of the corner of her eye, watching for any hint of deception. "Get close to them."

"Yes." His expression remained vague as the dusky woods.

Moonlight peeked through a break in the clouds, revealing the colony of summer cottages ahead. She slowed, not ready to surrender the freedom of the outdoors or her questioning just yet. "I'm curious about something."

"Hmmm?"

"You told the major you'd make it worth his while to let you speak with the prisoners." She stopped and faced him. She wanted to see his reaction full on. "What did you mean by that?"

"Any number of things."

"Such as?"

"Money. A favorable article on his prison.

Whatever I can provide that he wants."

"Like...oh, maybe...*me*?"

"You?" He glanced over his shoulder, then moved closer, his voice dropping to a cautious whisper. "I promised I wouldn't give you up to them. I always keep my word."

She got a quick picture of him making merry with the Yankee officers in the mess hall. Friendly. Accepted. One of the pack. "I just can't..."

"It's a little too late to be questioning your decision to play my wife, isn't it?" Lines furrowed his brow. "You've trusted me this far, Kitty. What's changed?"

She motioned at the surrounding woods. "This."

"This what?"

"This camp, this narrow spit of land." A dozen sharp-clawed hens took to scratching for bugs in her belly. "On the ride here, there was always a way to escape if need be. But, now..."

His frown deepened. "And what about *your* trustworthiness?"

"Mine?"

"Yes, yours. How do I know I can trust you? You've only given evasive answers regarding your reason for coming here."

She lifted her chin, letting anger soothe her unease. "You don't need to know my private affairs. It wasn't part of our agreement."

"I beg to differ. In case you've forgotten, I could be imprisoned for aiding and abetting a fugitive."

"Well then, I s'pose that leaves us at a draw, doesn't it?"

"I suppose it does."

Fury bubbled inside her at his haughty tone. "Perhaps we should just end this silly charade and be done with our doubts." Without waiting for his reply, she gathered her skirt and brushed past him.

As she stomped down the path, sanity pounded

behind her. Why, oh, why couldn't she hold her tongue? What if he decided to take her up on her foolish suggestion? Where would she be then? What about Lance and Jeb?

Frustrated with her rashness, she dashed up the stairs and pushed inside their cottage. Only a thin shaft of moonlight stabbed through the gloom. Shadows hung in the corners like ambushers waiting to attack.

A familiar fist of fear clamped around her throat. She skidded to a halt. The room remained quiet and still. The only sounds were the reassuring call of night insects drifting through the open door behind her.

She pushed out a breath. She'd always preferred the outdoors. But ever since Bart had trapped her in that shed, the need to be unconfined nearly strangled her.

A shadow fell across the floor.

She whirled, unable to contain a gasp even though she knew it had to be Porter. Her vision blurred. The figure in the doorway distorted, wavering and shrinking and changing to a man of smaller build. Dark hair turned light. Chiseled features plumped. Her mouth went dry. *Bart.*

Boot heels thudded across the floor, matching the rapid thump of her pulse. She stood there unable to move, her limbs frozen. Then came the soft hiss of a match, and golden lamplight flooded the room.

"Kitty."

Darkness turned to gray and slowly brightened. She blinked and blinked again. A taller, slimmer man stood by the sideboard, his eye covered with a patch. *Jack.*

"I am not your enemy, Kitty."

How could she be sure? Had something deep inside her twisted Jack into the image of Bart as a warning? Feeling returned to her legs. She took a step back, and another, until her thighs pressed into the side of an arm chair.

Jack shifted as if about to move forward, then stopped, hands clamped to his sides. A scowl rutted his brow. "You're not just angry, you are afraid of me. Why?"

She wanted to swallow, but her mouth was drained as a summer pond. "I...You..." She drew in a calming breath. "I just know so little about you."

His scowl softened. "What would you like to know?"

Everything. Nothing. Her wits were as muddled as how she saw words on a page. "I-I'm not sure."

"Well, you know about my profession." He pointed to the decanter of whiskey on the sideboard. "Would you like a drink?"

She shook her head. Spirits would only add to the scramble in her head. She stepped sideways and sank onto the chair.

The soft gurgle of pouring whiskey rose up. Jack faced her, drink in hand. "Just so there is no confusion, I do trust you."

Her fingers suddenly captured her attention. Hangnails were ever more fascinating than hawk-like stares. "Thank you," she murmured.

He went silent for a few seconds as if waiting for more. She didn't have more to give him. Not yet.

He cleared his throat. "As for learning more about me, I told you a little about my grandfather during our ride here."

"The odd one. Who said you squirmed worse than a worm in hot ashes. Is he still alive?"

"Very much so. He lives in Baltimore."

"And his wife? Your grandmamma?"

"She passed long before I was born. Grandfather says I have her coloring. The Halliday dark hair and dark eyes." Jack chuckled. "He called us his little gypsies."

His easy manner and openness tamed the paw scratching at her insides. She looked up and met his warm gaze. "Do you get to visit him very much?"

He took a sip of whiskey and then another. His attention shifted to the far window. His expression turned dark as if shadowed by a passing cloud. Did thoughts of his family cause him pain?

"I try to visit," he finally answered. "My job leaves me little time for social calls."

"What about your parents?"

"They died when I was just a boy. In an accident."

His tone warbled slightly, and her heart went out to him. She knew how painful losing a parent could be. To lose both of them at the same time? A bridge stretched between them, a connection she felt straight to her core. "I'm sorry for your loss."

"No need to be. It was a long time ago."

"You must miss them." She knew from experience that ache never fully receded.

"I do miss them. But I found other things to fill my life."

Things? Like a pet? "Such as?"

"Books, the theatre. My writing."

A woman? "Have you ever been in love?" The words darted out before she could stop them. She snapped her mouth shut with a click of her teeth. Now where had that notion come from? She had no reason to ask such a personal question.

His gaze brushed over her, slow and gentle with a whisper of heat. No ice filled her veins. No panic fluttered in her breast. Just a soft, pleasing warmth swelled inside her.

Jack might be educated like Bart. Might have the gift of gab like him. Yet instead of repulsion, he filled her with a sweet, tender yearning.

He opened his mouth as if to answer her question, but the bark of gunfire cut him off. The noise rattled the windows and sent her heart hurtling against her ribs.

Jack slammed his glass onto the sideboard. "Stay here," he warned, before sprinting out the door and down the steps, leaving her alone and defenseless and aching for his answer.

Chapter Six

Fifty-one. Fifty-two...

She stilled her brushing. What good would a hundred strokes do? She'd have shiny locks, but those green eyes in the mirror's reflection would still look the same. Haunted. Lifeless. Cheeks, once rosy with life, were pale and sunken. Papa had called her his little beauty. If he could see her now, would he make the same claim?

She shifted uneasily on the bench. Would any man think her pretty? Would Jack? She'd often dreamed of finding a man who would look beyond her flaws and love her for herself. Could Jack be such a man? Was he even capable of love? He never had the chance to reply to her question before dashing out the door. Now that some time had passed, she wasn't so sure she wanted to hear his answer. She couldn't handle any more disappointments.

Lamplight winked on the locket nestled between her breasts. Lance had given her the necklace one Christmas. Threaded onto a thin gold chain, it held her brother's picture and reminded her why she was here. She tightened her grip on the brush handle. She couldn't waste time on foolish notions. Lance and Jeb needed her. Her needs, her desires, would have to wait.

A flash of lightning lit the bedroom, followed instantly by the boom of thunder. Out of habit, she doused the lamp. Papa could easily calm rebellious slaves. He could beard the Lawrences in their den and come out unscathed. But he couldn't deal with thunderstorms. They terrified him. Whenever one approached, he made everyone sit in the darkened parlor, no talking, no playing. Noise and light drew the storm, he'd said. Odd reaction for a book-learned man. Belle told them as a child, he'd been knocked from an apple tree by a bolt from heaven. One minute he'd been swinging from a branch. The next, he was lying flat on the ground, looking up at the sky, the breath knocked from him. Reckon something that horrifying would put the fear into anyone.

The creak of door hinges rasped into her thoughts.

She froze as the chilling image of Calhoun, red-faced and stomping out of the mess hall, rose in her mind. She set down her brush and reached for the lamp, a sturdier weapon should she need it.

"J-Jack? Is that you?"

"Yes. I'm sorry if I frightened you. I should've called out." The door clicked shut. "I thought you'd be asleep by now and didn't want to wake you."

She relaxed her grip on the lamp. "I was too worried about those gunshots to sleep."

"There's nothing to worry about. Everything's fine. Go on to bed. I'll make a pallet here in the living room to sleep on."

Not just yet, Mister Dash-out-the-door Porter. She crossed to the open doorway. He stood near the settee, his attention focused on unbuttoning his shirt. She recalled his nakedness when she'd held him at knife point. Sleek muscles flexing beneath smooth skin. Dark hair dotting his broad chest. Her stomach did an odd little flip, and she pressed a hand to calm it.

She must've made a noise because he halted his task and looked up, his intense gaze finding her in the doorway. Heat surged up her neck and into her ears at being caught staring.

"The gunfire..." She licked dry lips. "What did you find out?"

"Guards shot and killed a prisoner."

A breath hitched in her throat. "Dear God. Was it..?"

"No, it wasn't your brother. Just some unfortunate soul caught outside his tent, looking to relieve himself but found a bullet instead."

"I'm sorry for the prisoner. But..." She clasped her locket, comforted by the warm smoothness. "I just don't know what I'd do if anything happened to Lance."

"I have no doubt you'd survive. Takes a strong woman to face what you have and not knuckle under."

Praise or slur? With Porter, one never knew. "I just do what I have to."

"And that's why you'll land on your feet. But there's no reason speculating about what you'll do without Lance. He's fine. I'm sure of it."

He fell oddly silent and sank with a groan onto the settee. His face and shoulders sagged. Exhaustion had clearly overtaken him. After a brief pause, he bent, unlaced and tugged off a boot, and began rubbing his arch.

Rooted in place, she stared at his sock-clad foot. In the evenings after dinner, she'd massaged the aches from Papa's overworked feet. She imagined herself sitting beside Jack, his leg draped across her lap, her fingers working the kinks from his toes and slender arches. Such an ordinary task, and yet her insides burned with rare heat.

His other boot thudded to the floor, and she jumped.

"Is there something else you wanted?" he asked. "To continue our discussion from earlier perhaps?"

And have to explain why she'd asked such a

personal question? *Best to let sleeping dogs lie,* Papa would say. "I think you've done enough soul baring for one night."

"Why don't you go on to bed then? Get some sleep. You must be exhausted after such a long day." He grimaced and stretched out his arms. "I know I am."

"Y-yes, I should get to bed." She gripped the edge of the doorjamb for support since her wobbly knees appeared loath to hold her up. "I'll need to be good and rested if I'm to get anything useful out of the guards."

"Get anything—" He shot to his feet, mouth pulled into a fierce frown. "You're not going to question the guards."

"Why not?"

"Because I am."

"Hmmph. I can cozy up to them just as easily as you can." She ran a suggestive hand over her hip. "Better, even."

"Absolutely not." He padded toward her, his unbuttoned shirt billowing open and baring more of his sleek abdomen. "It's best if I do the questioning. You don't have the experience."

She forced her focus upward. "I'm just as capable as you."

"Remember your reaction to Calhoun in the officers' mess?" His gaze slid to her lips. "Lovely though your mouth may be, it has an unruly tendency to brim over."

He thought her mouth was lovely? His wasn't so bad either. Pale and slightly pink, like the near-ripe innards of a watermelon. Would they taste as juicy and sweet?

"Go to bed, Kitty. I'll do my best to find out whatever I can about your brother. I promise." He leaned closer, those enticing lips mere inches from hers. "You *can* trust me."

Trust him? She couldn't even trust herself. All she could think about was his mouth on hers. "I-I want to trust you."

"Then do it." He straightened and moved back a step as though proving his word. "It'll make life easier...for both of us."

Easier. Somehow that just didn't seem likely. "You'll find out anything you can about Lance? And Jeb, too. I want to know how he's faring."

"I'll see to both of them."

"Their lives are in your hands, Jack. Please don't let us down."

"I promise I won't." He cupped her elbow, his voice softening. "Get some rest. You've had a difficult few days."

She stared at his fingers curled around her arm. So gentle and reassuring. She ached to find out if there was more to a man's attentions than the pain Bart had shown her. Something inside her whispered that Jack would be far gentler. But she couldn't take the chance that she might be wrong.

"Don't make me regret trusting you." She gave him one last pointed look and then fled for the safety of the bedroom.

Her hands trembled as she shoved the door closed and shot home the bolt. To lock him out, or herself in?

Never before had she felt such a forceful attraction. If only they'd met under different circumstances, before the War, before Bart. Perhaps then she could explore the sensations he created in her. Discover if she could trust Jackson Porter with her heart.

****

Jack stopped on the parapet overlooking the prison yard below. Row after row of Sibley tents stretched along dirt lanes that were ditched on either side. Slimy water filled the trenches, no doubt adding to the nasty smell drifting upward. Yet the condition of the inhabitants, not the odors, made his stomach revolt.

Thousands of men packed the enclosure, their ragged clothes hanging like tattered sails from gaunt frames. Some shuffled about; others sat in motionless heaps with clouds of flies swarming around them.

Fury raced through him. How could such treatment be condoned? Sure they were enemy soldiers, but they deserved to be treated like human beings, not pigs in a sty.

He called on the impartial journalist inside him. He had a job to do, and taking his anger out on his escort would gain him little ground. He forced an even tone. "That's quite a sizeable assembly of prisoners, Lieutenant. Looks like more than the stockade was designed to hold."

"We do what we can. Army keeps sending 'em regardless of our complaints."

"Any trouble keeping them in line?"

"Not at all." Whitlock patted the pistol strapped to his waist. "A well-placed bullet stops any riot in its tracks, whether they cross the dead line or not."

"Dead line?"

"See that boundary 'bout three feet from the base of the walls? Any prisoner who steps over it is shot. No warning. No questions." The officer hooked a thumb over his belt. "But those are rare instances. Most stay in their tents like they're supposed to. Trips to the cookhouses and the water closets are about all the stirring they manage."

"How often do they eat?"

The lieutenant pointed to the larger tents set at the end of each row. "Food is prepared in the cookhouses twice a day. That's the most we can handle with so many prisoners."

"What are they served?"

"Bread and a small portion of beef or pork in the morning. Soup in the evenings."

"And the quality?"

"As good as the government contractors can provide during times of war."

From the looks of the prisoners, not very good. He inclined his head toward a collection of buildings and tents set off from the rest. "What are those for?"

"The largest is the prison hospital. That sectioned-off area is the Officer's Pen. Commissioned officers are confined there away from the lower ranks."

"Out of courtesy, or to maintain order?"

The lieutenant shrugged. "A little of both, I suppose."

He jotted a note regarding the separation of the ranks and looked up. "Any fraternizing allowed with the guards?"

"Even if fraternizing were allowed, it wouldn't happen. Most of our guards are Negroes, and as you can imagine, they don't take to the Reb prisoners."

"I can well imagine." Gripes, even if he located Corporal Carleton, Kitty would have a hell of a time getting him out, bribery or not.

Whitlock gestured at the ladder. "Let's continue our tour inside. You can have a look at the hospital ward."

He followed the officer down the ladder, through the main gate, and into the bowels of the prison camp. The massive walls trapped the heat and gagging stench in a stagnant cloak. He breathed through his mouth, hoping his lunch would stay put. The last thing he needed was to show weakness. He knew from experience the soldiers considered any man who plied pen instead of pistol to be weak. They'd most likely even taken bets on when he'd puke. Remaining strong would gain their respect—and their cooperation.

The compound was surprisingly quiet. Only a low hum rode the air, interrupted by an occasional bark from the guards. Mosquitoes and flies hovered around the pools of stagnant ditch water. Though he'd only been inside for a few minutes, his innards still bunched. He couldn't imagine spending days on end confined in such a hell-hole.

"You were at Chancellorsville."

A statement, not a question. He swatted at a pesky mosquito, no less bothersome than where the lieutenant's conversation was headed. "I reported on the battle, yes."

"You did more than report on it, sir."

Memories surfaced of that clash nearly a year ago, the dense forest, the drifting clouds of gun smoke, and the panic. Chaos magnified by the undisciplined retreat of the Eleventh Corps as the Confederates launched an unexpected attack on the Union right flank. All caught up in the bedlam were forced to retreat, including him.

"I had to move back to safer ground along with the soldiers," he finally said.

"Begging your pardon, sir, but you *led* a confused platoon to safer ground after their commanding officer was killed." Whitlock's tone radiated with admiration and respect.

He remained silent. He'd only done what any other terrified human would do. Survive. If the soldiers saw fit to follow him, that was their business.

"My brother was one of those soldiers you saved," Whitlock added. "Newspaperman or not, I owe you a debt of gratitude."

He pretended to write a notation in his notepad. Let the lieutenant think what he would. Perhaps he could profit from the officer's misguided appreciation.

As they navigated the city of tents, vacant eyes

flicked in their direction, then looked away. Defeat lined the emaciated faces. What suffering they endured. Little food. Poor conditions. And even poorer clothing. The winter months would be pure torture in such rags.

He jumped over a slime-filled trench and poked his head through an open tent flap. Nearly a dozen prisoners packed the sweltering enclosure. Some sat on thin, ragged blankets while others had no such luxury and reclined on the bare ground. All were covered with dirt and filth. And stunk. His stomach, once again, rebelled at the stench. He scrubbed a hand over his mouth to keep from retching and backed out.

"They don't appear to be very well supplied, Lieutenant," he said once his feet and stomach were back on firm ground.

"We do the best we can with what we're given."

"Major Brady mentioned the families often send money or goods."

"Some do, yes." Whitlock motioned to several buildings situated near the hospital tents. "All packages sent to the prisoners are received and stored there. Would you like to have a look?"

"Yes, I would." His blood began to stir. Finally, an opportunity to see what dwelled beneath the soiled surface.

As they entered the plain, wood-plank building, a soldier seated behind the desk scrambled to his feet and snapped to attention as did the private standing beside him.

"At ease, men," Whitlock commanded. "Sergeant, this is Jackson Porter, journalist for *The New York Herald*. He's here to gather information for an article about Camp Hoffman. Answer any questions he may have."

The Sergeant dropped his hand to his side. "Perhaps Private Duncan could assist him, sir? I have an urgent matter I need to discuss with you."

"Very well. We'll be just outside if you need anything, Mr. Porter."

As the two men disappeared through the door, Jack crossed to the desk, greeting Private Duncan before pointing to a stack of journals. "What is kept in those?"

"Mostly prisoner transactions. Anything that comes in or goes out of this building gets recorded."

Just the information he was looking for. He tapped the ledger marked C-D-E. "May I?"

"Certainly, sir. You can look at all of them if you'd like."

"This one will do for now." He thumbed through the pages and found neatly written entries containing name, rank, and unit along with notations of items received. Even dollar amounts were listed.

"Everything goes in here?" He looked up, watching the soldier closely.

The corporal held his stare. "Yes, sir. Everything."

Either the soldier was a practiced liar, or he was telling the truth. He returned his attention to the journal, flipping through more pages. No entry for Lance Carleton. Not that he expected to find the boy's name listed. Kitty had sent herself instead of money or goods.

Lieutenant Whitlock filled the doorway. "If you're done here, Mr. Porter, we should be getting on with our tour."

He returned the journal to the desk, then followed Whitlock out of the supply building and into the nearby hospital ward. Though each end of the huge canvas tent had been propped open, the inside baked with a nasty cocktail of mid-afternoon heat, the sharp smell of antiseptic, and festering flesh.

Bile burned in his throat. He clenched his teeth,

pushing back the nausea and the memory of his own hospital stay after the loss of his eye. He would not give in. He'd promised to find out anything he could on Lance and Jeb, and by God, he would.

His stomach contained, he continued onward. Cots occupied by heavily bandaged patients lined either side of a center aisle. He stopped at the foot of one bed, the dark-skinned occupant clearly out of place among the sea of white prisoners. Odd how some slaves fled captivity, while others fought by their master's sides against the very army sent to liberate them.

The Negro lay on his stomach, head turned to the side on the thin mattress. His eyes were closed, but his sleep was fitful. Long legs jerked beneath the bed sheets as though he were running a footrace. Thick, white bandages swathed his bare upper torso.

Took a bullet in the back. Could this be Kitty's companion? He pointed his pencil at the patient. "What unit was this one with?"

Whitlock shook his head. "None that we know of. He was shot while fleeing from a Yankee Patrol about twelve miles north of here."

"Why was he running?" He pointed to the white scars fanning out from beneath the bandaging. "Looks like he might've been a slave."

"We're not sure what he was up to. He was in the company of a woman. A possible rebel spy." Whitlock prodded the Negro's foot, then frowned when he got no response. "He hasn't come 'round long enough for us to get any answers. Appears the fever's got him for now."

"And the woman?"

"Still looking for her."

"Major Brady mentioned you were searching for a female spy..." He flipped through his notepad, pretending to search his notes. "A Miss Lou Carleton?"

"Yes, that's the one. We had a Corporal Lance Carleton on the prison roster. This woman may just be a hysterical relative hoping to contact him. If that's the case, she's wasting her time."

Damn, that didn't sound good. "Is the corporal dead?"

"No, at least he wasn't two weeks ago. He and four hundred other prisoners were shipped to Elmira to relieve the overcrowding here."

"Elmira, New York?"

"Yes. Odd thing about that..." Whitlock lifted his hat and mopped the sweat from his brow with a neckerchief before continuing. "Just before the prisoners shipped out, the Major received a telegram from the Elmira Provost requesting we include Corporal Carleton in the shipment."

"Why was that odd?"

"Our initial instructions were to send officers first. Strange that the Provost would specifically request a corporal."

He nodded. *Strange, indeed.*

****

A salty tang rode the sun-warmed air. Gulls circled overhead, their shrill screeches melding with the crash of waves on the shore. A solitary figure ambled at the water's edge. One hand cupped her wind-whipped skirts; the other was clamped atop her straw bonnet. She paused and bent to reach for something in the sand.

She was calm now, but what would happen once he told her about Lance? He'd seen her volatility before. Had a scab on his throat to prove it.

He gave the surroundings a quick check. They were alone, but he knew better than to assume no one watched. If she became overly distressed, she'd draw unwanted attention. How would he explain her hysteria to the soldiers?

She straightened and turned, eyes gleaming as

she caught sight of him. A smile dimpled her rosy cheeks, and his heart sank to his feet. She'd risked life and limb getting to Point Lookout and her brother. And now Lance was gone. The news would break her heart, and the thought of causing her pain nearly strangled him.

Damn. When had he started to care?

"Jack," she greeted as he drew closer. "How was your day at the prison? Good, I hope."

Good? Not quite the word he would use. "It was productive. I gathered a lot of useful information for my newspaper article."

"Like what?"

"Well, I learned the prisoners are fed twice a day. That's as much as the staff can manage with so many mouths to feed." The real issue was not how often, but what they were fed. Pig slops from what he saw at the cookhouses. But she didn't need to know that. It would only fuel her anxiety.

"I suppose twice a day is better than nothing."

"It certainly is." He fished in his pocket. He was stalling, he knew, but he just wasn't ready to face her disappointment just yet. "I brought you something."

"Oh? What?"

"It's a necklace of seashells. The prisoners make them to relieve the boredom and to barter for goods at the sutler's store."

She took the necklace and fingered the tiny shells, her expression awed as if he'd given her a crown jewel. "How pretty." Her lips tipped into the sunny smile he'd come to adore. "Thank you, Jack."

"You're welcome. So, what did you do with your day? Did you visit the lighthouse?"

"I did. Sure is an interesting place. The keeper, Miss Edwards, was very sweet. Invited me to have tea." She leaned closer and lowered her voice. "I think she might be a Reb sympathizer. She didn't speak too highly of the Yankees. Said the conditions inside the prison were horrible. Are they?"

So much for keeping her sheltered from the ugly details. "Unfortunately, with so many men crowded into one small plot, it's hard to maintain an ideal environment."

"By that, you mean, it's bad." Her smile faded. "What else did you find out?"

She meant regarding her brother and Jeb. Dread roosted in his gut. No more delaying. He had to deliver the news.

He stepped closer and folded her into his arms. She tensed at first, then thankfully relaxed against him, her warmth seeping through the linen of his shirt. She felt so good, so right, as though she belonged in his arms.

He wished to God she did.

"Is someone watching?" she whispered.

She assumed he was playacting as he'd done at the farmhouse. If only he were. "I have some news, and I want you to promise to stay calm."

She stiffened. "Is it...is Lance..?"

"Your brother's fine."

"Oh, God. Jeb—"

"It's not him either. He's still alive and being well cared for at the prison hospital."

She sagged against him. "What is it then?"

"Lance is alive, but he's not here."

"Not here?" She tipped her head back. Though the brim of her bonnet shaded her eyes, it didn't conceal the worry-lines creasing her skin. "Where is he?"

"He and four hundred other prisoners were sent to another prison to relieve the overcrowding here at Point Lookout."

Color drained from her face. She opened her mouth, but nothing came out. She swallowed, then squeaked out, "Wh-what other prison?"

"The one in Elmira, New York."

"Oh God, no." She wilted, slipping from his grasp and sinking to her knees in the wet sand. A wave swept in and soaked her skirts. Yet, she merely sat there, silent and still as a pylon, letting the sea lap at her as she stared out over the water.

He blinked in confusion. What the hell? He expected her to be upset, but not this hopeless despair. He squatted beside her. "What is it, Kitty? What's wrong?"

"I'm too late."

Her forlorn tone stabbed his gut. He reached out and pulled her into his arms. "Shhh..." he whispered. "You're not too late."

Her reply was a soft sob. Warm tears dampened his shirtfront. He massaged her back, now rigid as a brick wall. "Don't be upset. Lance is still alive."

"H-he might've been alive...when he left here. But..."

"Lance is a lot stronger than you think. Look how long he survived at this prison."

"It doesn't matter how strong he is. Once he reaches Elmira, he'll die...or wish he was dead." She collapsed against him, her thin body wracked by vicious shudders.

He gave her a gentle squeeze. "Lance is not going to die, Kitty. You have to think positively."

"You're wrong. Let me go, Jack." She pushed away from him and reached for the water. "Let the tide take me under."

He yanked her back into his arms, his heart keeling over at her words. "Don't talk like that."

"Lance is dead. I might as well be, too."

Where was that spitting she-cat he so admired? She should be ranting and raving, holding him at knifepoint and demanding he take her to Elmira. There was more to her story than she was letting on.

And it was high time he found out what.

Chapter Seven

Elmira. It was just as she feared all along. She hadn't reached Lance in time. She'd failed. And he would pay the price with his life.

"Everything's going to be fine, Kitty."

Fine? Nothing would ever be fine again. A sob caught in her throat.

Jack's embrace tightened, then he pushed to his feet with her cradled in his arms. She should protest, but God help her, she could barely draw a breath, much less speak. It was as if someone had tapped her veins and drained every ounce of strength from her body.

He carried her the short distance to their cottage, and once inside, lowered her onto the bed. She lay there, unable to move, limbs heavy as snow-heaped logs. How would she go on without Lance? He was her twin, her other half. They shared everything together. Life without him would be bleak and empty.

The sound of pouring water trickled into her misery, then a cool, damp cloth bathed her forehead. "Kitty, talk to me."

She closed her eyes, refusing to meet his gaze. She didn't deserve his kindness. She was a worthless piece of human flesh, just as Mr. Lawrence had said. Tears of guilt and despair spilled from beneath her lids.

Smooth cotton swabbed her cheek. "Don't cry, honey."

Don't cry. He might as well ask the ocean tides

to stop rising.

Bed ropes creaked as he sat beside her. "Look at me."

"C-can't."

"Yes, you can." He cupped her chin and tilted her head toward him. "Open your eyes, Kitty."

His harsh tone goaded her to obey. She met his steady gaze.

"Would you like something? A glass of water? Wine?"

"I don't need anything." *Not anymore.*

His mouth flattened into a thin line. "What's going on? Why are you so upset?"

She stuffed down a groan. Here it comes, the relentless digging, like a hound after a rabbit burrow.

"You were so determined to get here," he continued. "Yet, now that you've learned Lance was moved to another prison, you've given up. Why?"

"I'll never reach him in time."

"In time for what?"

"Not what. Who."

"Who then?"

She gave a half shrug. "It doesn't matter."

"It does matter, and we both know it."

He brushed a stray curl off her forehead. The tender words and sweet gesture brought on a fresh pool of tears.

"Tell me why you're so upset, Kitty."

How could she tell him? He'd despise her, just as she despised herself. Despite her efforts to keep him at arm's length, Jack Porter had crawled under her skin, making her itch for things she could never have. No man wanted a soiled woman for a wife.

Best to end things now, before parting became any harder.

She shoved upright and grabbed her cloak from the foot of the bed. She'd at least make one thing right. She tugged at the hem until the seam ripped and coins and paper dollars spilled onto the counterpane.

"There," she thrust past the thickness in her throat. "Take what I owe you. You upheld your end of our bargain."

"I don't want your money."

"Take it." She shoveled the pile toward him. "Take all of it. I don't need it any longer."

He caught her hand in a firm but gentle grip. "I said I don't want your money. What I want is to know why you're so upset about Lance getting sent to Elmira."

She traced a path with her eyes from the tips of his fingers to the point where his wrist disappeared into a stiff white cuff. Such strong hands. Unusual for a man who used his mind to do battle. And right now, he was intent on dueling with her.

"Let me help you, Kitty."

She drew in a ragged breath. God how she wanted his help. If he could find a way to save Lance, she'd be forever grateful. But that would mean telling him what she'd done, and she just couldn't do that. She'd rather face a Yankee firing squad than see his tenderness turn to scorn.

She scooted off the bed and crossed to the window. A retreat, yes. But she just didn't have any fight left.

Unfortunately, the fight followed her.

Boot heels clicked on the floorboards, then his strong hands cupped her shoulders. "I won't stop until you tell me what's going on."

She closed her eyes, resisting the urge to turn into his comforting embrace. It would be wrong to encourage him. "You have to let this go, Jack."

"I won't. I want to help you."

"Why?"

He remained silent as though pondering an

answer. "Because..." He spun her around until she faced him. "I promised I would help find your brother, and I always keep my promises. In order to do that, I need to know what's going on, no matter how difficult it is to talk about."

Difficult didn't even begin to describe it. She focused on his perfectly-tied black cotton cravat. He was a gentleman through and through. He'd treated her with nothing but kindness and respect since agreeing to play her husband. Maybe he'd understand. Maybe.

"I-I don't know where to begin."

"Start with why the Elmira commandant specifically requested your brother, a corporal, be sent to his prison when officers are sent first."

Her knees weakened. A tiny part of her hoped Lance's movement to another prison had been mere coincidence. Clearly, it wasn't. She pressed back against the window sash, using the hardness to shore up her sagging strength. "The Elmira commandant is Mrs. Lawrence's brother."

"And that's a concern because..?"

"Because, before leaving Spivey Point, the Lawrences swore they'd get even with my family."

"Get even for what?"

She swallowed hard. "For a wrong they felt had been done them."

"What kind of wrong?"

The worst sort. "They blame us for a death."

"Was your family responsible?"

Not her family. *Her.* Had she not trusted the sweet-talking Bart... She dug her fingernails into the sash. "It wasn't his fault."

"Whose?"

"Lance's. He was only trying to—" The words wedged in her throat, jammed like logs in a river.

"Trying to what? You can tell me."

"He...I..." She broke off with a strangled sob. "I-I

can't. It's just too awful."

He reached out and cupped her elbow. "You don't have go into the details. I get the general idea. Something happened at Spivey Point and your brother got blamed."

Blamed for something she caused. "When I learned of Lance's capture, I knew I had to get to him before the Lawrences did."

"How would they have known he was at Point Lookout?"

Heat rose in her veins, for the moment dousing the iciness of misery. "Because the polecats had spies in Richmond. I knew they'd soon be warned of Lance's whereabouts."

"How did you know there were hired agents?"

"They weren't hard to spot. Like goats trying to hide in a herd of sheep." A pang stabbed her. "Also because of Papa."

"I thought your father was dead."

"He was killed just after we moved to Richmond." Her throat burned with the venom of hatred. "A runaway carriage...according to the authorities."

"I take it from your tone you don't believe his death was accidental."

She turned back to the window. A blotch on one of the panes claimed her attention. She wiped at it with her finger. The smudge only got worse and spread further. Just like her life.

"Papa hated the city," she finally managed. "Said there were too many people crammed into one small space. Crossing the busy streets near made him ill. He'd walk an extra block just to find a safer route and wouldn't go across until it was all clear."

She rubbed harder at the stubborn spot, her finger squelching on the glass. Dratted dirt. She drew in a breath, then pushed it out on a long exhale. "His death was no accident."

In the window's reflection, she saw Jack kneading his chin, his expression thoughtful. It was one of the gestures she'd miss most once he was gone.

"Well then," he said. "We'll just have to go to Elmira and make sure your brother doesn't meet with the same fate, won't we?"

We? He wanted to continue with their charade after hearing all that? She stilled her rubbing. A glimmer of hope cut through her gloom. "What about your assignment?"

"I've found no evidence of corruption here at Point Lookout. Visiting another prison would be the next logical step."

Logical. She was anything but logical. And the people she loved most had gotten hurt because of it. Outside the window, a breeze rifled through the treetops, lifting the leaves and revealing the hospital looming in the distance.

"What about Jeb?" she said. "I can't just leave him here."

"I took care of your friend."

"You did? How?"

"I called in a favor. When he recovers, Jeb will be sent to my grandfather's home in Baltimore. I told Lieutenant Whitlock we could use an extra hand around the place."

"I thought Jeb was being held for questioning."

"No charges have been brought against him. Besides, after seeing the scars on his back, the lieutenant felt a little more lenient. Figured Jeb had been forced to carry out his master's orders and might be interested in the opportunity at freedom and a new life."

Though his voice held no censure, she stiffened anyway. "He didn't get those scars at Spivey Point. Father didn't hold with whipping. Jeb was already marked when he came to the estate."

He held up his hands. "Whoa. I didn't mean to imply he'd been mistreated. I only wanted to explain why he wasn't being detained. He'll be released as soon as he's strong enough to travel."

"Jeb's getting better, then? He'll live?"

"He's fighting a fever, but the doctors say a man as strong and healthy as he is should recover just fine. He'll be up and about in no time."

Her shoulders lifted as if a great weight had been removed from them. "Thank you for seeing to him, Jack. I owe you...again."

"So, there's nothing to stop you from going to Elmira, then."

Nothing but the fear of finding a corpse at the end of her journey.

****

A tunnel of black encroached on his vision. He gripped the solid deck rail, anchoring himself, feet braced against the rise and fall of the steamer. Bile burned in his throat. He fixed his gaze on the beacon of light flashing on the shoreline and focused on maintaining his composure.

He shouldn't have agreed to travel by water. It would only feed the nightmares. But Kitty had insisted. Said the boat would get them to Elmira quicker. Those pleading green eyes and pouting lips had been damn hard to resist.

"Jack?" A hand settled on his arm, pulling him back from the darkness. "Jack, are you ill?"

He drew in a steadying breath and wagged his head. "I'm fine."

"Good. I wasn't sure. You sounded a bit edgy when Major Brady suggested we take this steamer."

"I said I'm fine," he repeated, a bit harsher than he intended.

She frowned, then moved her hand to secure her bonnet from the whipping wind. "I want to thank you again for offering to take me to Elmira. I don't think I'd be able to manage on my own."

Not for the first time, he wondered at his sanity in making such an offer. This woman had careened into his orderly world, knocking it clean of its axis. All he could expect would be more of the same, more chaos, more nightmares, and more longing for something that could never be. She'd made her intentions quite clear. This husband and wife business was just that—business. Nothing more.

"I imagine you'd do well enough on your own," he said.

"Hmmph. Most likely I'd end up in some smelly Yankee prison." She skimmed a hand over the railing, one finger tap-tapping the wood. "My mouth has a tendency to spill over, if you recall."

He managed a smile. He could never forget a mouth like hers. All pink and pouty. He didn't have enough fingers to count the times he'd wanted to silence those lips with a kiss.

"I'm relying on you to help me curb my tongue," she added.

Oh, he could help her with that. In more ways than one. "So, you trust me, then?"

She regarded him with those fascinating cat-eyes, now coyly hidden beneath half-masted lids. "Perhaps."

"I'll take that as a yes. What changed your mind?"

She shrugged. "Just the way you saw to Jeb, providing Socks for him to travel to Baltimore and leaving a note hidden in your saddle bag explaining my situation so he wouldn't worry. You're not such a bad egg...for a Yankee." She treated him to a quick smile, then leaned over the rail, face turned into the wind.

He clamped his teeth around a shout of alarm. It took every ounce of self-control he possessed not to haul her back to the safety of the deck. He didn't want to startle her and send her tumbling into the water.

"Papa once described the ocean to us, but words just don't come close."

"Don't let the water fool you," he warned. "It can be just as dangerous as it is beautiful...just like a woman."

She thankfully leaned back to a safer perch. "Sounds like you've had experience with both, Jackson Porter."

"I have."

"Who is she?"

"Who?"

She shifted from foot to foot as if unsure of the path she had taken. Her gaze flicked around the ship until it rested on him. She squared herself and finally answered. "This beautiful, yet dangerous woman. You said you didn't have a wife. So who are you talking about? Someone from back home?"

No. You. He peered out over the water to avoid her probing stare. If she discovered his feelings for her, she'd surely head for the hills. "I rather not discuss my personal life."

"I see. Well, if your personal life is forbidden, how about the sea? Where have you traveled? Europe perhaps? That's where all the privileged folks seem to go."

"I prefer my feet on *terra firma.*"

"*Terra firma?*"

"Solid ground."

"Oh." Almond-shaped eyes glinted with amusement. "Not afraid of the water, are you?"

"Let's just say I have a great respect for it."

A sailor drew next to them and tossed a rope over the rail. The weighted end plummeted into the swirling water and disappeared. The seaman let the rope play out in his hands until it stopped moving. He turned to the quarterdeck and called out, "Ten fathoms."

Sweat dampened Jack's armpits. Ten fathoms of cold, dark water, just waiting to suck him under. Any composure he'd garnered while bantering with Kitty sank at the thought.

She leaned toward him and whispered, "What's that sailor doing?"

Jack swallowed past the barnacles in his throat. "Measuring the depth. Those knots on the rope are six feet apart. He counts how many disappear into the water until the weighted end hits the bottom. We're sailing over..." He swallowed again. "Sixty feet of water."

"Lordy, that's near as tall as the granddaddy oak at Spivey Point. Is that why you're uncomfortable around the ocean? Because of its size?"

"It's not just the size."

"What then?"

Might be best if she knew. The nightmares would come no matter what he did. "I had a bad experience with water when I was younger."

"Oh? What happened?"

"Remember I told you my parents had died in an accident?"

"Yes, I remember."

"It happened one night during a rainstorm." He gripped the railing, drawing strength from the solidness. "Our carriage skidded on the wet road and crashed over the side of a bridge. It toppled into the river below. My parents..."

The macabre tale caught like a sliver of bone in his throat. He spun around, away from the water, away from her observant gaze. Away from the deaths that haunted his nightmares.

"Go on," she urged, her sweet voice lapping at his raw nerves.

"I survived the accident. My parents didn't. I

had nightmares for a long time afterward."

"And being around water makes you feel like a long-tailed cat in a room full of rockers."

He shook his head at her amusing turn of phrase. "That sounds like something Grandfather would say."

"It's one of Nanny Belle's." She glanced skyward, then gave him an encouraging smile. "Don't worry. There's nary a cloud in sight. We should reach Baltimore quite safely."

"From your pretty lips to God's ears."

She ducked her head, pink staining her cheeks. "Thank you for sharing that about your parents. I know it wasn't easy."

"You're welcome. And thank you for being so understanding...about my weakness."

"We all have weaknesses, Jack."

And she was rapidly heading to the top of a long list of his.

Chapter Eight

Louisa grabbed for her glass before wine sloshed onto the spotless, linen tablecloth. Dratted ship rocked worse than the rickety hobby-horse she'd found in the barn loft at Spivey Point. At least in the barn, she'd been pitched into a pile of straw. Here, it'd be onto the unforgiving plank floor.

She eyed the open doorway. Jack had politely declined the captain's dinner invitation. Said he preferred to stay on the deck where he could see the shoreline. Seasickness, he called it. She knew better.

"You and Mr. Porter haven't been married very long, have you?"

Her dinner companion regarded her from across the table. A mass of gray curls that must've taken some maid hours to shape framed a plump, rosy-cheeked face. Pearls decorated her ears and neck. Congressmen, it appeared, made good money.

"Um...no, ma'am, we haven't," she answered. "Just three weeks."

Mrs. Clark gave a knowing smile. "It shows."

Drat. What had she seen? Possibly overheard? She forced a smile of her own. "What shows?"

"The secretive glances you give one another. As though you're not quite sure about the other but are excited about the prospect of learning more." She ladled up a jiggling spoonful of pudding. "Not to mention your distraction since dinner was served."

Embarrassing heat flamed up her neck. "I'm sorry. I didn't realize I was being inconsiderate."

"No need to apologize. I was once newlywed

myself."

Louisa relaxed, reassured by the woman's shrewd yet warm expression. "And now?"

"Now, according to Arthur, I'm an old married hen who knows her husband's mind better than he does."

"And tells him so at every opportunity," added the man seated beside her.

Louisa hid her amusement behind her wine glass. That was the type of marriage she wanted. Comfortable. Respectful. Full of good humor.

"Are you staying long in Baltimore, Mrs. Porter?" asked the congressman.

She shook her head. "I wish we could. I'd love to visit the city. But we need to catch the next available train to New York." Not quite the truth, but close enough.

The captain cleared his throat. "I'm sorry to be the bearer of bad news, Mrs. Porter. But Confederate raiders destroyed the trestles north of town last week. I doubt you'll find any trains heading for New York any time soon."

Her heart plummeted along with the ship. If it wasn't for bad luck, she'd have none.

Mrs. Clark, her wide brow creased with a scowl, wagged her spoon in the air like a general wielding his baton. "This close to Washington, you'd think the Army could prevent such attacks."

While the captain and Congressman Clark nodded in agreement, Louisa merely dabbed at the wine that had sloshed onto her hand. Though she cheered Confederate victories, getting to Lance was much more important. If only the Rebs had postponed their raid for another week. Then she'd be well on her way to Elmira and not facing a frustrating wait in a city chock-full of Yankees.

She set her napkin on the table and rose. Her appetite, along with her enthusiasm, had fled.

"Thank you for dinner, Captain. The food was delicious." She forced a wan smile. "But I'm afraid I may be suffering the same difficulty with the sea as my husband. Perhaps a stroll on the deck will help. If you'll excuse me?"

Both men pushed to their feet, nodding and wishing her a quick recovery. She gave her good-byes and hurried out of the stuffy stateroom. Once in the corridor, she pressed a hand to her throbbing temple. Her ill-health was more real than contrived. Concentrating on every word, every movement, so she appeared a well-bred lady had taken its toll. A good dose of fresh air should help. And so should Jack. She could let her guard down around him. Speak and act without pretense. He was truly the perfect husband.

Her step faltered, and she nearly tripped. *Husband.* She never thought she'd call any man that after what Bart had done—much less find the word slipping so easily off her tongue.

As she pushed through the doors and onto the deck, a gust snapped at her skirts, and she reached to tame them. She'd better do the same with her silly thoughts. To consider more of her relationship with Jack would be pure folly.

All around her, sailors skipped in and out of the flickering lantern light. The weather had turned since she'd gone down to dinner. It was colder and much windier. The boat dipped and pitched, making walking an effort. Not a problem for the able seamen going about their duties. But what about for a man deathly afraid of the water?

She squinted into the gloom. "Jack?"

Only the wind whipping through the rigging answered her.

"Jack, are you out here?"

Still nothing. Perhaps he'd gone to their cabin. As she turned to leave, a faint moan rose over the creak of the ship.

On the other side of a stack of crates, she found him propped against a barrel, necktie unraveled, jacket and shirt unbuttoned, his hat planted atop a bent knee. Normally slicked-back locks stood at odd angles from his scalp. One hand gripped a half-empty bottle of whiskey; the other was fisted around the thick shaft of a nearby anchor.

"Land-sakes, Jack. What are you doing?"

He looked up, blinked, then supplied her with a lopsided smile. "G'evening, Kitty." He hefted the whiskey bottle into the air. "Having a drink. Care t' join me? Nish Scottish malt."

Her heart sank. She'd done that to him. Her insistence that they travel by ship had forced him to turn to hard spirits in order to deal with being on the water. It was up to her to right that wrong.

She bent and captured his arm. "Come, Jack. Let's get you to our cabin."

"Can't."

"Sure you can. Just stand up. Then you can lean on me while we walk."

He wagged his head. "Can't leave...need to shtay here. Safer."

Whiskey fumes assailed her, and she wrinkled her nose. "Phew. You smell worse than a brewery. After all that liquor clouding your head, I doubt you'll even notice where you're sleeping."

"I'll notish." He tipped to one side, barely catching himself from plunging head-first onto the deck.

She clucked softly and hauled on his arm. "You can't stay out here corned as you are. The boat's rocking too hard. What if you roll into the water?"

He glanced at the railing and shuddered.

"Please, Jack. For me?"

His bleary gaze returned to her, his expression softening. "Do anything for you, Kitty." He licked his lips. "But the dreams...bad..."

"You told me about the nightmares. No need to worry. I'll be right there with you."

He cocked an eyebrow. "In bed?"

Scoundrel. "No. But close by." She plucked his hat off his knee and plopped it on his head. "Come on now. Be a good boy and stand up."

He heaved a resigned sigh and pushed to his feet. Whiskey sloshed inside the bottle as he fought to right himself. A soft curse spilled from his lips. He was definitely not a seaman. And for sure, not a practiced drunkard.

"Here." She ducked under his arm. "Lean on me."

He latched onto her shoulders and slouched against her, his warmth searing through the thin muslin of her dress. Her insides nearly capsized. She braced herself against her reaction and his ungainly weight and propelled them both forward.

After a few stumbles and a narrow miss with a swinging rope, they made it across the deck and through the door to the staterooms. She panted softly as she slipped from beneath his arm and propped him against the wall.

"Stay there while I unlock the door."

He merely grunted and leaned his head back, eyes closed, lips thinned into a taut line. Hmmph. If he thought this was bad, wait 'til morning when his head and belly staged a nasty revolt. A stolen jaunt into Mr. Lawrence's corn mash had taught her that lesson quite well.

She unlocked the door and pushed it open. Before she could reach for him, he lurched forward and stumbled inside, careening across the floor and collapsing with a groan onto the shelf bed.

Bug-headed man. She closed the door, then went up on tip-toe to turn up the lantern hanging overhead. Golden light flooded the small cabin.

Barely enough room existed in which to turn around. No windows. Only one door. Her mouth went dry. Just like the Spivey Point tack room.

Blackness began to encroach on her vision. A shadowy image formed in the corner, slowly growing from mist to a solid shape. Ice filled her veins. She couldn't move. Could hardly draw breath.

A noisy belch punched into the darkness. *Jack.*

She sucked in several deep gulps of air then gave her head a violent shake. Jack needed her. The images would not win. Not this time.

She squared herself and anchored her focus on the man lying on the bed. Lamplight brushed his features in a golden hue. No monster there. He was her archangel. Her breathing evened out. Warmth returned to her arms and legs. A grimace lined his face, and tender concern for him cast out the last trace of panic fluttering in her breast. She smiled. There. Done. No more bad memories. For tonight, at least.

Jack tipped the bottle as if to take another drink. *Oh no, mister.* She crossed to the cot and reached for the whiskey bottle.

"I think you've had enough of this."

He tightened his grip. "Need—"

"You don't need it. Now, let go."

He slackened his hold and muttered something about mulish females beneath his breath.

She wagged the bottle at him. "You knew that when you married me, Jackson Porter."

"Shoulda thought that through a little better."

Though said in jest, the barb stung. Would he really regret taking her as his real wife?

The ship listed to one side, and he moaned. She stashed the bottle into the dresser drawer, then turned back, concern for him overriding her smarting pride. "Is there anything I can get you?"

When his gaze flicked to the bureau, she added,

"besides whiskey."

"No," came his clipped reply.

"Some water, a wet cloth?"

"Nothing. I'm fine."

"You don't look fine to me. You're as white as that bed sheet." She moved to the end of the cot and began unlacing his shoes. "Let's make you a bit more comfortable."

He tried to lift his head but only managed a couple of inches before he plopped back to the pillow with a groan. "You don't have to...not neceshary."

"I want to. Besides, removing shoes is a cakewalk compared to some of the things I've done for Fannie."

She shucked off one brogan, then the other. Her fingers skimmed over his sock-clad heel, across his high arch and down his long, perfect toes. Pleasing warmth fired through her. Cakewalk, her rosy behind. She dropped his shoes to the floor and buried her hands in her skirts to hide the trembling.

"There, all done," she said. "Is there anything else I can do?"

"Maybe."

"Tell me. I'll be happy to do it." *As long as it doesn't involve touching you.*

"Read to me."

That caught her off-guard. Her pulse dipped. "R-Read to you?"

"I need...a distracshion."

"Jack, I—"

"Tennyson's poems. In my knapshack. Under the bed."

She glanced at the canvas bag poking from beneath the cot. He might as well ask her to fly to the moon. "I'm sorry...but I can't."

"Why not?"

"I wish to God I could, but I can't read to you."

He regarded her through a half-closed, bloodshot

eye. "Never learned?"

"I know how to read." She averted her gaze, humiliation burning her cheeks. "I'm just not any good at it. The words...I don't see them like everyone else does."

"What if you try to—"

"I'm sorry," she interrupted. "I truly want to help. But I can't."

"No matter." He groaned again and shifted on the cot, turning his back to her. "Just wake me shoon as we dock."

Her stomach churned around the fish stew, now soured and heavy. He would suffer more than necessary due to her no-account reading skills. She didn't deserve to be called his wife, either in charade, or in truth.

****

A thud vibrated him to wakefulness. He slowly surfaced and tested the light before submitting his vision to any glaring brightness. The lantern was thankfully turned low, gilding the cabin in a soft glow. He blinked several times then mentally took stock of his body.

No hovering images. No nausea. Just a slight pounding in his skull. The whiskey had worked. Or had some other charm kept the nightmares at bay?

"Rise and shine," came a perky Southern drawl.

He gathered cramped muscles and sat, snatching up and sliding on his eye patch as he moved. His gut knotted at the thought of her seeing him without it. She knew more about him than he'd ever revealed to anyone. And that scared the hell out of him.

Haloed by the faint light, she crossed the room, her sunny smile a welcome treat. He'd rather walk the plank than see revulsion or pity for him etched on her lovely face. She carried a wooden tray on which sat a water pitcher, a plate of biscuits, and a steaming cup of what he hoped was coffee.

"You're awake. Good." She set the tray on the nearby dresser. "I was starting to get worried."

The heady scent of coffee invaded his senses. Rich. Strong. Real coffee. Not the weak chicory he'd been forced to drink while traveling with General Pope's brigade in Northern Virginia.

He swung his legs over the side of the shelf bed and ran a hand through his hair. "How long was I out?"

"Once you gave in, you slept through the night, though most of it was fitful."

"You stayed with me?"

"Of course." She poured water from the pitcher into the wash basin. "I said I would, didn't I?"

He eyeballed the tiny bed. Surely he would've remembered that soft body pressed against his. "Where did you sleep?"

"On the floor. I made a pallet with the blanket."

So his memory hadn't failed him. "I'm sorry you were inconvenienced. You should have woken me. I would've traded places with you."

She shrugged. "I've slept on worse. Besides, once I started moving around, the cricks disappeared."

It was then he noticed the calm, no listing, no slap of waves on the hull. "Have we docked?"

"Nearly two hours ago."

Two hours ago. "Gripes, Kitty." He pushed off the bed and stood, feet braced against the swimming in his head. "Why did you let me sleep? We need to get ashore."

"Don't get all in a pucker. After last night, I figured you needed all the rest you could get." She cocked her head to the side and studied him. "How's your head, by the way? Any backwash from the whiskey?"

He wagged his head, then groaned as pain harpooned his skull. Whiskey might've been his friend last night, but this morning, it was his enemy.

"Coffee will help that," she said with a wifely cluck. "Biscuits for your belly, too."

He kept his head still. "There's no time for food. We need to get to the station and secure passage on the next northbound train."

She fussed with the towel and soap, moving them around on the dresser until she had them just so. She always set to arranging things when upset or agitated. Not a good omen.

Her pretty mouth dipped into a frown. "We won't be traveling anywhere today."

"What happened?"

"Captain Ahern sent one of his men to the train station for me. It appears all the northbound trains are delayed."

The knot in his gut tightened. "Delayed? For how long?"

She adjusted the china cup on the saucer, twirling it around until the rosebud embellishment faced outward. "For a few more days. At least until the Army repairs the trestles the Rebs torched last week."

Damnation. He sank back onto the cot and cupped his throbbing temple. "This is not good."

"No, it isn't. But there's not much we can do about it." She abandoned her tidying and hefted her satchel off the floor. "Eat. Wash and get dressed. I'll meet you on the deck."

She was one resilient lady. If it weren't for her help the night before, he might've ended up as fish food. "Kitty..."

She glanced over her shoulder. "Yes?"

"Thank you for last night. I appreciate everything you did for me."

Her gaze flitted to his knapsack tucked under the bed. Her frown deepened. "I didn't help all that much."

She hadn't been able to distract him by reading aloud. She couldn't read well. That explained her odd reaction to the leaflet the major had given her. What other secrets did she conceal?

"You helped more than you know."

"I'm glad." Her sunny smile returned. "That's what friends are for." She turned and headed for the door, back straight, hips swaying gently against the rock of the moored ship.

Heat swelled in his loins. He wanted her. Wanted to uncover every one of her fascinating secrets. Perhaps once all of this was over, they'd see if there could be more between them than just friendship.

Fifteen minutes later, he headed for the deck, bathed, dressed, and a bellyful of invigorating coffee. Funny how his *fake* wife knew exactly what he needed.

He found her standing near the rail with Captain Ahern, one gloved hand holding down her straw bonnet, the other restraining her skirts from the wind. Such an exquisite figure should be gowned in silk, frilly lace, and jewels. Things he couldn't afford to give her; not on his meager income.

She caught sight of him and smiled. "Here he is now."

The captain turned and gave him a nod. "Good morning, Mr. Porter. Recovered from your bout o' seasickness, I see."

Seasickness? More like brain sickness. "Yes, I have. Thank you for allowing me to stay aboard and recuperate, Captain."

The seaman flicked a dismissive hand. "It was no bother. We had wares to unload. Besides, your wife is as persuasive as she is beautiful."

He nodded in agreement. "That she is."

A pretty blush stained her cheeks, and she tucked a hand on his elbow. "We should be on our way, Dear. Get settled at your granddaddy's house before suppertime."

Damn. He'd hoped she wouldn't remember him telling her his grandfather lived in Baltimore. Too late now.

Ahern lifted a quizzical eyebrow. "You have family living here?"

"My grandfather, Elias Porter."

"Ah yes, Elias. Freighted many a shipment for the man. Fine businessman, but a wee bit set in his ways."

You can say that again. He bent and plucked Kitty's satchel off the deck. "Yes, well, as my wife said, we should be going. Thank you again for your help, Captain."

"Glad I could be of service. Enjoy your stay in Baltimore."

Not likely. He guided Kitty down the walkway to the pier below. Broad-shouldered stevedores swarmed like ants around an anthill, loading and unloading cargo while the ship captains looked on, barking occasional orders. A noisy group of disembarking passengers filed down a nearby ramp, adding to the commotion.

"What's that?" Kitty pointed an object shimmering in the distance. "A fortress of some kind?"

"That's Fort McHenry. Fifty years ago, soldiers stationed there held off an invading British fleet. Sir Francis Scott Key wrote *The Star Spangled Banner* while watching from the shore."

"Ah, the Yankee war song. Not so popular down south."

He chuckled and steered her around a stack of crates. "When I was younger, Grandfather would take me on trips to explore the garrison. Fascinating place." His chest tightened as the memories rushed in, the long discussions, the picnic lunches. What he wouldn't give to have those idyllic days back again.

"What powerful fun you must've had. Lance and I would've been happy as clams at high tide in such a place."

He smiled at her turn-of-phrase. How had such a firecracker become his anchor? He didn't want to think about what he'd do when she was gone. "It was *powerful fun*, as you say. I used to pretend I was bombarding the British ships with cannonballs just as my great-grandfather had done."

"Your great-granddaddy was a soldier?"

"He commanded one of the artillery regiments. Unfortunately, he was fatally struck by shrapnel. He held on long enough to lead his men to victory. Died as the last of the British ships left the harbor."

"You must be proud of him."

"I am. I only wish I could have known him."

"I know what you mean. I wish I could've—" She tightened her grip on his arm, eyes going wide as saucers. "Oh, no."

He glanced around to see what had alarmed her. A small contingent of soldiers blocked the entrance to the pier and were ordering the approaching crowd to line up, papers in hand.

"Relax," he warned softly. "The soldiers are no threat. I have transit papers."

She shook her head. "It's not the soldiers."

"What then?"

She turned her back to the quay. "Over by that small shed on the mainland. The well-dressed man standing in the doorway. He knows who I am."

Gripes. He swiveled his head slowly as though taking in the wharf. A tall, slender man stood shouldered against the doorjamb, a glowing cheroot clasped between his lips. Dark trousers and a tweed jacket indicated a more refined gentleman, though the wary eyes scanning the crowd were those of a street-wise ruffian.

"Who is he?"

Trembling fingers adjusted the laces of her bonnet. "We sailed together on the blockade runner crossing the Potomac. Said his name was Smith."

"Did he say what business he had in Maryland?"

"He didn't say much a'tall. We parted ways when we landed at Tall Timbers." She stilled her fidgeting, the color draining from her face. "Do you think he'll give me away?"

"If he's here for illicit reasons, revealing your identity will reveal his. I don't think you have anything to fear from him." However, an anonymous note sent to the city Provost should arrest any potential problems.

"I pray you're right."

"I'm sure of it. Just act normal. We'll soon have our papers checked and be on our way."

As they moved forward, another batch of debarking passengers surged around them. Someone bumped into him. An elbow jabbed his back. Before he could turn, the barest hint of a tug jostled his jacket.

His skin rippled in alarm.

He yanked his head around. Out of the corner of his eye, he spied a pint-sized figure disappearing behind a pile of crates.

No. Hell no. He swiped a frantic hand inside his pocket. Nothing. He'd been robbed. Picked clean as a chicken bone at a charity kitchen.

Damnation. Bad enough he had to swallow his pride and ask Elias to put them up for a few days. Now he'd have to ask for money, too.

Chapter Nine

Though the doors were cast wide open, little air circulated in the stuffy parlor. The drapes hung like wilted fronds at the windows, in desperate need of a drink. Like her. She fanned her sizzling skin. Perspiration trickled between her breasts and further dampened her sweat-soaked chemise. Lordy, even at dusk, the July heat was suffocating.

Outside the doors, a maze of rose bushes, hedges, and summer flowers lined a graveled path that disappeared into the gardens. What she wouldn't give to grab a pair of gloves and a hoe and dive into the little oasis. Let the hard work take her mind off the heat and Lance and Jeb and her attraction to Jack Porter.

Yet, she knew better. Her troubles would intrude. They always did.

Footfalls sounded behind her. Then came the rasp of a glass stopper and the tinkle of pouring liquid. But no conversation. Not that she expected any. Jack and his granddaddy remained silent, just as they had since she and Jack had arrived at the townhouse, and all through the awkward supper meal. The only time they'd spoken was when the two men closeted themselves in the study. To discuss her.

Jack had decided it would be best if they told his granddaddy the truth. The shrewd badger would see right through their sham. He might grumble about being put in the position of housing a fugitive, but he wouldn't turn her in. He hated the War almost as much as he hated the politicians who started it. Louisa gave a soft grunt. Grumble about housing her? From the heated voices that'd poured through the study door, it sounded more like the roar of an angry bear.

She turned to find Jack standing near the sideboard, one hand fisted around a glass of brandy. Jaw muscles twitched beneath smooth shaven skin as he stared beyond her into the courtyard. He was definitely out of sorts. His face twisted into a scowl, then with a jerk of his hand, he downed the drink and reached to pour more.

She frowned. Surely such carrying-on wasn't good. Especially after his excess the night before. The quarrelling appeared to be equally unhealthy for Jack's granddaddy. The older man's face had a gray pallor, as if he'd recently taken ill. Rattle-headed men.

A slender Negro woman appeared in the far doorway, her gray hair scraped into a bun at her nape. Shrewd brown eyes scanned the room, then settled on the elder Porter sitting in a chair near the hearth. "'Scuse me, Mister P. Will you be wantin' yer usual game of checkers this evenin', sir?"

Mr. Porter glanced at Jack, gave an ill-humored grunt, then shifted his attention to her. "What about you, Miss Carleton? Do you play checkers?" He mashed his lips into a thin line. "It'd be nice to have someone else to play with. Usually all I have is Sally." He grunted again. "And the blasted woman cheats."

Her chest tightened with a familiar tug. Checkers. She and Papa had spent many an evening bent over a game board he'd fashioned from a discarded plank of wood. He'd taught her all about strategy and reading people. She wished he was here now to give her some pointers. He'd know how to deal with stubborn, feuding men.

"I'd love to play, Mr. Porter." She fanned at her face. "However, I am feeling a little warm. Perhaps Jack and I can take a stroll through the garden first."

"Wonderful," the elderly man replied. "You go ahead. Sally and I will set up the board while you're gone."

One Porter taken care of. Now for the other. Jack's piercing gaze tunneled into her, making the summer heat feel almost tepid. He set down his empty glass and in four stiff strides, reached her side.

He gave a brisk wave at the doorway. "After you, Miss Carleton."

Though his tone was cordial, the underlying tension was thick as month-old molasses. She brushed past him. This wouldn't do. Wouldn't do at all.

Once outside on the terrace, she rounded on him, hands planted on her hips. "What has you so prickly, Jack? You've been acting like a caged animal since we arrived, glowering at everyone, pacing the floor."

"It's nothing."

"Nothing my...Is it me?"

"You?"

"Is my being here causing you and your granddaddy to be at odds?"

"Our quarrel goes back many years."

She cupped his arm in a soothing gesture. "Is there anything I can do to help?"

Muscle twitched beneath her fingertips. He glanced down at her hand, then over at the open doorway. His frown deepened. "There's nothing you can do. This is for Grandfather and me to sort out."

"But I'd like to help. I owe you for all you've done."

"You don't owe me anything." He swept her

hand off his arm and tugged her forward. "Let's continue with that stroll you so needed."

She dug in her heels, slowing his headlong dash. "Stroll, Jack. Not a footrace."

He said nothing, merely adjusted his pace and continued down the path. Though improper, she let him keep hold of her hand. Something told her he needed an anchor. Lord knew she'd relied on his strength often enough.

They rounded a bend in the path and came upon a life-sized statue of a priest with a bird perched on his shoulder. Saint Francis of Assisi, if she remembered correctly from her stolen moments in the Lawrence library.

"I didn't realize you were Catholic," she said.

"We're not. The statue came with the property. Grandfather took a liking to the priestly saint who condemned violence and war and decided to keep it." He guided her around the leaning figure. "Don't get too close." He pointed to the crumbling base. "As you can see, it needs repair and is quite unstable."

"I do hope you're able to repair it. It reminds me of the statues at *The Louvre*."

"*The Louvre*? I thought Maryland was the farthest east you'd been."

"It is. I saw drawings in a picture book. It amazes me how anyone can carve such tiny designs in stone." She trailed a finger over a pink hydrangea blossom. "I wouldn't have the patience."

"Hmmph. I have little patience with many things."

The pathway opened up onto a small clearing with a circle of stone pavers at its center. Rose bushes of varying colors and sizes surrounded the quad. It reminded her of Mrs. Lawrence and the Spivey Point gardens. Woe to anyone who, accidentally or not, damaged her prized blooms.

Jack released her hand and motioned to a

wooden bench tucked beneath a vine covered arbor. "Please, have a seat. We should be able to catch a bit of the breeze coming off the water."

She hesitated. Trouble always seemed to find her in confined spaces.

"Kitty?"

"Um...sure." She moved to the bench and sat on the edge, ready to spring up if the need arose.

A warm breeze played through the canes, sending a sweet flowery aroma wafting around her. She drew in a deep breath and relaxed. Any place that smelled this nice couldn't be but so bad.

Hands tucked behind his back, Jack strode to the edge of the clearing, paused to stare at the distant harbor, then stalked back, his boot heels grinding into the pavers.

Man was definitely rattle-headed. She patted the space beside her. "Won't you join me, Jack? Surely you must be plumb tuckered out from all that pacing."

He stopped in front of her, a wry smile tipping his lips. "Ever the concerned wife."

"I am concerned. But I'm not your wife."

"No, but you play the part well." He sat beside her, his thigh pressing intimately into her skirts. "Very well, I might add."

Ill-at-ease with his closeness but unwilling to add to his fluster by moving, she worked at smoothing an imaginary wrinkle in her gown. "As you said, I *play* the part. Pretending is easy, if you put your mind to it."

"But you go beyond the call of duty."

Lordy, was he aware of her oh-so-wifely attraction to him? She kept her focus on the folds of her skirt, so her eyes wouldn't betray her feelings. "How so?"

"For one, you helped me through my attack on the ship when you didn't have to."

"I only did what needed to be done."

"You could've gone to Captain Ahern and requested one of the sailors to look after me."

His tender tone pulled at her. She looked up, her pulse jumping as it always did when their gazes met. "You were out of your head with drink. What if you'd jabbered my real name by mistake? Besides, I wanted to help. I know what it's like to be frightened of something."

"What could scare a tough, little Reb like you?"

"You'd be surprised."

"This I have to hear."

Perhaps if she opened up, he'd do the same. Then she could discover the reason for the quarrel between him and his granddaddy and maybe help them get beyond it. She owed Jack that much for all he'd done for her.

"I used to be a very curious child. Went full-chisel at everything."

A teasing glint lit his eye. "*Used to?*"

"Do you want to hear my story or not?"

"Please, go on." He lifted his hands in surrender. "I promise to be quiet."

Hmmph, just like the sun promised not to shine. She gave him a pointed look, then continued. "Fannie had boasted of staying in the root cellar overnight, a place the house servants claimed to be haunted. I decided if prissy Fannie Lawrence could face a ghost, so could I. So, I mustered up my courage and went down that dark, rickety stairway."

She grimaced inwardly. Going into that cellar was a picnic compared to what she'd endured in the tack shed. "I almost turned back twice, but I wasn't about to let Fannie win. My knees were shaking, and I had to hold onto the stair railing just to stay on my feet."

"That frightening was it?"

She shook her head. "I'd never put much stock

in all those stories, but at that moment, in the dark, I believed every one of them. And admitting that the demons must be real, made everything that much worse. I scrambled for the exit, only to find someone, most likely that mean, ol' goat Fannie, had bolted the door."

He gave a soft cluck. "Poor little chick. Is that why you always seek the exits when you enter a room?"

Lordy, he didn't miss a thing. "I imagine it is," she said, unwilling to reveal the truth about her fear of confined spaces. "I had nightmares for weeks afterwards. Belle would sit by my bed and hold my hand until I fell asleep."

"Like you did for me."

"Having someone nearby comforted me. I could only assume it would help you, too."

"It did. More than you know."

He leaned toward her, and before she could stop him, he pressed his lips to hers. Gentle at first, then more demanding when she didn't resist. How could she resist? His kiss was like a pirate ship running a blockade. Swift and bold. Unstoppable.

Tingles sailed delightfully along her neck and down her spine. Her lips, having a mind of their own, parted. His tongue delved inside with a daring swipe. He tasted of tobacco and after-dinner brandy. Her head swam. Potent stuff, his kiss.

A bluejay's shrill squawk brought her back to port. She stiffened. What was she doing? Giving her desires free reign with Porter was the last thing she needed.

She gripped the edge of the bench, using it as leverage to drag her lips away. Something sharp jabbed her finger. She flinched but remained silent. Better a splinter than a broken heart.

"What's wrong, Kitty?"

She brushed the back of her hand over her lips,

trying to scrub away the last trace of his kiss. She feared it was a taste she'd never forget. "You don't want to do that, Jack."

"Why not?"

He was the grandson of a rich and powerful man—lived in a world where she, the daughter of a poor overseer, didn't belong. Besides, if he knew what Bart had done to her, she doubted he'd want to kiss her, much less allow her to stay in his granddaddy's dignified home.

He took her hand in his. "You can't deny it, Kitty. I can see it in your eyes. You want me as much as I want you."

"You shouldn't want me. I'm not who you think I am."

"Look at me."

She moored her gaze on the pearl buttons parading down his crisp, linen shirt. If she got another glimpse of those tantalizing lips, she'd be lost.

"Look at me, Kitty."

His tender plea dug into her resolve. She lifted her head, making sure her gaze avoided his mouth. A wiser choice, but not by much. So much fire burned in his one eye, she'd worry if he had both.

He plucked a rose petal from her hair. "I know exactly who you are. You're strong and fiercely loyal. You know what you want, and you're not afraid to go after it, no matter what the consequences."

He was oh-so-wrong about her not being afraid. She had a mile long yellow streak when it came to him. "Jack, don't do this."

"I've tried, but I just can't fight it any longer." He leaned toward her as if to kiss her again.

She pressed trembling fingers to his lips to stop him. "Don't. Please. Our trip to Elmira will be difficult enough. We don't need the added strain of foolish emotions."

"Foolish…" His expression hardened. "You still don't trust me, do you? After all we've been through."

"Jack—"

"Fine. I won't push my attentions on you again. Ever."

****

The stomp of boot heels trailed her into the parlor. She slowed as Jack brushed past her and headed for the sideboard. Little good their stroll did. He was just as puckered now as he had been before they'd gone outside. Maybe more.

"Mister P had to go upstairs, Miss Carleton," the housekeeper said from the other side of the room. "Said he'd be back shortly for your game."

"Thank you, Sally."

"How was your stroll?"

"The stroll was lovely." It was when they stopped strolling that the trouble started. "Beautiful evening. The rose garden—"

"Badly needs pruning." Jack snatched up the brandy decanter from the sideboard. "Seems to have gone to hell like a number of things around here. Old man too cheap to hire a gardener, I guess."

"Here now." Sally planted her hands on her hips. "Don't you go disrespectin' your grandfather that a'way, Master Jack."

"Just pointing out the obvious."

"Maybe you ought t' be pointin' your attention inward."

"And maybe I ought not to have come here at all."

"Hmmmph. Sounds like some folks could use somethin' to cool down a mite. I'll go make up some lemonade."

He yanked out the stopper and poured a generous dose into a glass. "I need something with more bite to it than lemonade."

Louisa shook her head. Sally was right. He

124

needed to cool down. Maybe some time alone would help. "Sally, I need your help with something. I'll just come along with you to the kitchen."

She followed the housekeeper down the hallway and into a brightly lit chamber. Copper pots and baskets dangled from a rack suspended over a work-roughened table bearing knife marks and stains, but scrubbed clean. A black cast iron stove sat in one corner of the room, a pine hutch the other. It reminded her of Spivey Point and the happier times she'd spent cooking with Belle. But the Porter kitchen did little to cheer her now.

"What was it you needed, Miss Carleton?"

She held up her bloodied hand. "I cut my finger. Will you bandage it for me?"

"'Course I will. Pull that chair up to the table and have a seat. We'll see to it."

She scooted the ladder-back chair across the floor and sat while Sally gathered a basin of water, clean cloths, and a small basket. A sweet smelling pie cooling in the center of the table had her mouth watering. "That pie sure smells good. Apple, isn't it?"

"Yes'm. Master Jack's favorite. He'd eat the whole tin by hisself if I let him."

"It's my favorite, too. Add a dollop of cream on top...mmm-mmm."

"Got a crock in the cellar. We'll have pie and cream after your checker game." Sally set her supplies on the table, then turned up the lantern wick. "Let's see that finger."

She extended her hand, and Sally dabbed at the dried blood with a wet cloth. Her dark hands were gentle, yet firm, just as Belle's had been during the many doctorings she'd performed on her wayward charge. Her heart twisted. How was Belle faring? Were her new employers treating her kindly? She gripped the edge of the seat with her other hand. One day, they'd all be back together, her and Jeb and Lance and Belle. She'd see that happen, or die trying.

"Are you treated well here, Sally?"

"Better than most, I s'pose. Mister P's more bark than bite." Her brow furrowed like a freshly plowed field. "Why you askin'?"

"Jack arranged for a friend of mine to come and work here once he's well enough. I just want to make sure Jeb won't be mistreated. He's no longer a slave, and I'd like to see him stay that way."

"Well enough? Is he ill?"

"He was shot while trying to help me get to my brother." She swallowed around the lump that had sprouted in her throat. "He's recovering at the Yankee prison hospital in Point Lookout."

Sally gave her hand a gentle squeeze. "Don't you worry none. I'll see to it your Jeb is looked after."

"Thank you, Sally. That means a lot." She released her grip on the chair seat. Until she could come back for him, Jeb would have a comfortable home with good, caring people. It was one less worry to plague her thoughts.

The housekeeper stilled her wiping. Her frown deepened. "Looks like there might be a small sliver of somethin' just 'neath the skin. How'd you pick up a splinter? You was s'posed to be walkin'."

"The bench. In the quad."

"Hmmm?"

"Jack suggested we sit and enjoy the bay breeze. I was sitting there..." *Hanging on for dear life as he leaned in, big and close and strong, to kiss me.* Heat rushed into her face. "I must've slid my hand across the wood."

Sally, shrewd as an old fox, studied her for a moment, apparently considering the truthfulness of this account. She gave the finger a squeeze, and a hiss of pain escaped Louisa's lips.

The housekeeper glanced up. "Hurts you, does

it?"

The splinter she could handle. What hurt was the pained look on Jack's face and knowing she'd caused it. Knowing she had no choice. Tears stung her eyes. "A little."

Sally fished around in her basket, setting out bandaging, a needle, and a small pair of forceps. She clamped down on Louisa's hand. "Here we go. Hold still while I work out that splinter."

Poker hot pain seared her finger at Sally's probing, and she clenched her teeth to keep from yelping. It was one thing to be doing the doctoring, quite another being doctored on.

"Somethin' gettin' under your skin can cause all sorts of grief," Sally muttered while working.

You can say that again. There wasn't a pair of forceps large enough to pry Jack from under her skin.

Sally cut her a sly glance. "Best to get it out in the open where it can heal."

Clever. Very clever. But she had no desire to talk about her feelings for Jack. It would only remind her of what she couldn't have. She took the wisest course and kept her mouth shuttered.

Sally released her hand. "There, splinter's out."

Finally. She flexed her fingers, working out the soreness. "Feels better already."

"Good. We'll put some salve on it, and it should mend just fine."

"Salve? What kind? Seems like my nanny had a concoction for every type of injury imaginable."

"I have a batch of chickweed mixed with rosemary oil and a bit of comfrey. Eases the pain and helps with the healing." She gathered up the basin. "Look in my basket and take out the jar marked chickweed while I dump this."

Louisa slid the basket closer and eyed the multi-colored jars nestled inside. *Tarnation.* Why couldn't the woman just ask for green or blue? Colors she could handle. She shifted the jars until the labels faced up. As always, the letters bunched and twisted. She squinted and tried to make sense of the words.

"Hard to read my chicken scratchin's, ain't it?" The housekeeper wiped her hands on a drying cloth. "It's the blue one."

Cheeks flaming, she hauled the blue jar from the basket and set it on the table. Nothing was more frustrating and embarrassing than not being able to read. "Where'd you learn about medicines?" she asked, steering the conversation to a safer topic.

"I worked for a doctor before hirin' on with Mister P. Helped with his patients along with doin' the cookin' and cleanin'." She dabbed salve on Louisa's finger. "Good thing I learned such things. Master Jack got into more scrapes as a young-un. I remember one time he cut his foot on a piece of broken glass. Took eight stitches. Poor fella was green for days after that."

Glass had sliced his foot back then. Today, she'd cut him. Had him thinking she still didn't trust him, because she was too spineless to tell him the truth.

"He's lucky to have you," she managed past the guilty lump in her throat.

"Somethin' more than this little bitty cut has you upset. You want to tell ol' Sally 'bout it?"

She shook her head. "It's nothing."

"You shouldn't let things fester. Not wounds of the body nor the soul. No good ever comes of it."

The familiar words tugged at her heartstrings. Belle had said the same thing while trying to coax her to talk about Bart Lawrence. Hadn't done any good back then. Wouldn't work now either.

Strained male voices carried from the hallway. She glanced at the open doorway, her heart near to breaking at the thought of Jack in distress.

"Is it Master Jack what has you upset?"

Drat. She'd best take better care with her emotions, else she faced more pointed, personal questions. "He's part of it."

"Don't take his crustiness to heart. He comes by it honest. Let him be for a bit. He'll be smilin' agin by mornin'." Sally tore off a strip of bandaging and wrapped it around the now seeping wound. "He's a good boy, Jack is." She laughed softly as she tied off a knot. "Good man, I reckon I should say. Hard to think of him that way sometimes, 'specially when he gets that mischievous look on his face."

She knew the look. That captivating boyish gleam that had sparked in his eye when Socks tossed her on her backside. The look that made her stomach do odd little flips.

"I can still picture him clear as sunlight the day he left for college," Sally added. "He was so proud and cock-sure of hisself. Gonna take on the world, that boy was."

Just like the young men in Richmond on enlistment day. All fired-up and ready to march off to war. To save the world. Or at least their little portion of it.

Sally wagged her head as she gathered up her medical supplies. "I remember the last time he left here. He was gonna take on the world then, too, only it weren't so good a time round here."

"When was that?"

"When Master Jack took his job writin' 'bout the War. Mister P won't at all happy about it. They had a terrible row afore Master Jack—" She cut off with a frown.

Uh-uh. You're not clamming up now. "Is that what has them quarrelling? Jack's newspaper job?"

"It's not mine to say. Done said too much now, and I doubt either of them gentlemen would 'preciate it." She reached out and patted Louisa's cheek.

129

"You're just too sweet and easy to talk to. I can see why Master Jack brung you here."

"He brung...uh...brought me here because I needed a place to stay."

"Mmm-hmm."

"Jack's just helping me find my brother. I'm sure he'd be as kindly to anyone in need."

"Uh-huh. Kind ain't but half of it, if I know that boy at all."

"I admit we've become friends..." She let her words die off. That sounded feeble even to her own ears, and if that raised gray eyebrow was any indication, Sally wasn't fooled either.

Before the housekeeper could question her further, Louisa swung the conversation back around. "It's a shame about those two. Jack and Mr. Porter, I mean. Such a waste of time being angry. If my granddaddy were alive, I'd want to spend every possible moment with him."

"Oh they spends time together. Every now and agin, Master Jack comes round an' stays for a day or so. I swear it's just so they can sit and stare daggers at each other. Men. Hmmph. Makes you wonder what the good Lord had in mind."

A dull thud sounded, like the shutting of a door deep in the house. Time for her to face the music.

Louisa rose to her feet. "I ought to be getting back to the parlor. Don't want to keep Mr. Porter waiting. Thank you for doctoring my finger."

"Just like Master Jack, I'm always glad to help a person in need. Enjoy your game, miss." She grinned, her smile wide and bright against her rich coffee-colored skin. "But you watch Mister P...he cheats."

Chapter Ten

Fool. What had possessed him to take his anger out on Kitty? She had trust issues. He knew that. A few days in his company wasn't going to allay her fears, no matter what trials they'd overcome together. She needed time to learn to trust him. Why was it he could control his emotions around everyone except those closest to him? He shifted in the desk chair, seeking a more comfortable position for his rear and his conscience. He'd make it up to her—somehow.

He returned his focus to his journal and the notes he'd penned earlier. *Lawrence vendetta against the Carleton's. Why? When? Who involved? Still on-going? What of their father's death? Was it questionable as Kitty believes?*

He tapped the pen against his lip, thinking, then jotted another notation. *Any connection to the Lawrence involved in shady dealings at Fort Delaware and Camp Douglas?* He had a hunch there was. The more he learned about the Carleton situation, the more certain he was his article about federal prisons was about to turn into a full-blown unveiling of government corruption.

The soft pad of footsteps echoed in the hall, then a familiar gowned figure filled the doorway. His blood heated as it always did at the sight of her.

Kitty entered the study, toting a tray. "I thought you might like some tea and pie. It's apple. Your favorite, so Sally says."

She was all the sweetness he needed. He wanted

to tell her but held the words on his tongue. Such a confession would only send her scurrying for the door.

He closed his journal and stood. "Apple *is* my favorite. But you didn't have to bring it to me."

"It's no problem. When you didn't come back to the parlor, I offered to carry some dessert to you."

"Sally could've brought it."

Her chuckle skimmed in pleasant waves over his skin. "She was busy riding herd on your granddaddy. He tried to light a cigar in her parlor, and she chased him into the garden."

"I see you figured that one out."

"Figured what out?"

"Who rules the roost around here."

"Oh...yes." She placed the tray on the desktop. "Those two are quite an interesting pair."

"That they are." He glanced at her hand and spied a bandage wrapped around her middle finger. "Did you hurt yourself?"

She crooked her swaddled finger and gave a wry smile. "Just a little scrape. Wish I could use it as an excuse for my poor checker playing."

"You didn't fare so well against Grandfather?"

"He won all three matches." One corner of her lovely mouth wilted. "Papa would be shamed. I'm normally pretty good at checkers."

"Odd. Grandfather usually lets his opponents win at least one game before he starts cheating." He'd engaged in enough matches with the old fox to know.

"I didn't notice any plucking going on. But then again, I was having a hard time concentrating."

"Oh?" Was she thinking about him? His thoughts certainly centered on her.

She tipped the pot and poured tea into a cup. "Is your granddaddy a lawyer by any chance?"

"No. He runs a shipping firm. Why?"

"Man asks more questions than a magistrate. Figured he had to be a lawyer or something."

"Inquisitive was he?"

"If by that you mean he poked his nose where it didn't belong, then yes, he was inquisitive. He thinks I forced you into helping me. As if I can control what you do or don't do." She lifted the sugar bowl lid. "Sugar? Milk?"

"Neither, thank you. I'm sorry you were subjected to his cross-examination. He doesn't trust my judgment. Never has. Tries to run my life, and usually causes more problems than he solves."

"Well, he wants to keep me away from you and your money. I got that warning, loud and clear."

"Now that's a laugh." Her expression fell, and he held up his hand. "Not you. The money. I don't have any. I'm poor as a church mouse. At least until I get this prison article written and submitted."

She glanced around the room at the floor-to-ceiling bookcases lined with hundreds of leather-bound books. One lacy eyebrow lifted. "Poor as a church mouse, huh?"

"I don't own any of this." He gave a cynical grunt. "Or the money to have such luxuries. Old man cut off my allowance as soon as I accepted a job with *The Herald*."

"Why'd he do that?"

Gripes. Why was talking to her so easy? He'd confided more to her than he'd spoken of in years. Buying time, he gathered his pie and tea. "Let's sit on the settee where we'll be more comfortable."

She glanced at his closed journal. "I didn't mean to take you away from your work."

You are my work, in more ways than one. "I'm finished for now. Pour yourself a cup of tea and join me."

She wagged her head. "I had lemonade and pie earlier. I'm full up."

"Then just sit for a while. I'd appreciate the company."

"If that's what you want."

What he wanted was her lips on his, soft and pliable and showing him how much she desired him. But that wasn't going to happen. She'd made her feelings quite plain.

He sat on the sofa, and she settled in the chair across from him. She treated him to a sweet smile. "So, we were talking about your granddaddy."

"Were we?" He placed his teacup on the end table, then balancing the pie plate on one knee, forked up a healthy helping, stalling for time as he chewed. How much about his quarrel with Grandfather did he really want to divulge? He didn't want to worry her unnecessarily.

He poked at the flaky piecrust dripping with cream. "This is good. Haven't had pie topped with cream in a long time."

"It was my suggestion."

"And a good suggestion it was." He forked up another bite and moaned in contentment. His two favorite pleasures in one night. Apple pie and Kitty Carleton. What could be better?

"About your granddaddy..."

She wasn't going to give up. "Yes..?"

"Why'd he cut off your allowance?"

Maybe she ought to know the particulars, especially if the old man refused his request for a loan and caused further delays to their trip. "Just after the War started, I had an offer from *The Herald* to write first-hand about the fighting. It was a golden opportunity...a chance to get my name known outside of Baltimore."

"I wondered why you chose to be a newspaperman," she waved a hand, "when you could've enjoyed the easy life."

"I wanted to be recognized on my own merit, not

134

as Elias Porter's grandson. After living under his shadow for most of my life, I was ready to become my own man, a successful and sought-after journalist."

He finished off the last bite of pie and swapped the empty plate for the teacup. A few sips of tea soothed a throat gone dry as a summer field. He usually kept his deepest desires well-guarded. To speak them aloud felt like he was stripping himself naked.

"At the time," he continued. "I thought traveling with the Army would be a grand adventure."

"That's understandable."

"Not to Grandfather. It angered him that I wanted to leave a steady, safe job at the local paper. Said traveling with the Army was too dangerous. We argued. He finally told me to go and write about the War. But don't expect him to pay for it." Even now, his blood bubbled at his grandsire's high-handedness.

"Seems to me, he was worried about you." She rose and gathered his plate. "Would you like more tea?"

"No, that was plenty, thank you."

She crossed to the desk and placed the dish on the tray. Instead of returning, she wandered past the bookcases, trailing a finger along the spines as she walked. "You know, as much as your granddaddy's prying annoyed me, I understood he was only looking out for your best interests."

"Let's hope that *looking out for* includes giving me the loan I asked for."

"Loan?"

"To get us to Elmira. Having my wallet stolen has put me short on funds."

She skirted the table and returned to the settee. "That must've hurt."

"What?"

135

"Swallowing that massive pride of yours to ask for help." She folded herself beside him and rested a hand on his forearm. "Don't worry. I suspect he'd give you anything you ask for. It's obvious how much he cares about you."

Who was reassuring whom? "He sure has a strange way of showing it."

"Some folks aren't good at saying how they feel."

"Unlike you."

Pink stained her cheeks, and she ducked her head. "I'm sorry if I caused you any pain earlier in the garden. It wasn't my intention."

"No. No. I'm the one who should be apologizing." He set the tea cup on the end table, then shifted to get a better view around his nuisance of an eye. "From the beginning, you made it clear our relationship would be business only. I crossed the line and shouldn't have. Please forgive my churlish behavior when you...er...called me on it."

"There's nothing to forgive. You were upset with your granddaddy and not in your right mind."

And he still wasn't. He couldn't seem to get the taste of her lips out of his head. "It was inexcusable. I shouldn't have taken my anger out on you." He gave her an apologetic smile. "I want to make it up to you."

"You don't have to do that."

"Yes, I do." He scratched his chin, his mind whirling with possibilities. "What did you do for entertainment at Spivey Point?"

"Entertainment?"

"Fun. What did you do for pleasure before the War? Dancing? Games?"

"Work kept us busy most of the time, but we did have an occasional barn dance. Not as fancy as the Lawrence cotillions, but we had fun. As to games, we played checkers and mumblety-peg..."

Mumblety-peg. He chuckled. "Why am I not

surprised you played a game of knives?"

"I usually won, too."

"Again, not surprised. What else?"

A gleam lit her eyes. "Riding. I used to sneak into the back pasture and climb on one of Mr. Lawrence's racehorses. Those beauties sure could run. I'd imagine I was a jockey, riding at the Richmond racetrack."

"Did you win?"

"Of course. Everyone wants to win."

"Sometimes losing is more advantageous." Like yielding to a knife-wielding Rebel and finding out she's the one woman you could learn to love.

"What's that supposed to mean?"

"Nothing." He stood and crossed to the bookshelves, an idea percolating. "So, horse racing interests you, does it?"

"Very much. It's so fun and exciting. Papa once let me bet on a race at the track. Naturally, I picked the winner."

"Naturally." Smiling at her bravado, he ran a finger down the spines until he reached the one he wanted. He plucked the book from its slot and returned to the sofa.

"*Silk and Scarlet*." He held out the book to her. "One of Henry Dixon's better works on racehorses."

She eyed his hand as if he held a snake. "It's a book."

"Yes. And a very good one."

She looked up, her wounded gaze digging holes in him. "I told you I can't read very well. Don't you remember?"

"I remember. But I want to help change that."

"How?"

"By showing you how to read better."

"I don't think that's a good idea. Even Lance became frustrated with my stupidity."

"We'll have none of that. You're not stupid,

Kitty. Far from it." He turned up the wick on the table lamp, then sat beside her and pressed the book into her hands. "You just need to take a different approach."

"How do you know what I need?"

"I had a fellow school-mate who had a similar affliction. He trained himself to go slow and concentrate and was soon able to read as well as the rest of us students."

She licked her lips. "I tried that. But it doesn't work for me."

"Have you truly tried?" He leaned closer, forcing his gaze away from those pouty, moistened lips. "From what I've seen, I suspect you rush into the task and then become frustrated when it doesn't come to you as easily as everything else."

She glanced away, looking guilty as charged.

"Won't you at least give it a try?"

Myriad emotions played across her face—doubt, resentment, and finally resignation. "Very well. But I warn you, it won't be pretty."

"Pretty isn't necessary." He reached out and opened the book. "Now go slowly. Take your time and concentrate."

She frowned and bent over, her slender shoulders pulled tight. Perspiration dotted her forehead. He hated seeing her so distressed, especially when he took such pleasure in reading.

"What do you see when you look at the page?" he offered.

"Just a jumble of letters." She puckered her lips. "None of it makes any sense."

"See if tracing your finger under the words will help."

"What good will that do?"

"Just try it."

She heaved a sigh and pressed a finger to the page. Only the tick of the mantel clock and Kitty's rapid breaths broke the quiet. After a few minutes, she shifted uneasily and swiped her lips with quick stroke of her tongue. Fire shot into his groin. To have that lovely pink tongue caressing his own lips...

"I'm sorry, Jack." She lifted her head, cheeks and ears flaming. "I just can't do it."

"Yes, you can. Concentrate." *Like I'm trying to do to keep from pouncing on you.*

"It's not working..."

"Giving up already?"

Green eyes shot daggers at him. God, she was a beauty when riled. "Here, let me help you." He reached across her, his chest brushing along her shoulder. "This first word has an *h* and an *e*." He tapped a finger under each letter. "*He.* Can you see that?"

She leaned away, breaking the contact between them. "I think so."

"And this next one." He scooted his finger next to hers, letting them touch ever so slightly. "*w-a-s.*"

"Was." Her finger retreated. "And after that is an *a.*"

"Good." He couldn't help himself and countered her move by spooning her hand with his. "What's this one?"

Her eyes went wide, and she sucked in a breath. His pulse quickened at the thought of his touch arousing her. "Think about what you've already read, and picture the next word." *Like I'm going to picture you—*

She shoved the book from her lap onto his. "I believe I'll have some tea after all." She gave a clearly contrived cough. "My throat is a little dry."

Hell. What was wrong with him? She was uncomfortable enough with the reading. He'd made it worse with his little parlor games. Before he could put her at ease, she was on her feet and making a rabbit-dash for the desk.

The clink of china rang out, then came the soft gurgle of pouring tea. "I prefer honey with my tea," she said in a strained voice. "Unfortunately, Sally was fresh out."

"Sorry to hear that. If we're still stuck in town tomorrow, we'll make a trip to the market and get you some."

"I hope that won't be necessary."

"I hope not either." He wanted to be on the way to Elmira as much as she did. He missed the intimacy of traveling alone with her, of being her protector and provider. It made him feel wanted— needed.

She returned to the sofa with her tea, making sure no part of her body touched his as she sat. She took several sips, then supplied him with a reserved smile. "Much better."

"Good." He propped the book on his knees where he wouldn't be tempted to tease her. "Let's continue, shall we?"

Her soft grunt could've meant anything. He took it as acquiescence. "So, we've read '*He was a'...*" He pointed to the next word. "The one after that has five letters. See them?"

"Yes. *g-r-e*...great." She let out a frustrated breath. "I can read each letter by itself, but when I look at the whole word, it looks backwards."

"You're doing fine. Try the next one. It has five letters as well."

She scrunched up her face and leaned closer. Her soft breaths caressed the back of his hand. "Is that a *b* or a *d*? I can never tell them apart."

"It's a *b*."

Her mouth moved as she formed the letters. "*b-l*...Black."

"Good. Keep going."

"Lordy, another of those confusing letters. It's a *b*, right?"

"It is." *B as in softly rounded breasts...*

She leaned back, her expression wary. "Why are you doing this, Jack?"

Gripes, did she read minds instead of books? "Doing what?"

"Trying to help me read better."

Bullet dodged. "Because I want to. Reading is a big part of life, even for a woman."

"I've gotten by without it so far."

"Who read for you? Lance? Your father?"

Her expression sank, and he patted her hand. "Don't worry. I'm going to see to it you don't need to rely on anyone else ever again." His chest tightened. *Not even me.*

"But you've helped me so much already. Getting me to Point Lookout. Bringing me here. Why would you want to put yourself through this torture?"

The only torture was having her close and knowing it could go no further. "Helping you is no torture. I'm actually enjoying the challenge."

She lifted a dainty eyebrow. He wanted to kiss it back into submission.

"Let me put it to you another way." He leaned away from temptation. "You ride well and take pleasure in a rousing gallop. Am I right?"

"Well...yes."

"So, if some affliction caused me to ride poorly, and I feared horses, wouldn't you do all you could to help me find a solution?"

"Like your eye? I didn't notice you having any problems with Socks."

That hit a bit too close to home. Socks was well-trained for a reason. "It was just an analogy."

"A what?"

"An illustration. An example to explain why I want to help you."

She fingered the handle of her teacup. "You're just full up with those high-falutin words, aren't you?"

"You can learn them, too. Think of reading as a game of checkers. You have to think several steps ahead in order to beat your opponent."

She pushed a sigh past those luscious lips. "If only it was that easy."

"It can be, if you really want it. You have the drive, Kitty. I've been treated to it since our very first encounter. It's one of the things I admire most about you."

Silence descended as she stared at him, her pale eyes revealing little of her thoughts. Damn. He'd done it again. Shoe leather was fast becoming his steadiest meal.

The gong of the clock drew her gaze to the mantel. "It's growing late. I should be getting to bed." She rose and set her teacup on the end table. "I appreciate you helping me. It was very kind."

He stood and handed her the book. "Here, you keep this."

"I can't accept it."

"Yes, you can. I want you to have it. You'll be more likely to read if you're interested in the subject."

"Your granddaddy—"

"Would want you to have it as well. Keep practicing. Before you know it, you'll be reading like a scholar and enjoying it."

"Don't know about all that..." She clutched the book to her chest. "But I'll do my best to practice like you said."

If only he could be that book. Pressed against her soft bosom. Accepted. Trusted. No longer shirked out of fear.

Chapter Eleven

People jammed the sidewalk, rushing through their morning chores as though wanting to be done before the broiling afternoon heat set in. Carts, wagons, and hacks filled the narrow street, adding to the noise and confusion. No wonder Papa hated city life. Her nerves were strung tighter than a banjo, and they'd only just started their stroll.

She moved closer to Jack to avoid colliding with a passing couple. Her parasol tipped dangerously close to the gentleman's head before she yanked it upright. Sally had lent her the contraption, insisting a lady didn't venture outdoors without one. Who cared if the sun caused freckles? Papa had adored hers and called them her angel kisses. But she was in Jack's society now and expected to follow their rules.

An avenue of storefronts loomed ahead, their colorful awnings and busy window displays an eye-catching sight. Touring such new and fascinating places ought to have her giddier than a drunk with the keys to the tavern. Yet it didn't. Troublesome thoughts kept her from enjoying their outing to the market.

For one thing, the northbound trains continued to be at a standstill. Every minute spent in Maryland meant one less minute she had to save Lance.

And then there was Jack.

After a night of tossing and turning and being plagued by prickly thoughts, she'd come to a painful decision. Elias Porter was right to want to keep her away from his grandson. Not because of the money. She didn't care beans about his money. Her worry was the heartache she was sure to bring Jack. He was starting to care for her, had even admitted so in the garden. If she were honest with herself, she was starting to care for him, too.

And that couldn't be. She and Jack were worlds apart, in class and smarts. There was no future for them. No matter how painful, she had to free him from his promise to help her.

She could make it to Elmira on her own.

She had to—for both their sakes.

They rounded a corner and entered a less crowded and much quieter section of the city. Stately townhouses and tall oaks lined the street. Birds flitted through the treetops, one merry songstress piping out a cheerful melody from a branch overhead.

Louisa tipped back her parasol and spotted a splash of orange and black in the greenery. "What a pretty bird."

"It's an oriole. That one's a male. Females are duller, more yellowish-gray."

"Hmmph," she said, grateful for the distraction. "Unjust treatment, I say."

"You'll be happy to know the males don't get their brilliant plumage until their second year. They have to make due with drab coloring until then."

"Better, but still unfair." *Like a lot of things in life.*

"You can't tinker with mother nature, Kitty."

"Funny, Lance used to say that." She gave a sad sigh as the memories rushed in. "He'd sit in the meadow with his sketchbook on one knee, his pencil busy capturing nature on a blank page."

He patted her hand resting on his bent arm. "Don't worry. The trains will start running again.

We'll be in Elmira and with Lance before you know it."

We. Her belly knotted. It was time to tell him about her decision. No more shilly-shallying. "Jack, about that—"

"Shhh. Let's not talk about Lance or the train. It's too nice of a day to worry about things we can't control."

"But I have something I need to tell you."

"Later. The market is just ahead. Let's enjoy a brief sojourn from our troubles, shall we?"

By his cheery tone, a sojourn must be a good thing. She didn't have the heart to deny him this small pleasure. Besides, the walkway was filling with people again. Better to wait until they had more privacy.

He guided her into a long, open-air shed. From one end to the other, stalls displayed everything from ice-packed meat and fish to bins of apples, melons, and berries. There were as many people milling about as there were types of produce for sale.

She collapsed her parasol and drew in a deep breath, savoring the pungent hodgepodge of aromas. "Mmmm. Don't you just love that smell?"

"What?" He wrinkled his nose in distaste. "The odor of dead fish?"

"No, silly. The smell of earth's bounty."

"Smells more like earth's—"

"Jackson Porter!" A well-dressed man stepped into the aisle in front of them. "What a pleasant surprise."

A smile lit Jack's face, and he extended a hand in greeting. "Mr. Abell, so nice to see you again, sir."

The older man shook Jack's hand while eyeing her with friendly interest. "Are you in town visiting Elias?"

She shifted uneasily under the man's scrutiny. He appeared to know the Porters. Would that knowledge put her at risk?

"Yes, we are." Jack pressed a reassuring hand to the small of her back. "Kitty, may I present Mr. Abell, a long-time family friend. Sir, this is my wife."

"Well, well." The older man doffed his hat and gave her a welcoming smile. "It's a pleasure to meet you, Mrs. Porter."

She inclined her head. "Sir."

"Mr. Abell is the owner of *The Baltimore Sun* where I worked after graduation." His voice rang with respect. "Learned everything I know about journalism from this man."

"I can't take all the credit, Jackson. You appear to have done quite well since leaving us. By-lines in *The Herald*. Acclaimed as a brilliant War Correspondent. And not to mention a beautiful new wife."

Drat. Not the direction she wanted the conversation to drift. She adjusted the market basket on her arm. "I imagine you two would like some time alone to get reacquainted." *And talk about something else besides me.* She glanced at a nearby produce stand. "If you'll excuse me, I believe I'll have a look at those apples."

Jack gave her a loving smile. "That's fine. I won't be long, dear."

Dear. Was he still playacting? She couldn't be sure. The line between charade and truth was blurring faster than footprints in blowing sand.

She lifted her skirt out of the sawdust and crossed to the produce stall. Dozens of shiny red apples filled the wooden bin. She picked one out to test for firmness. It had a bruise near the stem that would only get worse and spread. Just like Jack's heartache if she allowed his feelings for her to grow.

"Only one," a stern female voice commanded.

A few feet away, a young boy stood on tiptoe over a pickle barrel, his guardian watching him like a mother bear with a cub. His sleeve shoved to his elbow, the youngster beamed with excitement as he fished in the briny water. Most likely groping for the largest pickle he could lay his fingers on, just as she and Lance had done at the General Store in Richmond.

"Got it!" The boy withdrew his dripping arm and held his prize aloft. And a grand pickle it was. One she and Lance would've been proud of netting.

Her heart lurched. Would she reach Lance in time so they could make more such fond memories? She could only pray she would.

As the boy and his guardian moved on, the prickling sensation of being watched raised the hairs at the back of her neck. It was the same eerie sensation she'd felt at Spivey Point, just before Bart had trapped her in the tack shed—and again in Richmond—days before Papa had been struck by a runaway carriage.

The marketplace buzzed with shoppers, none of whom appeared to be paying her any attention. Jack and Mr. Abell were still absorbed in conversation. Were her fears getting the better of her?

A gust blew across her face, hot and smothering, like Satan's breath. She drew in a belly-deep slug of air, trying to fill her starving lungs.

A hand closed on her elbow, and she jumped.

"Has something upset you?" Jack asked.

She swallowed. "No. Nothing. You just startled me is all."

"Sorry, didn't mean to do that. We should get your honey and be on our way. Sally will have our hides if we're late for dinner."

Fine with her. That strange sense of being watched still lingered. The sooner they left, the better. She angled closer to him as they continued down the aisle. Odd how she now trusted the man she'd once held at knifepoint.

"So, how was your visit with Mr. Abell?" she asked, using small talk to take the corners off her edginess.

"Very interesting. He offered me a job at *The Sun* if I decide to return to Baltimore after the War."

"Will you return?"

"I don't know. Haven't thought that far ahead yet."

"The War won't last forever...I hope."

"I hope not either." He stopped in front of a produce stand and fished coins from his pocket. "Crock of honey," he told the vendor.

The man ducked under the counter and returned with a small clay crock. "Anything else, sir?"

"That'll do." Jack paid the man, then placed the honey in her market basket. "Ready?"

"Yes." *More than ready.*

He reached up and brushed a piece of straw off her arm. "You wanted to tell me something earlier?"

The loud thud rang out. She flinched and jerked her head toward the sound. A vendor stood over a board he'd tossed onto the ground. Sawdust swirled around his feet.

"Kitty?"

She gave herself a mental shake. "It can wait."

"You seem skittish. Is something wrong?"

Lordy, the last thing she needed was to give him a reason to insist on accompanying her to Elmira. A pack of blue uniforms ringing an oyster stand caught her eye. She faked a shudder. "It's nothing. I'm just not comfortable being around so many Yankees."

The soldiers did make her uneasy. But not as much as the unknown, unseen threat.

****

She closed the door to the bathing chamber and headed back to her bedroom. The sinfully long bath had been just what she needed. Clean and refreshing, the lavender scented water had cooled her sun-warmed skin and soothed her tense muscles. For the first time in days, she felt relaxed and rested.

Clad in a borrowed robe, she stood before the bureau mirror and mopped her wet hair with a towel. The sweet scent of hydrangeas wafted through the nearby open window, reminding her of home and Lance. She'd give anything to be able to turn back the hands of time and be back at Spivey Point, enjoying the simpler, happier times with her family. Like the Christmas she and Lance had gathered and sold sprigs of mistletoe so they could purchase the fancy smoking pipe Papa had admired in a Richmond storefront. It was the same Christmas Lance had given her the lovely gold locket.

Feeling lost without her necklace, she set down the towel and rummaged on the bureau-top. It wasn't there. She pushed aside her brush, the desk clock, and the oil lamp. Nothing.

She pulled open a drawer and rifled through the neatly folded garments. Gloves, handkerchiefs, and stockings, but no locket. She searched the other drawer. Not there either. She bent and checked the floor. The necklace hadn't fallen. Where the devil was it? She'd set it on the bureau before her bath.

As she straightened, a movement in the mirror caught her eye. She whirled to find Lieutenant Calhoun shouldered against the end bedpost.

"Looking for somethin'?" Sunlight cut through the parted chintz curtains, framing him in a bright halo and sparking off the locket.

Her heart nearly leapt into her throat. With Jack and his granddaddy out running errands, she and Sally were alone in the house. And vulnerable.

She snatched the edges of her robe together, clutching the gathers against her thudding chest.

"How did you get in here?" she demanded in as stern a tone as she could muster.

He shrugged, a carefree gesture that failed to reach his steely eyes. "I walked in."

"You couldn't just...where is the housekeeper? Surely she didn't let the likes of you just walk in."

"Perhaps she went a visitin'."

"She wouldn't just up and leave without telling me."

"The behavior of Porter's servants doesn't concern me." He snaked a tongue over his lips as though anticipating a tasty meal. "I have better things to occupy my time."

Fear clawed at her spine. She took several steps back until she reached the comforting hardness of the bureau. Hopefully he was alone, but just in case, she'd make sure no one got the jump on her from behind.

"Why are you here? What do you want?"

He gave her a lazy smile and twirled her necklace chain around his finger. "I came into town on an assignment. Caught sight of you at the marketplace and thought we might have a friendly little chat."

Someone *had* been watching her at the market. A polecat of a someone. She glared at him. "You want to chat? In my *bedchamber?*"

"Why not? It's cozier in here."

Cozier. That didn't sound good. She squared herself, summoning a courage that was fast deserting her. "Get out. Before I call for someone to throw you out."

"Come now." He widened his slick smile but remained braced against the bedpost. "You wouldn't begrudge a war-weary soldier the pleasure of your company, now would ya, darlin'? You *do* owe me for those unkind words in the officer's mess."

"I don't owe you anything."

"You know..." He tilted his head to the side and studied her. "Ever since we met, I suspected somethin' was odd about you."

Her pulse skipped in alarm. "There's nothing odd about me."

"No?" His gaze roamed the length of her, leaving a slimy trail in its wake. "You don't appear to be the type a prominent newspaperman would wed. A mistress perhaps, but not a wife."

"How dare you say such a thing." She fisted the robe tighter to keep from slapping his smug face. Best not rile him and make things worse.

"I dare a lot of things, darlin'. Just like you."

"We're nothing alike."

"I beg to differ. We're both pretendin' to be somethin' we're not."

Sweet Mary. What did he know about her? She lifted her chin in a show of confidence while her stomach churned with rancid doubts. "I'm not pretending anything."

He glanced at her left hand and cocked an eyebrow.

She rubbed her bare ring finger and cursed her lack of forethought. "I don't owe you any explanations."

"No. But it sure does look peculiar. Rich man like Porter..." He looked around the bedchamber. "If you're married as you claim, where are his things?"

"Things?"

"A spare shirt. Cologne. I only see female trappin's in here."

"Our sleeping arrangements are none of your business."

"I doubt any man, includin' Jackson Porter, would allow a woman as captivatin' as you to sleep alone." He pushed upright and regarded her through narrowed eyes. "Miss Carleton."

Her heart slammed against her ribs. *He knew.*

151

"C-Carleton?" She shook her head and forced a reply past a throat gone tight and dry. "You're mistaken."

"I think not." He jogged her locket in the air. "Why else would you carry the picture of a captured Reb in your locket—a Corporal Carleton, if I remember correctly?"

He recognized Lance. This was bad. Very bad. "I know nothing about a Corporal Carleton."

"Are you denyin' this locket is yours?"

"No. It's mine." She held out a hand, keeping the other one fisted around her robe. "Give it to me."

He shoved the locket into his trouser pocket. "Soon enough, Miss Carleton."

"I am not that woman."

"Interestin' that patrols are lookin' for a Miss Lou Carleton, a purported spy and murderess." His pale eyes scoured her from head to toe, lingering on her breasts before returning to her face. "A scrawny woman with bright hair."

Her heart thudded so loudly she was sure he could hear it. Her ears rattled with the din. "Why do you keep calling me that? I'm not this Carleton woman."

"Didn't you sail across the Potomac with your black buck and land at Tall Timbers?"

How did he know about that? Ice swam in her veins. Had the Yankees tortured it out of Jeb? They couldn't have. Loyal, faithful Jeb would never willingly give up such information. He'd die first. She swayed on unsteady legs. Jeb couldn't be dead. He was strong and brave and full of life. He'd taught her so many things over the years. Like how to face-down a mean old badger they'd accidentally jumped up at Spivey Creek.

She drew on the memory of Jeb's courage to face the varmint in front of her. "I have no idea what you're talking about, Lieutenant."

"Maybe we ought to let the Baltimore Provost

determine the truth of your claim."

"You have no right to detain me."

"Oh, I have every right. The city is under military rule. Has been since the start of the War. I can hold you as long as I please."

Hold her. Confined. Trapped like an animal. The open doorway beckoned. Freedom was only a short dash away. All she had to do was get past a six-foot rattlesnake. She sucked in a breath and prepared to run.

"There's no one to hear your scream," he taunted, mistaking her intent. "I made sure of that."

He made sure of...

She froze as his meaning took hold. "What have you done with Sally?"

"Sally?"

"The housekeeper."

"Eh, she'll be fine."

Her fingers curled around an imaginary knife. Hers was across the room still sheathed in her boot. "Where is she? You'd best not have hurt her."

He hooked thumbs over his belt, fingers pointing to his groin in a suggestive manner. "We have more pressin' matters to deal with than worryin' about some old Negress."

Her stomach roiled at his oily tone. "Arrest me then," she spat out. "If that's why you came here."

"Oh, I will, darlin'. Make no bones about it." He eyed her with the ferocity of a cat stalking a kill. "But first, I thought we might get to know each other a little better."

Get to know each other. Bile seared her throat. Bart had uttered those same words, just before he had attacked.

"If you're nice to me," Calhoun added in a silky voice as he took a step toward her. "I could put in a good word with the Provost. Might make your incarceration easier to bear."

No. She would not be a victim again. Ever. She gathered herself to flee.

Calhoun anticipated her move and blocked her path to the door. "Ah-ah-ah," he clucked in warning. "You're not goin' anywhere just yet."

That's what you think, bluebelly. She reached behind her, grasped the oil lamp, and with a jerk of her hand, tossed it at him. As he hunkered down to avoid the blow, she darted around him and raced for the door.

The clatter of glass and Calhoun's angry bellow followed her into the hallway. Heart thumping, she hiked up her robe and dashed down the stairs as fast as her feet could carry her. At the bottom, she turned and sprinted for the parlor and the doorway to the garden.

Footfalls banged on the steps behind her. "You little whore. You'd best stop if you know what's good for you!"

She increased her pace and shot through the open doors and onto the terrace. The stone pavers lining the path bit into the pads of her bare feet. She pushed onward, ignoring the pain.

The bend in the path and Saint Francis loomed ahead. Behind her, she could hear Calhoun's labored breaths drawing closer. She risked a peek over her shoulder, then wished she hadn't. The sight of his angry, lust-crazed expression turned her insides to stone. If he caught her—

The glance cost her momentum. Calhoun dove for her. She thudded heavily to the ground, his hand clamped on her ankle. Her breath left her with a whoosh. Stars danced in her vision. Stunned, she worked to fill her lungs by taking rapid gulps of air.

Calhoun's hand raked up her leg, beneath her robe, fingers biting in the sensitive skin behind her knee. "Gotcha now, my feisty little filly." He pushed up on one knee and loomed over her. "I'm gonna enjoy tamin' you."

Bile again burned in her throat. *Get away. Escape. Now.*

She kicked out, and her heel connected with soft flesh. He grunted in pain and for a brief moment, his hold loosened. She wriggled free and scrambled to her feet.

Before she could move, he grabbed her waist and tugged her against him. Memories surfaced—of Bart's arms crushing her chest. His body grinding against hers. His mouth on hers, bruising and demanding. His rough hands ripping at her clothing, touching her, invading her, and then the pain...

No. No. No. Not again.

She twisted in his grasp, flailing her arms in an effort to break free. Her fist connected with his chin. As he jerked back, she lunged forward. The motion carried them colliding into a solid object.

She bounced to one side.

Calhoun stumbled. A loud scraping noise filled the air. His expression turned horrified.

"Get out of the way—" He threw up his arms, then careened into her, pushing her to the ground. Before she could roll free, he thumped atop her, his weight forcing the air from her lungs.

Everything went silent and dark.

Chapter Twelve

Prepare for the worst; hope for the best.

Jack pushed through the front door and into the foyer, his gut telling him to start preparing. While sending a telegraph to his editor in New York City, he'd run into one of the guards from Point Lookout. Private Duncan had come into town with a small detail to deliver a wagon-load of prisoners to Fort McHenry. A detail led by Lieutenant Calhoun.

"And very interested in you, Mr. Porter," Duncan had revealed of his squad leader. The young private had been easy prey. It took only one beer to loosen his tongue. "Talked of little else but you and that prison story you're writing." Duncan wiped foam from his scraggly mustache and grinned. "And your pretty lil' wife."

Calhoun might not have any ill intentions, but it was better to be safe than sorry. In the end, he decided it was better to tell Kitty her enemy was in town.

"Kitty," he bellowed from the bottom of the staircase.

Only the tick of the grandfather clock in the hallway answered him. Not upstairs, then. He combed the study, parlor, and kitchen. Nothing. And no Sally either. When he'd left earlier, the housekeeper had been working in the garden. Perhaps she was still there and Kitty with her.

He retraced his steps to the parlor. Late afternoon heat blasted him as he crossed the room and passed through the open doors. Nothing stirred in the stifling garden. Not a breeze, not a bird, not even a stray bee. And it was quiet. Too quiet. Unease rolled in his gut.

The path ahead curled around a tall hedgerow. He rounded the bend and froze. Beside the toppled figure of Saint Francis, two bodies lay unmoving. White cotton showed beneath a length of federal blue. A tangled mass of red hair fanned out over the ground.

Kitty! Fear unlike any he'd ever experienced exploded inside him. He sprinted the last few steps and rolled the unconscious soldier off her. He pulled her into his arms and crushed her against him, heartened by the faint rise and fall of her chest.

She was alive.

He loosened his grip and gently brushed a stray lock from her face. Dark lashes fanned her cheeks. So angelic. So beautiful. He wanted to hold her in his arms and never let go.

Blood streaked her forehead, the red stark against her pale skin. He thumbed away the smear and found no obvious wounds. The soldier's blood?

Though red stained the man's face, his features were familiar. *Calhoun.* The Texan lived—barely. Blood matted his hair and pooled beneath his head. He'd seen that much blood before. The battlefields had run red with it. Death wasn't far away.

He got a quick picture of a young soldier writhing on the ground and clutching his disemboweled innards. The figure shifted and swirled and became his father lying on the river bank. No smile. No laughter. Just mottled and bloated, his lifeless eyes staring skyward.

A hot breeze rifled over his face, jarring him back to the present. He tightened his grip on Kitty, holding onto her like a lifeline. He couldn't lose her, too. Not the only woman who made him look forward to the future instead of dreading it.

"Kitty?" With effort he pushed the word past the lump in his throat. The little nickname that started out as part of their scheme had come to mean so much more.

He gave her a gentle shake. "Wake up, Kitty." *Don't leave me. I need you.*

The thought startled him, like a stranger leaping out of the shadows. He hadn't seen it coming and wasn't the least bit prepared.

Had he ever really *needed* anyone before?

She made a small sound. Good, she was coming around. Her head rolled to the side. A twig had left a crease on her cheek. He traced the impression with a fingertip. Losing his fiancée because of his mangled eye had been merely a blow to his ego, if he were honest about it.

Losing Kitty would leave a hole in his heart.

She groaned. Her eyes fluttered open. "J-Jack?"

"Yes, it's me." She meant to eventually part company with him. He wouldn't think about that now. "How do you feel? Are you hurt?"

"Wh-what happened?"

"I don't know. I found you lying beneath Calhoun with the statue toppled over beside you."

"Calhoun..?" Her confused gaze flicked to the motionless soldier. She quivered in his arms. "Is he...dead?"

"He's still breathing, but it doesn't look good. Appears he took the brunt of the blow from the falling statue. Do you remember what happened?"

"I'm not sure. Everything's so...hazy."

Not good. "Do you remember me leaving to run an errand?"

"You went to the telegraph office."

"That's right. What did you do after I left the house?"

"I drew a bath, and..." Bewilderment turned to alarm. "Calhoun! He was in my bedroom."

Only a man intent on foulness entered a woman's bedchamber uninvited. His fingers itched to end what the statue had started.

"He came after me...j-just like Bart."

Gripes, did Calhoun have an accomplice? He tossed a glance around the deserted garden. Either the thug was long gone, or her memory was fuddled. With any luck, it was the latter.

"Who is Bart?"

"Wh-what?"

"Was there someone else with Calhoun?"

"I...uh...no. I didn't see anyone."

Calhoun was bad enough. They'd discuss Bart later. "How did you get out here in the garden?"

"He came at me, so I ran. I made it outside, but he was right on my heels. He grabbed me. We bumped into something hard." She eyed the statue and shivered again. "Dear Lord...I didn't mean for this to happen."

"Of course you didn't." He pressed a reassuring kiss to the top of her head. She smelled of soap and lavender. The scent of clean. And Calhoun had tried to soil her.

"Did he hurt you?"

"He didn't have time. I ran before he could...then the statue toppled. I think he actually tried to save me from it." She wiggled upright. Pain twisted her face. She lifted a hand to her temple. "My head. I must've struck it when I fell."

He parted her hair. A small lump protruded from her skull. "Just a bump. No blood, which is good. Does anything else hurt?"

She shook her head and then grimaced. "I shouldn't have done that."

"No, you shouldn't have."

"Jack, I'm sorry. Seems I'm always causing trouble of some sort."

"Shhh. You're not to blame for this." A bee

buzzed around her head. He shooed it away, then rose with her cradled in his arms. She didn't need a sting adding to her misery. "Let's get you inside where you'll be more comfortable."

Trembling fingers clamped around the back of his neck. She rested her head on his chest and melted against him, her warm tears soaking into his shirt. He ground his teeth around a curse and stepped over Calhoun. The swine deserved to die. Twice, if he had any say.

He set her on the settee in the parlor, then crossed to the sideboard and poured a shot of brandy into a glass. She needed a drink after all that. Hell, he needed one.

"Here, drink this."

She swiped away her tears and pushed upright. Her thin robe did little to hide her womanly curves. Not twenty-four hours ago, he would have delighted in a peek at that milky skin, but all he felt now was a consuming joy that she was alive.

"I don't need anything, Jack."

"Drink it."

She took the glass, downed the contents in one gulp, and thrust the tumbler back at him, eyes flaring with annoyance.

Good. That blow to the head hadn't dulled her lively spirit.

He set the glass on the end table, then sat beside her and took her hand in his. It was icy and trembling. He rubbed her with calming strokes. "Do you feel like talking, or do you need more time to recover?"

"I'm good."

"Let me know if you start feeling poorly."

She pulled her hand away and tucked it into a fold of her robe. "What did you want to know?"

"Calhoun. Any idea why he was here, besides the obvious?"

"He said he didn't believe our story...that we're married. He came to find out the truth."

"Damn. I didn't expect that. I just learned he was in town. Thought he might want payback for when you poked fun at him at Point Lookout."

"Oh, he wanted payback. But there's more. He knows who I am and that I crossed the Potomac and landed at Tall Timbers." She trembled like a rabbit caught in a snare. "Did they...could they have gotten that out of Jeb?"

He shook his head. "I doubt it. I'm sure if they had, Lieutenant Whitlock would've sent word to us. He's a good egg, as you would say."

"I hope to God you're right. Perhaps when Calhoun found my locket, he recognized Lance and figured out who I am."

"Could be. But it doesn't matter now." He glanced at the open doorway. "He'll soon be taking that knowledge with him to the grave."

She rubbed her upper arm as though it pained her. Had she injured it during her fall? "Let me see that arm."

"There's no need. It's only bruised."

"Then just humor me." He pushed the wide sleeve to her elbow and gently prodded her smooth flesh.

A faint moan rumbled deep in her throat.

"Pains you does it?"

She closed her eyes. "Not in the way you mean."

"How then?"

"I can't say. It's too..." Her voice trailed away on a desolate sigh.

"You can tell me, Kitty. I'm your friend." *And more if you'll let me.*

She eased out of his grasp and pulled a pillow against her chest, clutching it like a life buoy. What would make her trust him enough to seek comfort from him? He used Sally's favorite saying, hoping to coax her into opening up. "Things will fester if left bottled inside."

She looked up at him, those amazing green cat-eyes glistening with unshed tears. "Lord knows I want to tell you. I-It's been shut inside me for so long."

"Then let it out. You'll feel better if you do."

"You're wrong. I'll feel worse."

"Why will you feel worse?"

She drew in a ragged breath and averted her gaze. "'Cause you'll hate me."

Tears shimmered on her lashes. She sounded so forlorn, so dejected, his own eye burned. "I could never hate you, Kitty." He cupped her chin and gently tugged her head around until she faced him. Something more than despair shone in her eyes. His good opinion was important to her. She cared what he thought of her.

And that mattered more than he could ever have dreamed.

She sobbed and jerked out of his grasp. Her chest heaved as she tried to collect herself. Whatever she was holding inside was eating away at her.

He lifted his hand, moving slowly so he wouldn't frighten her. His fingertips hovered near her tear-stained cheek. "May I?"

Her lips parted. She drew in another less shaky breath. "Y-yes."

He wiped the wetness from her face with his thumb. "You don't have to talk about it if it's too difficult. I understand."

"Thank you, Jack. For understanding." A hesitant smile tipped her lips. "You've been so good to me."

"What have I done? Let you tag along to places I was going anyway?"

His attempt at lightheartedness failed. Her smile faded. "You let me tag along, as you say, even though it put you at risk. You brought me here. To your home. Introduced me to your family, to—" She gasped, eyes widening to the size of goose eggs. "Dear God. Sally."

Apprehension knifed into him. In all the confusion, he'd forgotten about the missing housekeeper. "Where is she?"

"Calhoun did something to her so he could be alone with me." Her fingers clamped around his hand. "We have to find her."

****

Louisa paused in the doorway and leaned against the jamb, waiting for the dizziness to subside. Her head felt as if a millstone had taken to grinding inside her skull. Added to that, muscles she didn't know existed argued when she tried to move. But none of that mattered. Sally was out there somewhere, possibly hurt...or worse.

Jack's frantic search of the house had uncovered nothing. When he'd dashed into the garden, she could no longer sit idle. She had to help. She'd never forgive herself if anything happened to the friendly housekeeper because of her.

After a few minutes, the swimming in her head receded to a mild paddle. She pushed away from the door and followed the path that ran alongside the house, careful not to disturb the agreement she and her body had come to.

She studied the bushes and hedges as she walked, looking for a splash of color among the greens and browns. *Blue.* The last she recalled, Sally had been wearing a dark blue outfit with a starched white apron tied at the waist. No gee-gaws or frills. Sally wasn't the frilly type. She dressed plain and simple. Just like the wisdom she parceled out.

A stiff gust rifled through the garden, pitching the treetops from side to side. Maple leaves twisted and flipped, showing their underbellies. The air was thick and heavy and carried a sharp metallic scent. A storm was brewing. She picked up her pace. They had to find Sally before the rain came and washed away her tracks.

Just ahead, Jack rounded the corner of the house, toting a shovel in one hand, the other clamped around Sally's upper arm. The housekeeper appeared to be unhurt. She walked upright, no limping or sagging. There was no blood that she could see. Her clothes were just a little rumpled and dusty. Louisa breathed a sigh of relief. Sally was safe and sound...

"Where is he?" the housekeeper demanded. "Where's that no-good Yankee polecat."

...And madder than a stirred-up nest of hornets.

Jack shook his head. "He's been taken care of."

"Not by me, he ain't. Thumpin' my skull and lockin' me in the cellar. Why I ought to..."

Thumping her skull? The knot in Louisa's belly pulled tighter. "Did he hurt you, Sally?"

Jack's head snapped in her direction, and his mouth flattened into a thin line. "You shouldn't be out here, Kitty. Go back inside."

"I came to help." She gave the housekeeper a closer look. Sally's skin was pale, like a batch of weak tea. "I heard you say he thumped you. Are you sure you're not hurt?"

"I'm fine, Miss Carleton. Little lump on the head ain't gonna stop me." Sally's gaze travelled over her and narrowed. "What about you? That's an awful lot of blood on your robe."

"It's not mine. It's Calhoun's."

"Calhoun?"

"The Yankee polecat." The vile feel of his body still clung to her. Like stink on dung. Her arms crawled with gooseflesh. "Saint Francis fell on him."

"Saint Francis did what?"

She didn't want to go through it all again, but

Sally deserved the details. She drew in a breath and explained as quickly as possible.

"Hmmph," Sally said when she was done. "Got what he deserved then. His worthless carcass still layin' out there?"

Jack ground the shovel tip into the dirt. "I'm going to bury him right now."

Clouds overran the sun and turned daylight into twilight. The wind kicked up, sending leaves and debris skating across the ground.

Sally glanced skyward. "You best get to it. Looks like we're in for a bad-un."

A chill raced down her spine, and Louisa folded her arms over her chest. *Bad-un had already hit. Calhoun was his name.*

Lightning flashed, followed a few seconds later by the rumble of thunder. "You two had best get inside," Jack urged. "I'll see to Calhoun."

"You want me to send for the authorities, Master Jack?"

"We can't risk them finding out who Miss Carleton really is. I'll take care of this mess."

Mess. Her mess. If she hadn't taunted Calhoun, he wouldn't have come after her, wouldn't have hurt Sally, wouldn't be dying in a pool of blood. Just another black mark to add to her growing list.

"Jackson," Granddaddy Porter's demand echoed into the garden. "Are you out here?"

Jack frowned and glanced in the direction of the house. "Damn. I'd hoped to have this cleaned up before he returned. Go inside and stall him, Sally. I'll be in shortly."

"Certainly, Master Jack. You comin', Miss Carleton?"

"I'm staying out here with Jack."

Jack hefted the shovel to his shoulder. "You should go inside, Kitty. That's a nasty thump you took to the head."

She pointed to her blood-stained robe. "If your granddaddy sees me like this, he'll know something bad happened. He'll be on us like a duck on a June bug. And I'm just not up to an interrogation right now."

"Fine. But let me know if you feel faint-headed." He planted a hand at the small of her back and guided her along the path.

He likely meant the gesture to be helpful, but it did just the opposite. Her head resumed whirling, every bit as muddling as the wallop to her skull. She had to concentrate on each step to keep from stumbling.

"Puzzling. Damned puzzling," Jack murmured.

"What?"

"Calhoun. If all he had were suspicions, why would he attack you and risk making trouble for himself? It just doesn't make sense."

"Reckon he had more than suspicions. He was very insistent about knowing who I am." Her step faltered as a thought took hold. "My locket. He slipped it into his pocket, before he lunged for me."

"Don't worry. I'll get it for you."

Fat raindrops began falling from the boiling clouds. She turned her face skyward, welcoming the soothing wetness. Nothing like a good shower to wash away dirt and filth. And blood.

She eyed the shovel. "You gonna bury him here on the property?"

"Don't see any other solution at the moment."

Neither did she. In order to keep her and Jack safe, Calhoun's secrets would have to be buried with him. Did he have family in Texas? A wife? Children? There'd be no body for a proper burial. No grave to grieve over and heal. They'd never even know what became of him. That he died trying to save her.

She swallowed her guilt with a hard gulp. "Will you try to move him later? Send his body home to his family?"

"Don't know. Maybe one day. We just can't risk it right now."

Seemed everyone connected to her risked one thing or another. Most of it bad. "I'm sorry I put you in this position, Jack."

"You didn't put me anywhere. I made my choice weeks ago when I agreed to help you."

"Bet you're regretting that decision about now."

He slipped his arm around her waist and gave her a squeeze. "Not one minute of it. Calhoun is an unfortunate tragedy, but he brought it on himself by attacking you."

Despite his reassuring words, unease slithered back into her belly. What was it that compelled men to assault her? Was she indeed a hussy as Henry Lawrence had claimed? Even Jack couldn't seem to resist touching her when he'd vowed not to.

They neared the curve in the path where Saint Francis had stood—before she and Calhoun had crashed into it—before the statue had toppled over and struck the Texan with a fatal blow. Nausea swept over her. She reeled to a stop, legs braced against the spinning in her head.

Jack tightened his grip on her waist. "Are you going to be ill?"

"I-I just need a minute." She pushed away from his too intimate hold. "You go on ahead."

"Are you sure? I can wait until you're feeling better."

"No. I'll be fine. Go on. Get started before the rain gets worse."

He handed her the shovel. "Here. Lean on this. I need to drag the body further out into the gardens before I dig. Bring it with you when you're back to rights."

She gripped the handle in a tight-fisted grip as Jack disappeared behind the hedgerow. A gale coursed through her at the memory of Calhoun's bloodied body. He'd come to—to what? Find out who she was? Arrest her? Had he really intended to rape her? Or had thoughts of Bart put the suggestion into her head? Whatever his purpose in coming here, he was dead.

The Yankees had suspected her of killing a man. Now she really had.

"Sonofa—"

At Jack's curse, she dropped the shovel and rushed around the bend. He stood beside the path, hands fisted at his sides, looking as threatening as the clouds gathered overhead. Across a rusty stain lay the broken statue. From where she stood, it looked like Saint Francis had bled out.

There was no sign of Calhoun.

"You're sure he was alone?" Jack didn't look up.

"I didn't see anyone but him." Which didn't mean he'd come by himself, or that he hadn't shared his suspicions with a companion. The possibility hadn't occurred to her until now, and it sent a flock of goosebumps fluttering up her spine.

Chapter Thirteen

Though stifling air clogged the hall, ice flowed in her veins. She stopped in the open doorway and pressed a hand to her churning belly. She'd rather face a Yankee firing squad than walk through that door. But she couldn't delay any longer. A cold cloth and a few hours rest had chased her dizziness to the fringes. Only a dull ache remained tapping at her temple. Pesky. But not enough to stop her from doing what needed to be done.

She took a hesitant step inside. Seated at the massive desk, Jack had his head bent over a journal. One lock of hair dangled devilishly over his brow. In contrast, the barest edge of a pink tongue poked from the corner of his mouth.

How sweet and boyish. Her heart lurched. She didn't want to cause him pain. But she knew deep inside, if she stayed with him, he'd get hurt much worse. A sob rose in her throat, and in spite of her efforts to swallow it, she must have made a noise.

He looked up, and a smile lit his handsome face. "Kitty."

Her courage retreated at his tender tone. "I see you're busy. I can come back later."

"I'm just jotting down a few notes. Nothing that can't wait." He closed his journal and stood. "Please, come in."

Well, there was nothing for it. Better to get this over and done with. She pasted on a smile and continued into the study. "I won't take up much of your time."

He slipped around the desk to meet her. "I'm yours for as long as you need me."

If only that were possible. She feared she needed him far longer than a mere trip to Elmira. A lifetime longer. He was like that little ragged blanket she'd hauled around as a youngster. As long as she had her *blankie*, she was safe and content.

"I see you bathed and changed," he said. "How are you feeling? Is your head still hurting?"

"My head's fine." Her heart was another matter. "How'd your granddaddy take the news about Calhoun?"

"Not very well. But he'll get over it."

Drat. Just as she thought. The ruckus with Calhoun hadn't set well with the elder Porter. That made carrying out her task all the more important.

He motioned to the pair of chairs facing the hearth. "Would you care to sit? There might be a breeze coming through the open windows."

"No, thank you. This won't take long." She hoped.

The mantel clock gonged the hour, reminding her time was running out. She twisted her hands together in a fretful ball. If she delayed any longer, she might never gather the nerve again.

"Jack..." She swallowed hard. "I have something I need to tell you."

He tilted his head to one side, training his good eye on her. Though he appeared to cope well with his deformity, it still ate at him. He lashed out when anyone tried to discuss it. How would he react when she told him of her decision?

"What is it, Kitty? You know you can tell me anything."

Anything but this, it seemed. Dread thickened in her throat. Would he go cold and silent? Or answer with angry fists? Neither seemed likely from the gentle man she'd come to know and—and what?

Love? The notion was as jumbled in her head as letters on a page. And she didn't have the time or the courage to sort it out.

She licked dry lips. "Promise you'll listen to what I have to say...all of it...before you answer."

His smile faded. "You're starting to worry me. What's this about?"

"Promise."

"Very well, I promise. Go on."

She buried her trembling hands in the folds of her skirt. If he thought she had any doubts, he'd use every weapon in his verbal arsenal to change her mind. She couldn't let that happen.

"I wish there was some way I could repay you for all you've done for me, Jack. You've been a Godsend." *And more.* He'd been her rock. Her port in a storm. To continue without him...well, she'd just have to weather that loss later. Right now, she had a more urgent tempest to sail through.

"It was my pleasure." He shrugged and gave a wry grin. "Well, maybe not at first, but you sorta grew on me. Besides, we shook hands on our bargain."

Sorta. Not a word she expected to cross his lips. She was definitely a bad influence, in more ways than one. "That's what I wanted to talk about." She stamped his face into her memory to savor once he was gone. The rakish eye-patch. His smooth, strong jaw. His firm mouth. Brandy. His kiss had been like that expensive spirit everyone was forever plying on her. Smooth and bracing, leaving a trail of fire wherever it touched.

Heat flamed in his gaze as if he'd read her mind. Too bad he couldn't read what she was about to say and save her the trouble. On the down side, that passionate heat would most likely turn into icy coldness.

She squared herself, preparing for his reaction.

171

Difficult or not, she had to do this. "I've decided I no longer need your help getting to Elmira."

His lips thinned, but he remained mute. Man kept his word, just as he always said. Was it any wonder she admired him?

"I can make it there on my own," she added.

More silence. The tick of the mantel clock sounded like boot heels pacing off an early morning duel. The marble busts of Washington and Jefferson perched on a nearby shelf watched in quiet disapproval.

Jack cleared his throat. "Are you finished?"

With hurting him? Yes. Caring for him...not even close. "I mean what I say, Jack. I can make it without your help. I'll leave tomorrow. Find a place to stay until the trains are running again."

"What about your..." His gaze slid to her lips, devouring her inch by painful inch. "...Mouth. It has a tendency to spill over."

Longing flared deep inside her, an ache fueled by the sweet memory of his lips on hers. "I'll just have to make sure my mouth behaves." *As well as the rest of me.* "I can do it. I know I can."

"I know you can, too. But you don't *have* to do it alone."

"Yes, I do. I release you from our agreement."

"What if I don't want to be released?" He moved closer, bringing all that heat and maleness to muddle her wits. "I'm not going to Elmira just for your benefit. I have a stake in this as well. My editor is expecting a front page article. And I intend to give him one."

"Then go. But not with me." She retreated to the middle of the room, putting a small round table between her and temptation. No telling what her traitorous body might do if she stayed near him.

"What brought on this sudden change of heart?" He countered her retreat and joined her beside the table. "Is it Calhoun? I know you're worried about his blood trail playing out at the edge of the property. But it's been six hours since he disappeared, and no one has come to question or arrest you."

"That could change at any moment. I can't allow you or your granddaddy to be pulled into this mess— my mess—any further. You could be arrested for concealing me." *And if found guilty—hanged.* She'd never forgive herself if that happened.

"We're aware of the consequences."

"But, what if—"

"Shhh." He reached out, his hand skimming her arm from shoulder downward until he cupped her elbow in a gentle grip. "Calhoun is most likely lying dead in a ditch somewhere. No one can lose that much blood and live."

Her skin twitched, more from Jack's teasing touch than her mind filling with image of Calhoun dead. "Even so, he has my locket with Lance's picture."

"I doubt anyone can link it to you."

"I can't take that chance." She eased out of his grasp and crossed to the open window. Lightning bugs flashed in the growing darkness, like the sparks of guilt winking on her conscience. So many people hurt because of her. Bart. Lance. Jeb, and now Calhoun. Despite Jack's assurances, she could no longer put him or his granddaddy in danger.

The heady scent of sandalwood enveloped her. Lost in thought, she hadn't heard him approach. "I won't let you go by yourself, Kitty."

Anger and frustration rose inside her. Why did he have to make this so difficult? Couldn't he see it's what she wanted? What *he* needed?

She turned, latching onto her anger like a lifeline. "Stop calling me Kitty. It's over."

"It's not over. Not by a long shot."

She folded her arms over her chest, closing herself off from him. If he found one crack in her blockade, she'd be done for. "Don't do this, Jack. You have to let me go on alone."

"No, I don't. I care what happens to you."

"Why?"

"Because..." His expression softened. "I have feelings for you. Feelings I can't stop. Don't want to stop."

Joy trilled like a songbird inside her. She plugged her ears to the noise. "I'm not who you think I am."

"I know exactly who you are."

"No, you don't. But you should." She took a step back to give herself some breathing space. His nearness made thinking, much less talking, difficult. "Earlier, I was too upset to tell you. But now that things have calmed down, it's time."

"You don't have to do this."

"You deserve to know the truth." She dropped fisted hands to her sides, holding onto her dwindling courage before it slipped away. "As I said before, my father was overseer at Spivey Point. Fannie refused to be attended by a Negro, so Papa offered my services as her maid."

"That must've rankled."

"I wasn't happy about it. But I did what I had to. Papa depended on me." And she'd let him down. Let everyone down. She reached behind her and gripped the window ledge, using the solidness as a brace for what was to come.

"The Lawrence sisters were mean and spiteful, always looking down their pointed little noses and calling me names. But not Bart. Not at first."

"Bart is the owner?"

"The owner's son. Or, he was." She wet her dry lips and went on. "He was nice to me. Always had a kind word and even gave me small gifts from time to time. He was my only friend at the main house." She dug her fingernails into the wood. "So I thought."

"What happened?"

Lamplight flickered on the columns of books standing in formation like soldiers. How different would her life be if reading wasn't her enemy? Would she have made smarter choices? Not hurt the ones she loved?

"Kitty?"

She shook off the ugly thoughts and continued. "When the fighting drew close, the Lawrences decided to tuck tail and run. Everyone was busy with the preparations, rushing here and there. It was total bedlam. Bart asked me to help him with something in the tack shed. H-he...I wasn't expecting him to..." As the memories rushed in, shame boiled in her chest and bubbled up to burn in her face and ears.

"You weren't expecting him to attack you," Jack finished for her.

She ducked her head and averted her gaze, unable to bear his scorn.

He slid a finger under her chin and tenderly lifted her head. "There's nothing to be ashamed of. You're not to blame for the actions of another."

No matter how many times she heard those words, they still failed to cheer her. "I should've known better. No woman goes alone into a shed with a man. No *decent* woman."

Jaw muscles twitched beneath his smooth skin. He was angry. At her? The thought sent an arrow zinging into her heart.

"Where is the brute now?"

"Jack—"

His voice hardened. "Where is he?"

"Dead."

"Your doing?"

If only. "No. Lance heard me struggling to get

175

free and charged inside the shed." Guilt pounded on her, a hammer striking an anvil. Her chest ached from the force. "They scuffled, and Bart fell back onto a pitchfork. My sweet, gentle brother, who wouldn't hurt a fly, killed a man. Because of me."

"Lance did what any civilized man would've done. Hell, I'd do the same if the swine was still alive."

"But if it weren't for my stupidity, Lance wouldn't have needed to enlist in the Army to escape the Lawrences. Wouldn't now be in prison, facing God-knows what tortures. And Papa..." She couldn't go there. The pain squeezing her was so fierce, she could hardly draw a breath. "So you see...I'm soiled. In more ways than one. You deserve better than me."

"What I deserve—"

A sharp rap on the front door interrupted his reply.

His expression blackened. "Gripes. Who could that be at this hour?"

Another knock sounded, louder and more insistent.

She nodded at the doorway. "Best see who it is before the knocking wakes Sally."

"Fine. But don't you go anywhere. This conversation isn't over yet."

Her heart thumped in tattered beats as she watched him cross the floor and disappear into the hallway. He now knew all about her past. Every ugly detail. Surely those feelings he claimed to have for her had withered.

Her knees went weak, and she had to grab the table edge for support. She'd never again feel his hand, warm and comforting, on her elbow as he guided on an exciting adventure. Or hear his deep voice as he related some fascinating tidbit. Her life would be dark and hollow—like the shed she'd died in.

The creak of hinges echoed into the study. "Private Duncan," Jack said. "What can I do for you?"

A bluebelly. Would Jack protect her now that their pact was over? He had no reason to do so. Probably had a better reason not to. She crept to the doorway and stopped just inside the threshold to better hear the men's conversation.

"Sorry to bother you, Mr. Porter," the soldier replied. "I've come about Lieutenant Calhoun."

Fear punched the breath from her. The Yankees had found Calhoun. They'd come to arrest her. She had to leave. *Now*. Before it was too late.

She craned her neck around the jamb. Jack stood at the far end of the hall, his tall form blocking her view of Private Duncan. Good. That meant the soldier couldn't see her either. She eased out of the doorway and tiptoed toward the rear staircase.

"You sound worried," Jack said. "Is there a problem, Private?"

Problem? Try a disaster. And if she didn't get out of this house, it would become a horrible tragedy.

****

Tall lamps lit the street corners but did little to brighten the dark pockets dotting the walkway. She gathered her cloak tighter around her. Unfamiliar city streets teeming with riffraff were not the place she wanted to be, especially at night. If she remembered correctly from their trip to the market, the *Federal Inn* should be somewhere in the next few blocks. The sooner she reached it, the better.

Footsteps thumped behind her.

She glanced over her shoulder. A figure moved from the darkness into the light. Though a slouch hat hid his features, his blue uniform was unmistakable. The breath lodged in her throat. *Calhoun*? Couldn't be. He'd been near death. She quickened her step anyway.

The click of boot heels kept pace, and panic galloped inside her. She couldn't let him catch her. Not alone and unprotected.

An open door beckoned. She darted through the entrance and into a well-lit mercantile filled with a maze of shelves and bins. Perfect hidey-holes. She ducked behind a tall shelf and peeked around the edge.

Her pursuer paused in the doorway. Lamplight lit his rugged features. Not Calhoun. But that intent expression on his face suggested a threat just as great. He scanned the inside of the store, frowned, and then moved on.

She released her pent-up breath. A near miss. But what if she wasn't so lucky the next time? She had to find lodging and get off the streets. Soon.

"Can I help you, ma'am?"

She turned to find a gray-haired woman peering up at her, a welcoming smile dimpling her cheeks. "I...um..." *Drat.* She hadn't thought beyond escaping her stalker.

A rack of ready-made dresses caught her eye. Just what she needed. "I'd like to purchase an outfit. Black if you have it." She bowed her head and laced her tone with sorrow. "For mourning."

Sympathy softened the woman's expression. "I'm sorry for your loss, ma'am."

Not the kind you're thinking, but a loss nonetheless. She supplied a slow nod. "It happened so suddenly. My husband and I were on our way to visit relatives in New York, and..." She swallowed around the lump in her throat that was more real than contrived. Would lying about a death make it come to pass? "I-I was totally unprepared."

"You poor dear. We were about to close shop, but we can make an exception. Considering your circumstances."

"Why, thank you, ma'am. That's mighty kind of you."

"Glad to be of service. I'm Mrs. Sloan." The shopkeeper gestured at the aproned man standing behind the far counter. "And that's my husband. We own this shop."

"Mrs. Porter. Kitty Porter."

"Porter, you say? There's an Elias Porter who lives up on Federal Hill. Any relation?"

Tarnation. The Porter name wasn't hers and never would be. She'd have to take better care with her identity, else she faced more trouble than she bargained for.

She flipped a dismissive hand. "Oh, no. We've no kin in Baltimore. Just passing through."

"Well, Jonas and I will do whatever we can to help you."

"You're sweet to offer. As you can probably tell by my accent, I'm not from around here. Your kindness makes this big ol' city seem a little less frightening."

"I'm happy to help." Mrs. Sloan motioned at the clothes rack. "Why don't you look through those? I'm sure you'll find one to suit."

She began rummaging through the outfits. Her fingers drifted over a lovely lavender. The cottony material would hug her in a soft embrace, gently molding her figure, a welcome change from the sagging sack she currently wore. Would Jack like—

She stiffened. No. She had to stop thinking of him. He was no longer part of her life. She had to accept that. Just as she'd asked him to accept it.

She forced her fingers past the gown. It was pretty enough but not quite the grieving image she wanted to portray. She selected a plain, black muslin and held it up to her front-side. The ample dress nearly swallowed her whole.

Mrs. Sloan gave a soft cluck. "Goodness, you're a

slender one."

Bread and broth did little to fill out a person's bones. "Times've been hard. Especially with War."

"They certainly have." The shopkeeper patted her ample girth and chuckled. "Though you wouldn't know it from my spreading figure."

"More of you to love, so my nanny would say."

"Wise woman, your nanny." She pointed to the gown. "I can alter that if you'd like. Where are you staying?"

Too many questions for which she had too few answers. "I...um...haven't found lodgings yet. I was on my way to the Federal Inn."

Mrs. Sloan's smile faded. "With the Army in town, I doubt you'll find any available rooms there."

Bad luck appeared to be stalking her as well. "Do you know of any other place I can try?"

"Nothing near here. Or anywhere else, I suspect."

Louisa glanced at the darkened window, worry returning to chew at her insides. What would she do now? Going back to the Porter house was out of the question.

"You're more than welcome to stay with us," the shopkeeper offered. "Our apartment above the shop has a spare bedroom you can use."

"Oh, I don't...I couldn't impose." She couldn't keep eagerness out of her voice. Staying at the mercantile would be the perfect solution. Neither Jack nor the soldiers would think to look for her here.

"It's no imposition a'tall."

She gave one last half-hearted try. "I don't want to put you out."

"You wouldn't be putting us out. Besides, I welcome the company." Mrs. Sloan leaned closer and lowered her voice. "Jonas is a sweet man, but he isn't much of a talker."

"I'd be happy to pay for the use of your spare room."

"Heavens, no. You'll be our guest." She nodded at the black muslin. "Is that the one you've decided on?"

"Yes. This is perfect."

"Good." Mrs. Sloan whisked the gown into her arms. "Let's get supper cooked, and then we can see to taking it in for you."

She followed her savior across the floor, her heart much lighter than when she entered the store. This fortunate outcome was much more welcome than the less-than-kind cards life had dealt her so far. Would her luck hold out?

****

Thor's hammer pounded inside his skull. His eye burned as if coated in sand. Even his teeth hurt. But he couldn't stop. Kitty was out there somewhere. Alone and vulnerable. He had to find her. Bring her home. Much as he wanted to strangle her for leaving, he prayed he'd find her safe and unharmed.

Two heads were tucked together, one capped with fine gray hair and the other salt and pepper hued. Conspiratorial whispers carried to the doorway. The proverbial saying *thick as thieves* came to mind. If he wasn't so damned drained, he might've been concerned.

Elias glanced up, caught sight of him, and jolted upright. Rather quick for a man of his age. What other secrets did he conceal?

"Master Jack," Sally blurted, worry lines adding to the wrinkles on her face. "Did you find her?"

Jack shook his head. "Not a trace. I searched all night. Every nook and cranny in this moldering city."

"Lord have mercy, where could that chile be?"

"I wish I knew. I thought for certain she'd go to the Federal Inn. We passed by the place on our trip to the market. She even commented on the architecture."

Elias grunted. "Good riddance, I say. She's caused enough trouble as it is."

Heat charged through his veins. He fisted his hands at his side to keep from doing something he'd later regret. "How can you be so callous? She's a stranger to this city, much less a woman alone. Anything could happen to her."

"She's a smart bird. Like our Sally. She's likely roosting somewhere safe and sound."

In a city filled with Yankee soldiers? She was likely scared out of her wits. A sharp pang lanced his chest at the thought of ill befalling her and him not there to offer protection.

Sally crossed to his side and rested a hand on his arm. "Come, Master Jack. Get some breakfast in your belly. I cooked up a rasher of bacon. And your favorite buttermilk biscuits."

How could he eat when Kitty was out there possibly without food or shelter? "I'm not hungry."

"You have to eat. To keep up your strength. You won't do yo'self or Miss Carleton any good if you give out." Sally tugged on his sleeve. "Have a seat. I'll bring you a platter."

"I don't want anything, Sally. Truly."

"Hmmph. Best let the woman fix you something, boy. Or you'll never hear the end of it."

Now wasn't that the pot calling the kettle black. "I only stopped by long enough for a change of clothes. I'm going back out soon as I'm done."

Sally wrinkled up her nose. "Phew. You smell worse than skunk spray. What you got into?"

"I was looking for her down at the docks. Slipped and fell into a bilge pit." He pulled up his trouser legs stained from the knees down to reveal bare feet. "I left my socks and boots on the back stoop. Didn't want to track muck into the house."

"Lands sake, Master Jack. You sho' do get into more muddles." She turned, clucking like a mother hen. "You change and get somethin' to eat while I clean up them boots. Then you can go back to looking for Miss Carleton."

"Thank you, Sally," he called after her as she sped down the hall. "You're a Godsend."

She didn't stop to answer, merely waved a hand in the air and kept going. Jack turned back to the parlor. His grandfather had moved to one of the armchairs in front of the hearth. A small fire burned in the grate. The temperature had dropped to an unseasonable chill during the night. Much like his spirits had dipped as search after search for Kitty turned up nothing.

"Perhaps it's a good thing Miss Carleton left. You're shed of her now. There won't be any ugly scenes."

"What do you mean *ugly scenes*?"

"When the two of you part ways. It's going to happen sooner or later."

If their parting was inevitable, he'd preferred it happened later. After he girded himself for the pain. A chill rattled his bones. He crossed to the hearth and rubbed his hands in front of the fire, though no heat could penetrate the coldness that filled his soul.

He knew he shouldn't put himself back in the line of fire by going after her. She'd left without a fare-thee-well. Had stolen out of the house like a thief in the night, taking his heart with her. But he couldn't stop himself. He couldn't give up on something that felt so real.

He turned to face his grandfather who eyed him like a hawk from a perch. "You're right about one thing; she *has* probably found a place to lay low until the trains start running again. When that happens, she'll emerge and I'll find her."

"What will you do when you locate her?"

"I'll resume our arraignment. Travel with her to Elmira to free her brother."

"And after that? Will you make her your wife in God's eyes?"

His heart bucked. Kitty had made her wishes quite clear. She didn't want a relationship with him. Felt she wasn't good enough for him. He hoped to eventually change that notion. He had to find her first.

"I haven't thought that far ahead."

"I have." Elias pounded a hand on the armrest. His bushy brows snapped together. "You must give up on this woman, Jackson. She's all wrong for you."

Heated blood rushed into his skull at his grandfather's condescending tone. "Wrong how? She's not of our privileged set? She's got more class in her pinky finger than many of the ladies you've tried to foist on me. She's smart and funny and makes me feel alive."

"God save us." Elias grimaced and held his temple as though it pained him. "You're in love with her."

Jack blinked and blinked again. Did a twinkle flash in those hard gray eyes before Elias had ducked his head? No. Couldn't be. His exhausted mind was merely playing tricks.

"I don't know what I am. I just know I can't give up on her."

Elias looked up, head shaking. "Mule-headed. Just like your grandmother, God rest her soul."

"Grandmother would take you to task for your hard-heartedness, and you well know it."

"Hmmph. How would you know?"

"I might not have known grandmother, but if my mother was anything like her, she would have found the good in a person. Any person. Of any station."

Elias stared into the fire, jowls and mouth sagging. He looked every bit of his seventy years.

Jack's heart sank. He hated being at odds with his grandfather. Their quarrels sapped all of his strength. He knew it had to be much worse on the older man.

"Grandfather—"

Elias gave himself a shake. Hardness returned to his eyes. "You're a fool, Jackson. Miss Carleton will only bring you heartache."

Anger replaced his concern. "I'm going to find Kitty and go to Elmira. And there's not a damn thing you can do about."

"And how will you pay for this addlepated undertaking?"

"I'll find a way. Once my article is submitted, I can honor my debt. Mr. Abell—"

"Will be disinclined to provide you with any kind of assistance. I reminded him of my generous patronage of his newspaper."

He speared Elias with a barbed look. "And warned all your other wealthy acquaintances as well, I'd wager."

"A wager you'd win."

Gripes. Jack reached up and yanked his cravat lose. Little good it did. The strangling sensation wrapping his throat remained. He didn't have to work hard to force gravel into his tone. "You go too far, Grandfather."

"Perhaps." Elias steepled his fingers under his chin and regarded him through narrowed eyes. "I've given it some thought and have decided that I shall lend you the funds you require...on one condition."

His stomach fell. "Do I even want to ask?"

"As soon as this assignment is over, you will return to Baltimore and accept the position Arunah Abell offered."

"That's not a problem. I had already considered accepting that offer."

"You will do so *without* Miss Carleton in tow."

****

"You're in luck, ma'am. Tracks were cleared for northbound trains just this morning."

Louisa slumped against the ticket counter. *Hallelujah.* She'd soon be out of Baltimore and no longer looking over her shoulder in fear of being spotted by the soldiers—or by Jack.

"I'll take one passage to Elmira, New York."

The clerk nodded. "That'll be four dollars, ma'am."

She fished a handful of coins out of her purse. The silver one with the eagle was a dollar. She plunked it on the counter. And another. Plus a half dollar. That's...drat. She counted even worse than she read. Avoiding the clerk's stare, she shoved the coins across the countertop.

He counted the money and slid one coin back. "You gave me too much, ma'am."

She covered for her wretched adding skill with a wry smile. "So, I did. I'm so excited about the trains running again, I miscounted. Thank you for catching my error."

"We'll be boarding soon." He handed her a ticket and dipped his head toward the far end of the lobby. "You're welcome to wait over by those benches."

Satchel in hand, she crossed to the row of wooden benches and squeezed into the only vacant spot left. Despite the early hour, nearly two dozen customers milled about the small, high-ceiling stationhouse. A young mother worked to calm her fretful baby. Another pursued a runaway toddler. A group of men stood near the clock tower, chatting sociably. All were well-dressed. None wore an eye patch.

Relief warred with disappointment. She'd fully expected to find Jack waiting for her. A raw ache speared her chest. Had he accepted her decision to end their pact? It was the right thing to do, she knew. But Lordy, why did it feel so wrong?

Something moved behind a large potted fern tucked in one corner of the station. Brown trousers and a tweed jacket were just visible through the thick fronds. The man appeared to be hiding. From who? And why?

She leaned forward for a better view. The man shifted and buried deeper into the shadows. *Tarnation.* The only way to see him would be to get up and—

A shout rang out followed by the thud of hurried footsteps. Half-a-dozen soldiers rushed through the front entrance, expressions fixed, rifles at the ready. Another group scurried in through the rear entry, effectively trapping their quarry.

Her pulse stampeded. Her, perhaps?

She grabbed her satchel. They wouldn't take her that easily. As she leapt to her feet, gunshots erupted from the potted fern. The soldiers hunkered down and returned fire. Screams and shouts filled the chamber. Ears ringing from the noise, Louisa swarmed with the equally frightened crowd toward the platform just outside the open doors. Their flight provided the perfect cover, but not without a price.

A boot heel ground her toe. An elbow jabbed her side. She pulled up with a yelp and cupped her throbbing ribs. Before she could resume her escape, someone crashed into her, sending her sprawling forward.

She landed on her hands and knees, gasping, the breath knocked from her lungs. Out of the corner of her eye, she caught a glimpse of tweed trousers. A second later, blue uniforms engulfed the man.

The platform echoed with angry shouts, the scrape of scuffling boots, and the muffled thuds of fists striking human flesh. A heavy clunk sounded, then a pistol went skidding across the planks. The thrashing brawlers quieted and grew still.

Her breath restored, she rocked back on her haunches. The soldiers had backed away from their quarry, giving her a clear view. Familiar brown eyes met hers. She froze. *Smith*. The man from the docks.

A hand clamped around her arm. "Ma'am?"

Startled, she jerked her head around and looked up at the solider standing over her. Sweet Mary. Her luck had finally run out. She was caught tighter than a rabbit in a snare.

"Ma'am?" he said again, his tone oddly polite and spiked with concern. "Are you hurt?"

Blue uniforms surged around her. Well, there was naught for it. To resist would be pointless. She gave a resigned nod and with his help, stood upright. As she reached for her satchel, her knees wobbled, and she had to hold onto his arm for support.

"Let me get that for you." He hefted her satchel and straightened. "Can I help you back into the stationhouse?"

Help her? Weren't they going to haul her off to prison along with Smith? The soldiers had secured his hands with rope and were herding him across the platform.

Her helper nodded toward the procession. "I'm sorry you were caught up in that. But we couldn't let him get away."

"Get away?" Her voice squeaked in spite of her effort to keep it steady.

He leaned closer and whispered, "He's a Rebel spy."

It was just as she suspected. Smith had come to Maryland with ill intentions. Would he tell the soldiers she'd sailed with him across the Potomac? Brown eyes once again met hers. He gave a brief nod, then clamped his lips shut.

Maybe her luck hadn't run out after all.

"All aboard," the porter announced. "All aboard for destinations to York, Harrisburg, Williamsport and Elmira."

Praise the Lord. "That's me." She eased her arm out of the soldier's grasp and took her satchel from him. "I can make it from here. Thank you for your help." Though her feet itched to run, she forced a slow, steady pace. No need to call attention to herself. The soldiers weren't after her. Not yet, at least.

She found a seat in the forward coach and before long the train pulled out of the station, leaving Baltimore, the soldiers, and Jack behind. She focused on the passing landscape and not on the pain clacking like train wheels inside her chest.

After an hour of staring out the window, she pulled *Silk and Scarlet* from her satchel and tried to read. Thoughts of Jack, not her poor reading skills, blurred the words. Had he succeeded in dodging Private Duncan's questions, or had he been arrested for concealing her? Poor Granddaddy Porter would surely suffer apoplexy if that happened. And Sally. She didn't even want to think about what Jack's arrest might do to the kindly housekeeper who loved him like a son.

If only she could go back in time, back to the night she and Jack had met. She'd take her chances with the Yankee patrol and run right past that canvas-covered haven. Then he would never be involved in her life, would never have found his way into her heart.

An excited yelp cut into her thoughts. On the other side of the aisle, a young boy crawled beneath the benches, a wide smile dimpling his dirt-smudged cheeks. A harried woman, presumably the child's mother, made a grab for the boy. He squealed again and darted out of reach. The little scoundrel threaded his way around trousers and skirts, sending the disturbed passengers leaping to their feet. A soldier seated a few rows up nabbed a handful of britches and hoisted the child off the floor.

The boy flailed arms and legs, trying to escape. He scowled at the soldier and gave a cub-like growl. "Lemme go, you snake."

Louisa hid a smile behind her hand. If she ever had children, she hoped they would be as game and spirited as that one. Her heart fell. But that would never happen. She'd left behind the only man she trusted enough to touch her, trusted enough to give her children.

Her gown became too tight, too warm. The coach windows had been pulled shut, keeping out the soot and cinders spewing from the engine's smokestack, but caging in the heat. Hades couldn't be any hotter. She struggled to draw a breath. Thick air clogged her throat. She needed fresh air. Now.

She shot to her feet and rushed toward the exit, grasping the seat backs for support against the sway of the railcar. From her seat to the door seemed like miles, yet the blast of smoky air that greeted her on the platform was a relief. She leaned against the handrail and sucked in several deep breaths, much preferring the smoke to the heated staleness inside.

"I didn't realize I had died."

She whirled around at the familiar voice, heart skipping as she met Jack's penetrating gaze. "Wh-what are you doing here?"

He cocked an eyebrow. "What? No tearful greeting for your dear, departed husband? That *is* why you're wearing widow's weeds, I assume."

The train lurched, throwing her against him and cutting off her reply. His arms curled around her, warm and steadying, and for a moment, she ignored the warning bells in her head and simply basked in the comfort of his embrace.

Hold me, Jack. Hold me and keep me safe.

The train jolted again, and the moment burst

like a fragile soap bubble. With a sigh of regret, she pushed away.

He clamped a hand on her upper arm. "Let's go back inside where it's less noisome and safer."

She opened her mouth to refuse but stopped at the deadly expression that crossed his face. She'd best give in to his demand or risk being dragged, or worse, carried back inside. She ground her teeth together and shoved past him into the coach.

He followed her, his fingers fastened like a shackle around her arm. After only a few steps down the aisle, he tugged her to a halt. "Right here will do."

"But my satchel—"

"Will be fine. It's less crowded back here. Less chance for you to evade my questions."

"Jack, I—"

"Sit," he growled.

Her stomach gave an anxious roll at his tone. He was far angrier at her leaving than she thought he'd be. But she'd only done what she had to do, and he had no right to question her actions. He had no hold over her.

She jerked out of his grasp, resentment replacing her unease as she slid onto the bench. She glared up at him as he sat beside her. *Have at it, Jack Porter.*

He narrowed his gaze. "Why, Kitty?"

"Stop calling me that, the charade is—"

"Over. Yes, you said that. Now tell me why you left."

"Hmmph. You know perfectly well, why."

"Would I ask if I knew?"

"You might, given your newspaperman's nature. Always asking questions. Always picking somebody's brain. Can't you ever just let things be?"

He stared at her for a second and then pressed his lips into a hard, impatient line. "Tell me why you ran off. We were in the midst of a fairly serious discussion before we were interrupted, and I thought—" He froze, mouth agape as the pieces fell into place. "It was Duncan wasn't it? Gripes, he was no threat to you."

"No threat!" She glanced at the nearby passengers, who either couldn't hear, or were ignoring their conversation. She lowered her voice anyway. "He was looking for Calhoun."

"Yes, he was. The lieutenant didn't show up for the return ride to Point Lookout. Duncan thought he might've stopped by for a visit, seeing as how interested Calhoun was in my article. If you had stayed around long enough, you would've known that."

"I couldn't take that chance."

"Even if he had come for you, I wouldn't have let him take you."

"That's just why I had to leave, Jack. I couldn't let you ruin your life for me."

"My choice, not yours." He raked a hand through his hair, mussing the neatly combed locks. "God, Kitty, when I think about what could have happened to you last night. All alone in a city filled with soldiers and riffraff."

"Nothing happened. I was perfectly safe."

"Where did you stay?"

She plucked at her skirt. "At the general store where I bought this. The storekeepers insisted I stay with them."

"I'm glad you found a safe place. We were worried about you."

We. Sweet, kindly Sally. Granddaddy Porter, who had a heart of gold beneath that gruff outer shell. And Jack. No she wouldn't think about Jack missing her. That would only bring on a fresh round of regret. "I'm sorry if I worried everyone. But I had no choice."

"You could've come back after Duncan left."

"No, I couldn't. You clearly weren't happy with my request that we part ways. I had to make a clean cut. It was for the best."

"For the best." He shifted on the bench, angling all that bone-melting maleness closer. "You're not thinking this through, Kitty. Getting your brother out of prison is going to be difficult at best. You need the help of someone familiar with the ways of the Army."

"I'll manage." Hopefully better than she was dealing with her feelings for him. "So, I'm guessing since you're on this train, your granddaddy gave you that loan."

His mouth went taut as a bowstring. Something flickered in his gaze. Anger? Pain? Both?

"We're not talking about me, right now." His voice turned low and pointed. "Have you thought about Calhoun?"

"What about him?"

"You don't know whether he's dead or alive. What if he recovers and comes after you?"

It was one of many fears that plagued her. "I hope Lance and I will be long gone from Elmira by then."

"And if you're not..."

"Then I'll take care of the polecat myself."

"I doubt you'll be lucky enough to find another unstable statue."

She stiffened. "If you're trying to frighten me—"

"Damn right, I'm trying to frighten you." He leaned toward her as if pressing home his point. "This is not a simple jaunt, Kitty. You could be hurt, or worse."

"So could you. I don't want you to be involved in this mess any longer."

"Well, I'm sorry to disappoint you, but I'm here to stay, whether you like it or not."

Chapter Fourteen

She stepped off the railcar stairs and onto the depot platform. Passengers streamed around her, eager to fill their bellies during the brief stop. Her own stomach rumbled its need for food, good wholesome food like the pot roast the portly gent had been going on about for the past hour. But she'd have to make do with an apple and crackers just as she had for the noon meal. After the necessary, but expensive, purchase of her traveling outfit, she needed to conserve her funds. A lavish dinner meal was a luxury she couldn't afford.

She sensed someone behind her and knew by the captivating sandalwood scent who it was. She tightened her grip on her satchel handle. The mule just wouldn't listen to reason, wouldn't accept her decision to part ways. And he called his granddaddy stubborn? She blew out a frustrated sigh. Not much she could do about it now.

Once she reached Elmira however...

Jack fell into step beside her. "The porter suggested *The Dumm House Inn* for a quick meal. Why don't we go there?"

"Can't. I need to make a purchase at that mercantile across the street. You go on. I'll find something to eat in the store."

"I'll walk with you. Besides, I need another journal. The one I'm working on is nearly full."

She shrugged and used his earlier words against him. "Your choice." As she stepped off the curb, two blackbirds swooped in front of her. She halted midstride, heart thumping like one of Belle's hide-covered drums. *No. Please not that.*

Jack's hand closed on her arm. "What is it?"

"Blackbirds."

"What about them?"

The pair circled overhead. One cawed three times. Dread soared in her belly. "Dear God, no."

Jack moved closer as if to protect her. Not that it would do any good. "What's wrong?"

"Someone's going to die."

"Die? Why do you say that?"

"Those birds are omens. Three caws and..." A quiver rumbled through her. "I heard them the day before Papa—" She cupped a hand to her mouth, refusing to say more. Uttering the words aloud might curse someone else.

"Settle down, Kitty. It's just a silly superstition. No one is going to die."

"It's not silly. I know what those birds mean. Something bad is going to happen."

"Nothing is going to happen." He gave her arm a gentle squeeze. "I won't let it."

She pulled out of his grasp. "For a newspaperman interested in everything that goes on around him, you sure are narrow-minded."

"I just don't hold with superstitions. I need tangibles, real things I can touch and see."

"You can see those blackbirds, can't you?"

"They're just birds. Nothing more."

If only she could believe that. But she'd been raised by Belle Fontaine, a wise spiritual woman who knew to heed such signs. "You believe what you want. I know better." She glanced skyward, then picked her way carefully across the street. Only thing to do now was keep an eye out for danger.

Inside the mercantile, a balding clerk standing behind the counter gave them a cheerful greeting. Jack, ever the nosey journalist, struck up a conversation with the man, so she wandered toward the back of the store where she found a bin of apples. Thoughts of the blackbirds faded as she searched for a big, ripe one to fill her grumbling belly.

A few feet away, two women flitted around at a table littered with bolts of cloth. A stout lady held up a length of deep purple velvet. "What about this one?"

The other woman eyed the fabric. "No, no, Edla. That's much too bold for a bedchamber, a parlor maybe." She pointed to another bolt. "This gold would look much better."

Edla pursed her lips. "I don't know. That color is so...dreary." She shook her head and looked up, her gaze finding Louisa near the apple bin. "What do you think, ma'am?"

They wanted *her* opinion? The only curtains she'd ever fashioned were made from sackcloth. "I'm sorry. I'd like to help, but I don't know much about fabrics."

Edla tilted her head to the side and studied her. "You're not from around here, are you?"

Lordy, the last thing she needed was to call attention to herself. She shook her head and offered a vague, but safe, explanation. "No, I'm not. I'm heading north to visit with relatives. The train made a brief stop for supper."

The older woman gave her a warm smile. "Welcome to Williamsport. I'm Mrs. Elam and this is my friend, Mrs. Spicer."

She plucked an apple from the bin and moved closer. She couldn't very well be rude to such friendly women. Besides, the urge to inspect the lovely fabrics tugged at her. Perhaps one day, she'd be able to sort through similar bolts to decorate her own home.

"Pleased to meet you, ladies. I'm Mrs. Porter." Drat. She did it again. She needed to come up with a new fake name.

Martha ran a finger over the purple velvet. "So, what do you think, Mrs. Porter? This or that dreadful gold?"

She eyed the two fabrics, then envisioned sunshine pouring through a window framed by pleated curtains. Images always came easier to her than words on a page. "Did I hear you say this was for a bedchamber?"

"Yes, it is."

"Would you mind describing the room?"

"Certainly. The furnishings are dark walnut with brass hardware. Wallpaper printed with spring flowers covers the walls. The floor is pine. The ceilings are swirled white plaster."

Sounded like the stately bedrooms at Spivey Point. She tapped a finger to her bottom lip as she considered her answer. She glanced at the two women, each sure their selection was the right one. Best to offer a tactful solution, else she risked hurt feelings.

She lifted a length of olive green velvet. "Personally, I like this. The green would bring out the white and browns and accent the flowers in the wallpaper. It'd give your room a light, outdoorsy feel."

Mrs. Elam regarded the green for a moment, then draped the end over a nearby table. "This wood is similar to mine. What do you think, Martha?"

"That just might do," the woman answered. "Try it against that painted vase behind you."

She moved back several steps and held the bolt up to a vase decorated with flowers and vines. "Well?"

"Perfect." Mrs. Spicer cut Louisa a sly glance. "And you said you know little about fabrics."

She shrugged, pleased by their obvious delight with her suggestion. "I don't. But I can picture the room with all the colors."

"Yes, my wife has quite the eye for decorating." Jack eased beside her and placed a hand at her lower back.

She arched to escape his touch. "Ladies, this is my...er...husband."

After exchanging greetings with the two women, he grasped her elbow, fingers pressing lightly into her skin and making her stomach do those unnerving little tumbles. "I'm sorry to intrude, but I must collect my wife. We don't want to miss our train and further delay our trip."

Mrs. Elam wagged her head. "Good thing you weren't traveling north last week or you would've found your trip delayed anyhow."

"Oh? What happened?" Jack asked.

The woman's expression grew grim. "One of the trains carrying prisoners to Elmira collided with a freighter just east of Shohola. Horrible crash. Fifty prisoners were killed."

Fifty...killed. Her knees turned to mush. If it weren't for Jack tightening his hold on her elbow, she would've collapsed.

"How terrible. It appears we're fortunate to have missed such a tragedy." Jack dipped a nod to the two women. "I wish we could chat longer, but we need to be going. Good-day, ladies."

Louisa mumbled her good-byes and followed him to the front of the store where he paid for their purchases. Once outside, her gaze went immediately to the sky. No birds. No bone-chilling caws. But that didn't matter; they'd already delivered their message.

"It doesn't mean a thing, Kitty."

"How can you say that? The birds. The train wreck. Lance..."

"May not have even been on that train."

"You don't know that."

"And you don't know that he was. Don't go inviting trouble."

"I don't invite it. It finds me." First there was Jeb getting shot, and then Calhoun's attack. Bad things come in threes, so Belle had said. Was the train wreck the third evil waiting to rip into her world?

She gathered up her skirts, the need to get to Elmira and discover the truth near strangling her. "I'm going back to the train."

"You should eat something first. That meager lunch you had wouldn't nourish a bird. Pun intended."

"My meals are none of your concern. Besides, I'm not hungry." Her belly rumbled, giving lie to her words.

His eyebrow lifted in mocking disbelief. "Your stomach says otherwise."

She glared up at him, annoyance replacing her edginess. "Hmmph. Didn't your granddaddy teach you it's rude to comment on such a personal matter?"

"He taught me a lot of things. Some I learned on my own."

"You missed the lesson on rudeness."

"Did I?"

"And arrogance."

"Perhaps I need a new tutor. Care to volunteer?"

"We both know how that would end." She stepped off the curb and sailed for the train depot. "I may be many things, but patient is not one of them."

****

The clack of iron wheels slowed, the noise becoming less deafening, less annoying. All around him, sleepy-eyed passengers began to stir. Jack remained still, reluctant to awaken the beauty snuggled against him. Kitty had finally given in to her exhaustion and fallen asleep. Her head now rested on his shoulder, her warm breaths fanning

199

his neck.

He closed his eye and savored the pleasant sensation. A soft ache filled his heart. What he wouldn't give to always have her at his side, her indomitable spirit lifting him from his ever-present gloom. Only two obstacles stood in his way. Convincing Kitty to make their sham marriage real. And countermanding his grandfather's demand that he return to Baltimore, *alone*. Each were equally daunting prospects. Yet one way or another, he'd overcome them. He had to. A future without Kitty held only bleakness.

The train lurched to a stop, jarring him from his thoughts. He opened his eye and wiggled his shoulder. "Kitty," he called out softly. "It's time to wake up."

She lifted her head, taking her warmth with her. Hooded green eyes drifted up to meet his. His loins stirred at the dazed, lover-like expression sketched on her face. He sucked in a soft breath.

As though she realized his ardent interest, the corners of her mouth dipped into a frown. She blinked the sleep from her eyes and pushed upright, glancing around the busy railcar as she moved. "Have we arrived?"

"Yes," he replied, ignoring the disappointment that flooded him. "We just pulled into the Elmira depot."

"Good. I've had enough of this hard bench." She grimaced and arched her back in an easy cat-like stretch.

His mind filled with a sudden shocking vision of her naked, arching beneath him, his hands drifting along the curve of those smooth, limber muscles. He forced a dry swallow and shoved the image away.

"Uh, yes...me too," he croaked as he stood and moved into the aisle. The bench wasn't all that was hard. His lack of control embarrassed and annoyed him. "It's near midnight," he went on, his tone still husky. "We should find a hotel and get some proper rest. I suspect tomorrow will be another trying day."

She gave him a searching glance, then grasped her satchel. "Yes, I suspect it will." She eased past him and headed for the exit along with the other passengers.

Wondering if she'd noticed his rusty tone, he gathered his knapsack and followed her, his gaze riveted on the gentle sway of muslin-encased hips. He felt his throat close further and hoped for a few extra minutes before he had to speak again. Not that time would matter. The woman could entice words from a mute.

Once on the platform, she stopped and pivoted around. "Drat, I forgot my book. I'll have to go back and get it."

He held up a hand to stop her. "Stay here. I'll get it for you." The task would give him more time to rein in his body.

He retraced his steps into the railcar, found her book, and made his way back to the dimly-lit and now deserted platform. Though he had himself under control, he couldn't stop his heart from leaping in alarm. Where had she gone? He knew in his gut she planned to give him the slip once they reached the city. But now? In the middle of the night where anything could happen to her?

"Kitty?" he called out, unable to keep the worry out of his voice.

"Shhh," came her reply from the shadows. "Over here."

Relieved, he joined her in the darkened pocket. "What are you doing?"

"I saw something, so I moved over here out of the lamplight."

"What did you see?"

She pointed to the far end of the station. "People

climbing out of the boxcars."

In the faint light spilling from the stationhouse, he could just make out a slender man assisting others out of a baggage car. The dark-skinned figures glanced from side to side, then trotted across the platform toward a waiting wagon.

The journalist in him stirred. He'd heard about the Underground Railroad. Hadn't seen it in action until now. "Runaway slaves."

"Runaways? Here?"

"Apparently so." He tugged her forward. "Let's find out more."

As they approached, the conductor of the operation barked a sharp command, and all movement stilled. The man eyed them cautiously, shoulders pulled back, head raised.

Jack gave him a friendly smile. "Don't be alarmed, sir. We mean you no harm." He held out his hand. "Name's Jackson Porter. I'm a journalist with *The New York Herald*, and this is my wife."

The man's dark face sagged with relief. He grasped Jack's hand in a firm handshake. "John Jones, suh. Ma'am."

Jack nodded at the boxcar and the shadowy figures crouched inside. "I'm assuming these are fugitives from the South."

"Yes, suh, they is."

"I'd be interested in hearing about their journey and your part in helping them. It would make a mighty fascinating article for my paper."

"I'm sure it would, Mista Porter." Jones gave a wry smile. "But I hope you understand that I has to keep this part of the operation secretive. Some folks 'round heah don't cotton to aiding slaves."

Kitty stepped from the shadows. "Do I detect a Virginia accent, Mr. Jones?"

"Yes'm, you do. I was born on a plantation in Leesburg. Belonged to the Elzy family. I 'scaped in forty-four and made my way heah where I been livin' eva since."

"And now you're helping others find their freedom," Jack added. "I applaud your generosity. Perhaps after the War, we can have a long chat, Mr. Jones."

The conductor smiled, his teeth white against his dark face. "Yes, suh. I'd like that."

"Well then, we'll let you get back to your work." He pressed a hand to Kitty's back, urging her forward. "We should be going as well, dear. Find us a hotel for the night."

Jones pointed at the far end of the street. "Try the Depot Inn on the corner. Mista Silas runs a simple, but clean establishment. He might have a room 'vailable."

Jack thanked the man and guided Kitty across the street.

She glanced over her shoulder as they walked. "I often worried about the slaves who escaped from Spivey Point. Where did they go? What became of them? I can only hope they met someone as charitable as Mr. Jones."

"I'm sure there are others like him out there, else the operation wouldn't be so successful."

Kitty fell silent for the rest of the walk, most likely agitating over her dark-skinned friends. She had a big heart, bigger than most. Was it any wonder he loved her?

They reached the end of the street and entered the three story wood-frame inn on the corner. Lamplight lit the front counter and the clerk bent over a registration book.

The elderly man looked up and smiled. "Welcome, sir. Ma'am. Are you just off the train?"

Jack nodded. "We are."

"Well you're in luck. I have one room left."

One room. Gripes. He cut a glance to the side.

Slightly pursed lips were the only outward sign of Kitty's displeasure at the news. He shrugged inwardly. Not much they could do about it now. It was far too late to search for another hotel. Besides, he was too exhausted to be troubled with the notion of sharing a room with a woman, no matter how enticing.

He slipped his wallet out of his pocket. "We'll take it."

After paying the clerk and signing the registration book, he escorted her up the stairs to their room. Lamplight from the hall spilled into the small bedchamber and onto a quilt-covered four poster pushed against the far wall. His loins stirred at the thought of her stretched beneath him on that bed, her smooth skin pressed against his heated flesh.

Damnation. He'd never make it through the night if he kept this up. He tossed his knapsack onto a chair and busied himself with lighting the lamp. Not such an easy task when his groin twitched at every enticing swish of her skirt.

Bed ropes creaked, and a soft, feminine sigh sent his pulse bucking. "I'm so exhausted. This could be a mattress of moldy straw, and I wouldn't care one whit."

He knew he shouldn't, but he turned to look. She reclined across the bed, eyes closed, lips parted in silent invitation. God, she was beautiful. He fought the urge to join her. One day, they would share a bed. But not now. First, he needed to earn her trust.

He reached for the blanket folded at the foot of the bed. "I'll just make a pallet over by door. Then you can ready yourself for bed."

She sat up, a frown tucking more lines on her weary face. "A pallet? You shouldn't sleep on the hard floor after that horrid train ride."

"Where else would you have me sleep?"

She glanced at the bed, and pink stained her cheeks.

"Thought so." He crossed to the door and unfurled the blanket onto the floor. "I'll face the wall, so you can have all the privacy you need."

"Here." She plucked a pillow off the bed and tossed it to him. "At least you can rest your head on something soft."

He caught the pillow and smiled. Ever the thoughtful wife, even if she wasn't his. Not yet, at least. He lowered himself onto the makeshift pallet, removed his boots, and then lay back, facing the door, head cradled on the down-filled pillow.

Soft sounds caressed his ears—the faint pad of bare feet on the wood planks, the shush of fabric as she undressed, and the snick of brush bristles sliding through unbound hair. He didn't need to see her. His mind created a picture of that glorious mane tumbling around bare shoulders and down her slender back. Embers he'd successfully banked flared to life. It'd been a while since he'd been with a woman. Not by choice. The War had kept him focused on staying alive. Now that he was away from the battlefields, need charged through him like a Confederate incursion.

He swallowed hard and mentally recited the Lord's Prayer. Minute by agonizing minute, he confined his desire until the overriding lust diminished to a flickering flame. He shoved out a relieved breath. Perhaps he wouldn't make a fool of himself after all.

He relaxed and congratulated himself on his victory. Until the tantalizing rustle of bed sheets reignited his desire. He recalled the feel of her soft curves as he'd carried her from the garden after the Calhoun debacle. It seemed inappropriate at the time to lust for her, but now...

The moan he'd caged escaped.

Bed ropes squealed. "Jack? Is something wrong?"

His pulse leapt at her velvety tone. Hell, he must've been mad to think he could sleep in the same room with her and not go crazy with want.

"Jack?" she whispered again.

"Everything's fine. Go on to sleep."

"I thought perhaps...it sounded like you might be having another of your nightmares."

Oh, he was having a nightmare. But this one wouldn't be banished so easily come daylight. He shifted on the hard pallet. "No nightmares," he assured her. "Just trying to get comfortable."

"Would you like the quilt for some extra padding? It's warm enough that I don't need it."

He stuffed down a groan at the thought of her uncovered on the bed, a feast waiting to assuage his hunger. "No. What I have will do."

"But it wouldn't be any trouble for me to—"

"Goodnight, Kitty."

Her softly muttered, "mule," drifted across the room. He smiled. He would endure the torture of unfulfilled desire and a sleepless night, if it gained her trust.

Chapter Fifteen

The clatter of hooves on street cobbles rattled into her sleep. She opened her eyes and blinked at the brilliant sunlight streaming through the window. Was it morning already? Had she even been asleep?

Though exhausted from the long train ride, she'd found it difficult to drift off the night before. Tormenting sounds kept her wakeful, and oh-so-aware of the man sleeping a mere eagle's wingspan away. His soft, even breaths. His faint groan as he'd turned in his sleep. Even his tantalizing scent had wafted across the room, making each breath a torture.

When she finally did fall asleep, her dreams had been plagued with images of him joining her in the bed, his hands and mouth roaming her body and finding those secret places that ached for his touch. Heat coursed through her at the memory, and she couldn't hold back a moan of pleasure.

Mortified by her wantonness, she bolted upright. The pallet on the floor was gone. So was Jack. Embarrassment turned to dismay. Had he sensed her plan to slip away and decided to strike first?

A folded note propped on the dresser caught her eye. She rolled out of bed, grimacing as stiff muscles screamed in protest. Too many nights of hard earth and harder railcar benches were taking their toll.

She hobbled to the bureau and picked up the letter. Though printed in neat even strokes, the writing still looked like a hodgepodge of letters. How was it other people read without difficulty? Surely they cheated in some way.

She concentrated on each word, sounding them out in her head as she read. *Thought it best...* Lordy, he was always thinking. Her brain would be mush if she pondered as much as he did.

Thought it best...if I...checked...out the prison first.

She tightened her grip on the note, resentment curling inside her like a prickly vine. He had no right to make such a decision without her.

You stay...here...and rest. Be back soon. J.

Stay here and rest. Infuriating man. Treating her like some silly goose of a girl who needed to be looked after. She balled up the note and tossed it onto the bureau. Let him think he was the cock of the henhouse. He wouldn't find this hen waiting for him when he returned.

She shook the dust from her new dress. Widow's weeds, Jack had called it. Sanity settled over her. Running off half-cocked to the prison might put Lance in danger and make the mourning outfit not just for charade. Her recklessness had hurt too many people. Time now to practice a little restraint, no matter how much it galled.

She dressed and made her way to the lobby where she learned from the desk clerk of a suitable eatery across from the train station. Might as well get something to eat, even if all she could afford was a biscuit and tea. Besides, the outing would make the wait go by faster.

The walkway was surprisingly deserted for so late in the day. Only a few people braved the mounting heat. A shopkeeper sweeping dirt from his stoop gave her a nod. Another store owner was busy adjusting the colorful awning perched over his door. A pair of youngsters rushed past, each toting an armful of newspapers. It was a quiet, peaceful morning and just what she needed to keep her mind off Jack and Lance.

Sunlight glistened on an assortment of china dishes arranged in a display window. Plates, bowls, cups and a large tureen, all edged in feathery blue trim. So elegant and pretty. And most likely horribly expensive. It had cost her two weeks wages to replace a similar dish she'd dropped and broken in the Lawrence dining room. Wedgewood, they'd called it. Fine bone china. Might as well've been made of gold. She gave the dishes one last look and moved on. Such luxuries were well beyond her means.

The Silver Spoon loomed ahead. She entered and found the eatery filled to the brim with lively, chattering women. So much for peace and quiet. Once seated, she found her attention drawn to the conversations flowing around her.

"Blueberries, Gertrude. Use blueberries in your muffins. I'll bet those Southern boys have never tasted anything as fine as our sweet Northern berries."

"I just don't understand why we must provide for them. Seems to me there are more worthy folk in need of aid than heathen, slave-owning Rebels."

"Now, Jennie," another woman said. "Whether we agree or disagree with their views, it's our Christian duty to see those prisoners are treated with kindness."

"They don't deserve our kindness."

"Only God can make such a judgment."

Louisa nodded. *Amen, lady*. It was a shame more Yankees didn't have such charitable attitudes. Maybe they could've avoided war altogether.

"Imagine your Henry confined in some Confederate prison," the wiser woman went on. "Wouldn't you want someone to help ease his suffering?"

"Hmmph. If they can mistreat slaves, how do

you expect them to be kind to an enemy soldier?"

The woman's words struck a sore spot. Louisa angled around in her chair. "Excuse me for meddling, but you're wrong, ma'am. There are decent Southern folks who do their best to look after your men."

Hazel-colored eyes looked down a pointed nose. "And you are..?"

"Louisa Carleton. Of Virginia. I know for a fact many Richmonders took food and supplies to the soldiers being held at Libby prison."

"You were one of them?"

"My family didn't have the means to donate, but we helped where we could." She held her head high, proud of their charity, no matter how modest.

Taut lips slackened. "Well, that's certainly heartening to hear."

A round-faced woman with a wide, friendly smile patted the empty chair beside her. "Won't you join us, Miss Carleton?"

Louisa shook her head. "I wouldn't want to intrude on your gathering."

"We insist. Please, come tell us about your hometown. Richmond, did you say?"

She shrugged. Why not? What could it hurt? Besides, talking with these ladies would be a sight better than being alone with her thoughts. She took the offered seat, greeting each of the ladies as they introduced themselves. They were members of the Elmira Women's League and were holding their weekly business meeting.

"What brings you to Elmira?" asked Mrs. Gardner, the sweet-natured lady who'd invited her to join them.

"My brother. He's one of the prisoners sent here from Point Lookout."

"You came all the way from Virginia to see your brother? How courageous of you."

Courageous or mighty stupid. There was a fine line between the two, and she was beginning to wonder which half she'd crossed into. "It really wasn't a question of coming or not. I had to. My brother's not a strong man. He could easily fall prey to disease or infection." *Or worse—a madman's bullet.*

Mrs. Gardner motioned for the waiter to pour more tea. "Unfortunately, being captured is one of the consequences of soldiering."

"That's just it. He's not the soldierly type. Never was. I'm afraid he joined for all the wrong reasons."

"Many a young man got caught up in the excitement and later regretted his decision." Mrs. Gardner ladled cream into her cup, the spoon tinkling against the porcelain as she stirred. "Perhaps you should have a word with Senator Morgan."

"Morgan? Can't say I know the man."

"He's our New York congressman. He'll be in town tomorrow to tour the prison facility. I heard he'll give pardons to prisoners if they swear loyalty to the Union."

Her pulse quickened at the news. A pardon. It was just what Lance needed. All he had to do was survive captivity long enough to take that oath. "Thank you for the suggestion, Mrs. Gardner. I'll be sure to find a way to see the good senator."

"We're planning to hand out donated supplies to the prisoners during the senator's visit. Why don't you join us? You might even catch a glimpse of your brother."

Her meager breakfast had just turned into a banquet of options. If Jack's visit didn't work out, she had the Women's League to fall back on. "I just might take you up on that offer, ma'am. Thank you."

"Good. Meet us tomorrow at one o'clock in front of the prison."

****

The chair rungs bit into his back. His rear end had gone numb hours ago. He shifted to a more comfortable position, not that there was any to be had in the hard wooden chair. But he wasn't about to give up. Not after waiting so long. The Provost Marshall would see him, or he'd become a permanent fixture in the commandant's headquarters.

For once, the waiting room was quiet. The last of the numerous visitors had been ushered into the major's office. Lieutenant Gaines, the Provost's adjutant, sat behind a desk near the closed door, his bulbous nose buried in a mound of paperwork. Gray hair dotted his temples. Wrinkles lined his eyes and mouth. Had age loosened the man's lips or taught him how to keep them shut? Only one way to find out.

"So tell me, Lieutenant," he ventured. "Where were you assigned before Elmira?"

The officer scratched pen to paper before looking up. "Washington."

"What unit?"

"Eighty-third New York."

A militia unit with the Army of the Potomac. "You saw a lot of action then."

"Enough."

Definitely not loose-lipped. "Quite a change from the big city to this backwoods town."

"I go where they send me."

Jack pointed to the paperwork stacked on the desk corner. "I imagine there'll be a lot more of that as additional prisoners arrive. How many do you have now?"

"'Bout eight hundred."

That matched with what the supply clerk had told him. He'd met Sergeant Johnston outside the prison. Chatty fellow. Appeared to enjoy the sound of his own voice. Unlike this terse officer. "I heard about the train collision in Shohola. Fifty dead. You lose any more prisoners besides those?"

"A few."

"Only good Reb is a dead one, huh."

Gaines grunted and returned to his scribbling, lips clamped tighter than a Chesapeake clam. Jack reeled in his line. Might as well save his breath. This one wasn't biting.

Outside the window, short shadows lined what he could see of the prison yard. Noon or shortly thereafter. Was Kitty eating another of her modest meals? He turned a deaf ear to his own grumbling belly. His hunger would have to wait. This fishing expedition was more important than food. If he didn't return with information on Lance, Kitty would surely go off on her own to find it. He ignored the little voice in his head saying she'd probably already done just that.

The far door opened, and the lieutenant shot to his feet. Jack rose as well. He wouldn't be denied an audience. Not this time.

The major's visitor sauntered out of the office and into the waiting room, cupping a gold-handled walking stick in one hand, a top hat in the other. Rich duds. And from the looks of his girth, richer food.

"Supper, tomorrow night, seven o'clock," the man said. "Don't be late."

Major Beale filled the office doorway. "I wouldn't think of being late."

"Your sister will have your hide if you are." The visitor slapped on his top hat. "I'll have a look at that supply building before I leave. Make sure construction is coming along as planned."

"Very well. Good-day, Henry."

Lieutenant Gaines gave the passing man a brief nod, "Good-day, Mr. Lawrence."

Jack straightened with awareness. *Lawrence?* As in Kitty's Spivey Point Lawrence? She'd mentioned the commandant was a relation by marriage. Could there be more than just a family connection between these two?

As the door clicked shut, the major's gaze lit on him. The officer frowned and flicked a glance at his adjutant.

Thought you'd gotten rid of me, didn't you? Jack crossed the short distance in four strides and stretched out his hand in greeting. "Major Beale, I presume."

The officer nodded and took his hand.

"Jackson Porter, sir." He gave the major a firm shake, letting him know he wasn't some limp-wristed Nancy. "Journalist for *The New York Herald*. As I told your adjutant, I'm here to do an article on your prison."

"Sorry for the delay, Mr. Porter. It's been a hectic morning. We're in the midst of planning for Senator Morgan's visit."

Previous Governor of New York and now United States Senator, Edwin Morgan was a force to be reckoned with. No wonder Beale was in a lather. "Then I won't keep you, Major. If you'll just assign someone to escort me around the prison—"

"That won't be possible," the major blurted. "Not only are we extremely busy, but I have strict regulations regarding civilian visitations."

"Surely you have allowances for newspapermen?"

"Only for the select few accompanying Senator Morgan tomorrow."

"I see." Jack slid a hand into his pocket as if reaching for his wallet. "Any possibility you could add me to that list of journalists?"

The major's gaze narrowed. "I'd have to check with the Senator's people first. But I don't expect there'd be a problem."

"I would surely appreciate any effort on my behalf." He gestured to the office door. "In the interim, perhaps we could have a little chat?"

"I imagine I could spare a few minutes. In the interest of the news."

And in the interest of padding your wallet. If Beale wasn't averse to a little money greasing his palm, what other underhanded activities could he be involved in?

Lieutenant Gaines cleared his throat. "Excuse me, Major, sir. With your permission, I'd like to head to mess for a bite to eat."

"Very well. Permission granted." Beale turned back to his office. "This way, Mr. Porter."

Jack took the chair across from the major's desk and slid a notepad and pencil from his pocket. Cardinal rule of journalism—*Interview first, money later.* "I understand many of your prisoners came from Point Lookout."

"They did."

"And most were officers," he added, watching the Provost for a reaction.

Beale's expression remained stoic. "Most, but not all. Some officers weren't healthy enough to travel. Others were sent to fill the quota."

Jack flipped through the notebook as though reviewing his notes. *Damn.* No holes in that defense. *Let's try a flanking maneuver.* "I was allowed to tour the Point Lookout facility which holds over ten thousand prisoners. You only have eight hundred. Why restrict visitations?"

Beale leaned back in his chair, arms folded over his chest in a classic I'm-in-control exhibition. "This is a newly formed prison, Mr. Porter. Construction is still on-going and could be dangerous to civilians."

"Dangerous if you go where you're not supposed to." He let that sink in, then added, "It'd be helpful to my article if I could talk with some of the prisoners, get a few quotes. Like the group that just arrived from Point Lookout. I could have them compare the two facilities."

"Why don't you just make those up? That's what you newspapermen do anyhow, isn't it?"

Only the corrupt expected corruption in others. "Now, Major, that'd be dishonest."

"Sorry, Porter. But I just can't allow you direct contact with the prisoners."

"What about the civilian who just left?"

"Mr. Lawrence? He's a government contractor paid to supply food, clothing, and housing for the prisoners. It's his job to inspect the facility."

A government contractor. He had to be the same Lawrence suspected of shady dealings at Fort Delaware and Camp Douglas. Was the major also part of Lawrence's corruption? "I overheard him speak of a dinner party. Are the two of you personal acquaintances as well?"

Beale stiffened ever so slightly. "We are."

Ah, not comfortable with this line of questioning, are you? He smiled and set the hook. "Care to elaborate, sir?"

A loud boom rattled the window.

Startled, the Provost leapt to his feet and darted for the doorway. "Stay here," he shot over his shoulder.

Jack trailed after him. "I'd like to go with you. See what happened."

"No. You stay out here in the waiting area. Lieutenant Gaines will be back shortly." Beale shoved open the door and was gone before Jack could open his mouth to reply.

Stay in the reception area. Not damned likely. *One, two, three...*

Jack wheeled around and returned to Beale's office. No sense looking this gift horse in the mouth.

He cocked an ear to the door. Only the faint thump of distant hammering broke the quiet. Good. For now, he was in the clear.

He crossed to the desk and rifled through the paperwork stacked on the desktop. Command directives and daily reports. Nothing out of the ordinary. He pulled open the top drawer. It too was filled with harmless official documents. As was the next drawer, and the next. Perhaps Beale was smarter than he thought.

The distant hammering knocked loose a memory. He smiled. Some interviews were more useful than others.

Working quickly, he removed the papers from the bottom drawer and tapped on the underside. Hollow. A hidden cavity. He widened his smile. *Thank you, Alan Pinkerton.*

Using the major's letter opener, he pried up the false bottom. Several documents lay nested in the hollow. A quick scan revealed supply requisitions from two weeks ago. It was incriminating enough that the major had seen fit to secret the papers away. More importantly was the amount of goods listed. It was triple what the supply clerk said he'd received.

He peeled a ten-spot out of his wallet and tossed it onto the desk. A little lard to smooth the way for tomorrow. He folded the documents and tucked them under his shirt. And some honey to sweeten the pot of revenge.

He had the leverage he needed to free Kitty's brother.

Now he just had to make sure the boy was still alive.

Chapter Sixteen

"Well, well. Will wonders never cease."

Louisa ignored the dig and turned away from the window. She was too anxious about his findings to get plucked by his verbal jabs. "You're back."

He closed the door behind him and strode to the bureau, his bland expression giving little hint as to how his day went. "And you're here. I fully expected to find you gone."

"The notion crossed my mind a time or two. Especially after finding your note." She wagged a finger at him. "You sure got some gall, Jack Porter."

"I apologize for not talking with you first. But I thought it best if I went alone. Get a feel for the lay of the land, so to speak."

His sincere apology soothed her temper. Some, but not all. "I could've gone with you. Probably should have. You don't know the Lawrences like I do."

"Everything turned out just fine. You'll find your wait was more than worthwhile." He shrugged out of his jacket, then unraveled his necktie and yanked it free. "Whew, hot as Hades out there. What did you do with your day? You ate, I hope."

Her mouth went dry at the sight of him undressing. For a moment, she forgot what he'd asked. "Um...I did. And learned something that might be useful."

"What's that?" He unfastened the top few buttons of his shirt and loosened the collar, baring his neck and a pie-slice portion of his chest.

Warmth that had nothing to do with the summer heat bubbled through her. She reached for the fan she'd fashioned from a discarded leaflet she'd found and gave her face several sweeping whiffs. Not that it'd do any good. Her whole body burned, inside and out.

"A Senator Morgan is visiting the prison tomorrow," she said. "Lady at the eatery told me he'll give pardons to prisoners who swear loyalty to the Union. I'm sure Lance'd be more than willing to take such an oath. We just need to get him away from the Lawrences."

"That might be easier than you think."

She stilled her fanning. "What? How?"

He unbuttoned the rest of his shirt and pulled out a folded wad of papers. "An explosion in one of the cookhouses provided me an opportunity to search the Provost's office. I found these secreted in his desk."

Sleek muscles peeked through the open folds of his shirt, just like the teasing images from her dreams. She swallowed and resumed her whisking. "You stole from him? That was awful risky, Jack."

"It was a chance I had to take." His expression softened. "For all of us."

He'd done it for her. And Lance. Was it any wonder she'd fallen for him, body and soul? "What's in those papers that you'd risk getting caught?"

"Evidence proving the major and Henry Lawrence are embezzling."

"Embezzling?" She snapped her fan shut. "What good will their fondness for drink do us?"

He scrubbed a hand over his mouth as if smothering something. "Er...embezzling means they breached someone's trust and took money for their own use. Appears they're skimming from prison funds."

Her cheeks burned at her blunder, but he didn't

219

seem inclined to push. A welcome change from weeks ago when he would've jumped at the opportunity to goad her.

She moved to the bureau and busied herself with pouring lemonade to hide her embarrassment. "I had the desk clerk send this up here. Thought you might like something refreshing after such a long, hot day."

He tossed the papers onto the bureau and took the glass from her, his fingers grazing hers in the exchange. "That was thoughtful. Thank you."

She watched as he lifted the glass to his lips. The nick on his neck had healed. Had the ache in his heart? She'd rather die than hurt him again. "So, how will we use this embezzling evidence to free Lance?"

He set his empty glass on the bureau. "Ahhh. That hit the spot. As you said, Senator Morgan will be visiting the prison tomorrow. With a little friendly persuasion of the monetary kind, I convinced Major Beale to add me to the list of journalists touring with the Congressman."

"Hmmph. No surprise there. The Lawrences are greedy as pigs at the slop trough." Papa's pitiful wages were proof of that.

"And it'll be their downfall. The senator's a bulldog when it comes to investigating government corruption. I'll find an opportunity to approach him with what I've found. The Lawrences won't know what hit them."

"What if Morgan's in on their scheme?"

"I sincerely doubt it. But in the off chance he is, there'll be other newspapermen present. He won't risk doing anything stupid."

Man thought of everything. She traced a finger over the stolen papers, still warm from being tucked next to Jack's body. Lance said words were powerful weapons. She always believed it took more than that.

"I s'pose you'll want me to stay here while you meet with the senator."

"It'd be helpful if you did. That way, I can concentrate on Lance and not have to worry about your safety."

Understandable, but still darned frustrating. She wanted to be the one to free Lance—to take down the Lawrences. But if staying behind brought her brother back safe and sound, she'd bow to Jack's sensible judgment. After all, he had asked for her cooperation this time instead of demanding it. "Fine. I'll wait here."

"Good. I know waiting is hard on you. But before you know it, this'll be all over, and you and Lance will be reunited."

"And Jeb and Belle, too. It's hard to believe we might actually all be together once again..." A cloud darkened her enthusiasm. "Provided Lance is still alive."

"Oh, he's alive."

Blood rushed from her head. She had to brace herself against the bureau to keep from swaying. Deep inside, in that dark place she tried to ignore, she expected to find Lance dead and buried. Even now, she mistrusted what her ears had heard.

"H-how do you know? Did you see him?"

"I did, but only from a distance."

"How did he look? Is he well?" The words rushed out on a frantic breath. "Lord, Jack why didn't you tell me straight off?"

"Whoa, sweetheart, slow down. One question at a time." He grasped her arm. "Let's sit on the window bench. You look like you're about to collapse."

He guided her across the room, then sank beside her on the padded bench. His hand remained cupped on her elbow, strong and reassuring, but not enough to curb the riot wallowing inside her.

"Tell me, Jack. Tell me everything."

"I will. I promise. First, take a deep breath and settle yourself." He nodded as she did so. "That's a good girl."

Good girl, her sore backside. She clutched his arm, fingernails digging into his sleeve as if to pry the words from him. "Please, Jack. The wait is near killing me."

"Fine. Guess you're as settled as you're going to get. I was able to convince the Provost's adjutant to let me speak with the recent arrivals from Point Lookout. Lance was among them."

"Praise be. How was he?"

"He looked fine from what I could tell. A little thin and dirty, but otherwise healthy."

Dirt and thinness she could handle. "I wish I could've seen him. Did you speak with him?"

"There wasn't time. Besides, he'll be safer if he's unaware of who I am and what we're up to."

Fear slithered back into her belly. "In case the guards get suspicious. How is it the major hasn't done anything to him yet? As commandant, he certainly has the power and the opportunity."

"Probably hasn't had time. Your brother was on the train that wrecked in Pennsylvania. He only arrived a week ahead of us."

"I knew it. I knew he was on that train." She slumped over. It was too much. The ups, the downs. The constant, gut-eating worry. It was just too much to bear.

Jack slipped an arm around her shoulders and gave her a comforting squeeze. "Lance is alive and well. And we're going to see he stays that way."

We. Tears stung her eyes. He was such a good man. Who would've thought an arrogant, pig-headed Yankee would turn out to be her champion?

"Thank you, Jack," she whispered past the lump

in her throat. "You don't know how much this means to me."

"I'd do anything for you, Kitty. You know that."

The air went out of her at his sweet words. She leaned against him, no longer able to fight her feelings. She loved him. Loved his sincerity, his unwavering devotion.

Devotion she didn't deserve.

She swiped away her tears and pushed upright. "I can't do this."

"Do what?"

"I have to leave." She shot to her feet. "Find another hotel room." Something she should have done earlier. What had she been thinking? Her fussy sleep the night before should've been warning enough. And just now, her reaction to his undressing...

He stood and tucked his hands behind him. "There's no need to do that. There's plenty of room here."

"I can't stay."

"Why not?"

"I...you..." She swallowed back the words. What if she was wrong? What if he'd lied about caring for her? And here she was about to lay her feelings on the chopping block.

His concerned gaze tunneled into her. "What is it, Kitty? Why must you leave?"

"I-I can't stay here with you...and not want..."

"Not want what?"

Misery tightened like a noose around her neck. She blinked back a fresh batch of tears. "It doesn't matter."

"Of course it does." He reached up and thumbed her chin, tracing a fiery trail over her skin. "Everything about you matters. Tell me."

If she told him, she risked rejection. If she didn't, she'd wonder for the rest of her life what might have been. Lordy, how had it come to this?

"Tell me what you want."

Nothing ventured; nothing gained, Papa would've said. She wished Papa could've met Jack. He would have approved of the straight-shooting journalist, a man cut from the same cloth as himself.

"I want you, Jack," she finally answered. "Your kisses. Your love. I want to be your wife, in every sense of the word." There it was out in the open. Her heart thudded in anxious beats as she waited for his response.

He studied her with that deep, thoughtful stare, the one that made her insides quiver. "Why did you think you couldn't have those things?"

"Because you deserve a well-bred lady. Someone of your own class." She picked at the wrinkled folds of her store-bought skirt. "Not some poor, uneducated, backwoods hoyden."

"I don't care about your up-bringing. All I care about is you."

"But I'm soiled and—"

He pressed a finger to her lips, stopping her. "What Bart Lawrence did doesn't lessen what I feel for you. I'd kill the man myself if he was still alive." He leaned forward and covered her mouth with his. His kiss was gentle and sweet and over far too quickly.

A bonfire burned in the dark depths of his gaze. "I want you, too, Kitty. Your kisses, your touch. Your body next to mine. But only if that's what you truly want."

"I do. More than you know." She smoothed a crease in his sleeve with her fingertip. "But, I don't know if I can. Bart was..." Her throat closed around the words. Kisses were one thing. What would happen when Jack touched her naked body? Would she fight and scream like a mad woman as she'd done when they first met and he'd rolled atop her?

Or would she freeze? Either seemed likely. How could she give him pleasure if she couldn't take pleasure herself?

"Look at me."

She glanced from the painting on the wall to the mantel to the fire poker leaning against the hearth, anywhere but his all-seeing gaze. It'd kill her to see pity for her etched on his face.

"Look at me, Kitty," he repeated, more forceful this time.

She briefly closed her eyes, gathering her courage, and then looked at him. Her breath caught in her throat. His expression was full of love and tenderness.

"Who do you see?"

"You, Jack."

"Me. Your friend. Not Bart Lawrence. Not Calhoun. I would never hurt you." He gently thumbed the corner of her mouth. "Ever."

"I know you wouldn't, but what if I can't stop the memories of what Bart did?"

"Do you trust me?"

With all my heart. She managed a nod.

"Your body will recognize the difference. I promise." He again captured her mouth, this time, teasing her lips with his tongue and tormenting nips of his teeth. Heat unfurled in her lower belly, and she couldn't hold back a moan.

He lifted his head. "What do you feel?"

"I-I..." She pressed fingers to her lips that still burned from his assault.

"Pain? Fear?" His gaze narrowed. "Disgust?"

She shook her head. "None of those. It was very..." Embarrassing warmth climbed up her neck. She'd never spoken so openly with a man. Not even Lance with whom she shared everything. "...Nice."

"Hmm. Nice. Not quite the word I was looking for. But it will do for now." He lowered his hands to his side. "Would you like to touch me?"

Her pulse tripped in a rousing mixture of alarm and excitement. "Wh-what?"

He glanced down at his exposed chest. "Slip your hands under my shirt if you'd like. Feel the warmth of my skin beneath your fingertips. The beat of my heart."

Tingles shot down her spine. Oh, what a delight it would be to explore his smooth, satiny skin. Slide her fingers over all that firm muscle. But she knew deep inside once she started down that path, she could never turn back, whatever the outcome.

She pressed trembling hands against her stomach. "I can't."

"Yes, you can. Come. See how pleasurable touching can be."

A soft ache filled her. She wanted—needed—to do this. To know she could touch him and not be afraid.

At his encouraging nod, she took a hesitant step forward and reached out. Downy hair brushed her fingers as she eased her hands under his shirt. A tremor rippled through her. She pressed harder, relishing the feel of heated skin and solid muscle. Her breasts grew tight with want.

"Not so bad, was it?"

She smiled and shook her head.

"Why don't you pull off my shirt? It'd be easier to explore with it out of the way."

She swallowed her last bit of moisture and eased the shirt off his shoulders. It fell to the floor and pooled at his feet, baring his smooth chest and rippling stomach. She drank in the sight of him with greedy gulps.

"Roam where you please, my sweet."

She played her fingers over his skin, from the dip at the base of his neck, across his broad shoulders, and down his muscular arms. He remained still, allowing her to explore at will, when she knew from his fisted hands and taut muscles he ached to join in. Her heart soared. Only a man filled with loving patience could do such a thing.

Encouraged, she traced a path across his rock-hard stomach to his navel and down the dark column of hair that disappeared beneath his waistband. The soft hiss of his indrawn breath drew her gaze upward. Jaw muscles twitched under flushed skin as though he clenched his teeth.

"Jack...?"

He shook his head and muttered a gravelly, "Don't stop."

She hooked a trembling finger in his buckle, then stilled. Clothes fastenings were her bugaboos. "I'm not sure I can do this." She swallowed again. "Will you help me?"

"With pleasure." He cupped her hand and like a skilled puppeteer, manipulated her fingers over buckles and buttons until his pants joined the shirt on the floor. He stood before her, legs braced apart, his engorged staff rising from a dark nest.

She sucked in a breath, pulling air into her starving lungs. Magnificent. Absolutely magnificent. The prime stud of the stable.

"Take me in your hand," he whispered.

She wanted to hold him, to explore in pleasure what had been thrust at her in violence. But such a desire was surely unseemly and wanton. She fisted her hands and shook her head.

"Go on," he urged. "It's perfectly acceptable for a wife to touch her husband."

"But I'm not your wife. Not in the eyes of God."

"You will be."

Was he just saying that to mollify her? Pretty words offered in hopes of a romp between the bed sheets? "Jack, you don't have to make any promises."

"Shhh. We'll talk later. Right now, just focus on

the pleasure we give each other." His chest rose as he drew in a deep breath. "Hold me, Kitty."

Her pet name riding his ragged exhale nudged her onward. Wife, mistress, concubine, she didn't care which, as long as this delight didn't end. She reached for him, then hesitated. What would happen when she touched his most intimate part? Would he turn from an unmoving statue to a raging beast?

"Go ahead," he encouraged. "Feel my desire and know you control it."

Heartened by his steady gaze, she curled her fingers around him. Velvety heat scorched her palm. She tightened her grip, and he pulsed in response. Warmth flooded her and pooled at the juncture between her legs.

The only beast that needed taming was the one flailing inside her.

****

Want ricocheted through him like a careening bullet. He pulled in a deep breath and called on every ounce of willpower he possessed. His release would have to wait. Kitty needed to control their lovemaking, to see for herself how pleasurable joining with a man could be—on her terms.

Her hand slid up his shaft, fingers brushing his tip in mind-shattering strokes. Fire exploded inside him, and despite his efforts to hold strong, he groaned and leaned into her grasp. Gripes, she learned fast. Teaching her new things was going to be pure delight.

He fisted his hands at his sides to keep from hauling up her skirts and taking her against the wall. "Why don't you take off your clothes?" he asked instead. "Get out of that stuffy dress."

Hooded eyes that could tempt a saint lifted. His control slipped a notch. "But only if you want to," he rasped. Better his voice cracking than his willpower. "No one's forcing you to do anything you aren't comfortable with."

She licked her lips, then released him, giving him some much needed time to collect himself. Trembling fingers fumbled with the buttons at her collar. Her hand slipped, and she grimaced. Fasteners sure did give her fits.

He reached up and gently covered her hand. "May I?"

She nodded and with a flick of his fingers, he made quick work of the tiny buttons. Her dress slipped away, revealing dusky nipples just visible beneath her cotton undergarments. He ached to caress her tantalizing mounds, taste those taut peaks. But he held back. She needed to make the offer, give herself to him of her own accord.

As if reading his mind, she peeled off her underthings and stood before him, chin lifted, shoulders back. Not a cowering bone in her sweet, naked body. The breath hung in his throat. She was perfect. A Goddess sent from the Heavens. He could span her tiny waist with two hands. And her hips. They were wide and inviting and just made for cradling a man—him.

She freed the pins from her bun and shook her head. Fiery locks tumbled around her bare shoulders. A timid smile tipped her lips. "Your turn."

Desire slammed into him, fast and hard. He wanted to touch her. Wanted to feel her heated skin against his. But he had to be certain this was what she wanted. If it wasn't, he needed to leave—now—before he reached the point of no return.

"Are you certain?"

"I want you to touch me...like I touched you."

Her lips trembled as she spoke. From fear or desire? A sheen of perspiration glistened on her brow. Her pert breasts rose and fell with each breath she took.

Probably a little of both.

He nodded at the four poster. "Would you like to lie on the bed?" He held up his hands to show her he meant no harm. "It's only a suggestion. Your choice whether we do or not."

She glanced at bed, then at him, her gaze dark with desire and near-to knocking him off his feet. "Yes, I'd like that."

"Good." Damned good. His legs were growing far too wobbly to keep him upright. He crossed to the bed and lounged back, hands laced behind his head in as casual a pose as he could summon, considering his body was pulled tighter than a bow string.

A breeze sifted through the open window, lifting the gauzy curtains and carrying with it the faint odor of roasting meat. Dinnertime was nearing. And so was his feast. Creamy mounds jiggled with each step she took. Her stomach was pancake flat. And those legs, slender and milky...

She was all the sustenance he needed.

He remained motionless as she eased onto the bed, letting her decide how close to get. To his surprise, she scooted next to him and pressed her body along his length. Flames licked at his loins. He ground his teeth around a moan and stared at the ceiling, tracing the swirls in the plaster to keep from pouncing on her.

She reached up and pulled his hand free. Smooth fingers pressed delightfully into his palm. "Find the places that ache for your touch."

He'd dreamed of her secret places often enough he could find them blindfolded. But it'd be best to have her lead the way. He shifted onto his side. "Show me."

She guided his hand to her breast, and he cupped the satiny mound. "Here?" he asked.

Her quick exhale caressed his neck. She closed her eyes and nodded.

He kneaded the supple flesh, his hunger for her

rising with each stroke. A rosy nipple beckoned. Unable to resist, he leaned over and latched onto the bud. Sweet, ever so sweet. Like a summer ripened berry.

"Oh, Jack..."

He lifted his head at her soft plea. "You liked that?"

"Yesss. I never knew..." her voice trailed away on a contented sigh.

"There's more. Much more. Do you want me to continue?"

"Yes, please. I want..."

"What? Tell me what you want."

She ran a pink tongue over her lips. "I want all of it, all of the pleasure you have to give."

Those words were manna from Heaven. He claimed her mouth, this time sweeping his tongue between her lips and plunging inside. Her tongue met his, tentative at first, then with more daring as she grew bolder.

Lava flowed in his veins. He didn't know how much longer he'd be able to keep his lust corralled before he'd explode like a Fourth of July firecracker.

****

Louisa curled her hands around Jack's neck and grazed her fingers through his wavy mane. So satiny. It was the only softness on his rock-hard body. She skimmed her fingernails down his spine and relished the deep moan that rumbled at the back of his throat. It appeared she pleasured him as much as he did her.

He moved his tormenting lips to her breast and flicked her nipple with his tongue. Heat blossomed inside her like a bud opening up to the sun. It was the most delightful sensation she'd ever felt.

His fingers trailed a scorching path over her ribs, past her navel, and down to the juncture of her legs. He brushed her curls in slow, maddening caresses. She arched against his hand, wanting more.

He obliged, plunging his fingers into her flesh in an intimate invasion that left her gasping for breath. He dipped deeper, stoking her desire into a bonfire of need. She thrust her hips to meet him.

"You're ready, sweetheart." His voice came out in a hoarse whisper. "More than ready."

She met his blazing gaze. "Ready?"

"Hot and slick with want. As am I." He cupped her hips. "Sit up and straddle me."

Straddle him. Like a horse. Her heart went out to this gentle man who cared enough to let her control their lovemaking. How could she not love him?

She slid her leg across his stomach until she sat astride his lower belly. His shaft pulsed against her backside. "What now?"

"Lift your hips and guide me inside you."

She shifted and slowly fed his length into her until all she felt was his incredible fullness. A deep sense of completeness filled her—as if she'd finally come home after a long journey. "Oh, Jack..."

He bent his knees, throwing her forward and intensifying the delightful sensation. She rocked back and forth, pursuing the thread of something new, something wondrous.

He slipped his fingers between them and stroked her sensitive flesh. Heaven. Pure, heaven. She rocked faster, her body aching for more. Fire roared inside her, building and building, until finally cresting in pleasurable tremors that engulfed her.

Groaning, Jack grasped her hips and pushed deep, spilling his warmth inside her. Her breath coming in soft pants, she clung to him, riding the final wave of pleasure.

Chapter Seventeen

She opened her eyes to find faint sunlight streaming through the open window. A cool draft wafted across her bare skin. She shivered and cuddled closer to the solid warmth beside her. Jack lay on his stomach, one arm stretched over his head, the other draped between them and heating her skin where they touched.

Head burrowed in the pillow, he faced her, his eye closed, dark lashes fanning his tanned cheeks. His lips were parted in a boyish pout she knew to be deceiving. Not after last night. Not after all the enjoyable things he'd done to her with that very grown-up mouth. And she'd responded. Totally. With only the barest hint of hesitation.

A happy glow bloomed inside her. She was whole again—no longer tortured by what Bart Lawrence had done to her. And she owed it all to this man.

The memory of his skillful lovemaking surfaced. The breath-robbing nips from his teeth. His hands finding and caressing her secret places. His staff filling her. A ribbon of pleasure pulled through her, and she shook from the force of it.

"Chilled?"

He was awake. Was he aware of her lustful thoughts? "A little," she whispered, unsure how to greet him after a night of intimacy.

He shifted onto his side and pulled her against him. "Does this help?"

Pleasing heat banished the cold and her

uncertainty. Her body sure knew how to greet him. She tipped her head back and smiled. "Mmm. Much better."

An answering grin dimpled his cheeks. "Thought it might."

She noted the absence of his ever-present eye patch. A grayish colored lid covered the sunken socket. Jagged white lines fanned out from the corner and disappeared into the hair at his temple.

"You said you did this in a bar fight." She traced the scar with her fingertip. "How did it happen?"

His arms tightened around her, but he didn't move to grab for the patch. He trusted her. And that meant more than she could ever have imagined.

"It happened because of my own stupidity."

"Everyone makes mistakes."

He shook his head. "I should've known better...should've listened to my grandfather. He warned me to keep to the straight and narrow." His chest rose as he filled his lungs with a deep breath. "And I disappointed him."

She knew all about disappointing the people you love. "I wouldn't begin to judge you, Jack. I have many regrets of my own."

"Am I one of them?"

"Heavens no." She smoothed down a dark, unruly lock. "You're the one thing in my life I did right."

His troubled expression softened. "I have to admit your reaction to last night had me worried."

"There's no need to worry. I have no regrets." Well, maybe one. She'd fallen into an exhausted sleep far too soon. She nuzzled his neck and drank in his scent. Sandalwood. It was a smell she'd cherish for the rest of her days. "Tell me about the bar fight."

A sensual growl rumbled in his throat. "I'd rather do more of what you don't regret."

"Uh-uh. After your story."

"After?" His warm breath teased her ear. "You're sure?"

Tempting. Real tempting. But the reason behind his mangled eye pricked her curiosity. "Yes, I'm sure."

"Waste of a nice, quiet morning."

"Jack..."

He heaved a sigh and rolled onto his back. "Guess you won't be satisfied until you know." He stared at the ceiling as if seduced by the plaster swirls. When he spoke, his voice came out in a harsh mixture of anger and sadness. "When Grandfather became my guardian, he sheltered me from the worst in life, thinking he was protecting me."

"Of course he wanted to protect you. He loves you." *As I do.*

He shook his head. "It was a recipe for disaster. When I finally got out from under his thumb at the university, I went feral. Drinking, carousing." His jaw twitched as though he ground his teeth. "A fight broke out at one of the taprooms my friends and I had gone to. I was drunk and full of myself. Someone smashed a chair against my head. The wood splintered and...well, you can guess the rest."

Sorrow knifed into her at the pain and suffering he'd gone through. Was still going through, it appeared. "You were just feeling your oats like any other young man. It could've happened to anyone." She gave his arm a comforting squeeze. "Look at what you've accomplished since then. You have nothing to be ashamed of, Jack."

He shook his head. "You're nothing like her."

"Her?"

"My fiancée."

He'd never mentioned a fiancée before. Her heart took a nose-dive. How could he offer marriage if he was spoken for?

"Not to worry," he said. "Felicity ended our

engagement after learning of my disfigurement. Said she wouldn't marry a reckless, deformed man." He shrugged. "Not that I could blame her."

Anger at the unknown Felicity welled inside her. "It was a horrible thing to do. A person should be loved for what's on the inside, not by their pretty outer shell."

"Which philosopher said that?"

"No philosopher. Just another of Nanny Belle's words of wisdom."

"I think I shall enjoy meeting this Nanny Belle of yours." He shifted back onto his side and draped an arm across her waist. "We'll send for her, of course."

"Send for her?"

"For the wedding and to live with us afterwards." He grasped her waist and rolled her atop him. "I love you, Louisa Carleton. And once we take care of the Lawrences and free Lance, we'll make this sham of a marriage real. If you'll have me, that is."

So he hadn't been plying her with sweet words just for a night of pleasure. Her heart took flight. Oh, she would have him. Every minute of every day. And by the feel of his growing hardness, pretty darn soon.

"The entire Yankee army couldn't keep me from marrying you, Jackson Porter."

"What a news headline that would make." He twirled a stray tress around his finger. "Flame-haired Reb takes on Union battalion."

She dug an elbow into his ribs. "I prefer to keep my battles private, Mister Newspaperman."

"What? Don't you want to see your name in ink? Become all rich and famous with notoriety?"

"Don't know what notoriety is, but from the sound, I don't think I'd like it much. I'd rather have a simple, humble life. With you."

"Simple, I can do." His mouth twisted into a lopsided grin. "Not so sure about humble."

She pressed her lips to his in a quick, tender kiss. "You can be whatever you set your mind to. I knew from the day we met you were someone special. I love you, Jack Porter. And I can't wait to start our lives together. In New York, or Baltimore, or wherever we decide."

The color faded from his face. His grip on her waist dropped. "There's something I need to tell you." He pushed out a ragged breath. "About Baltimore and grandfather."

****

Louisa slowed her pacing and glanced at the mantel clock for seemingly the hundredth time. It'd been four hours since Jack had left for the prison, far longer than he said he'd be gone. Was everything going as planned? Had Beale figured out the plot against him and arrested Jack?

She slumped onto the window seat. Silly to let such gloomy thoughts hold sway. Jack was a very capable man, always thinking two steps ahead of everyone, her included. It was one of the things she loved most about him. He'd triumph over Beale. And also over his stubborn grandfather.

The elder Porter had agreed to lend Jack travel funds in exchange for him giving up on any type of relationship with her. Although his disapproval of her stung, she understood that love drove him to make such a steep demand. She'd just have to trust that Jack would find a way over that hurdle.

As she started to stand her foot struck something. She bent to find she'd kicked over Jack's knapsack. His journals had spilled onto the floor. Curiosity nipped at her. What exactly did he write in those ledgers? He sure labored over them often enough. Why just this morning, he'd sat at the window seat, brow furrowed, his pencil scritchscratching as he logged his thoughts onto a page.

She picked up one of the journals. Surely he wouldn't mind if she took a peek. He was always pestering her to practice her reading. Besides, what could he have to hide?

She flipped the ledger open and concentrated on the muddle of marks, plucking out a word here and there. *Henry Lawrence. Fort Delaware. Camp Douglas. Shady dealings?*

So, he suspected Lawrence of wrong-doing at other prisons as well. It wouldn't surprise her if his suspicions turned out to be true. A more crooked man she couldn't imagine.

She skimmed her finger beneath more letters. *Em-bez-zling.* There was that word again. Embarrassing heat flamed in her ears at the memory of her earlier blunder. At least she knew what it meant now.

Sergeant Johnston, supply clerk. Dis-parity with Re-quisi-tion. More high-falutin words. She might not know their meanings, but she got the general idea. He had a source at the prison. Some supply clerk he'd wrangled information out of. Jack was plumb good at his job, she'd give him that.

Since there were no other notes in that journal, she selected another and thumbed to the middle, expecting to find remarks about Point Lookout or Elmira.

What sort of man is Lance Carleton? Driven and determined like his sister? She blinked in confusion. Why had he written about her and Lance? They had nothing to do with the operation of Yankee prisons.

Include their father's questionable death in article.

Her head reeled as if she'd been struck. Jack had been using her all along—gathering information on her family's troubles for some damned newspaper article. A pang knifed into her heart. Had he used her for his pleasure as well?

A shout clambered through the open window, drawing her attention to the street below. Melons, corn, and tomatoes littered the roadway around a mule-drawn wagon. A bearded man in a straw hat paced through the clutter, waving his hands at the young Negro hurrying to gather the scattered produce. Poor fella. Probably wasn't even his fault.

An aproned woman stood in the doorway of a nearby mercantile, hands planted on her hips as she watched the two men. Above her, a banner attached to the store fluttered in the breeze. *Annual Women's League Parade and Charity Fair. Saturday.*

The Women's League. Of course. She'd nearly forgotten about their visit to the prison. She gathered the journal detailing Lawrence's wrongdoings and crossed to the bureau. She'd deal with Jack's deceit later. First she had to make sure he was safe.

Then she'd kill him.

She tore out a blank page and began copying his notes. Writing was near as troublesome as reading. She gripped the pencil tightly, forming the letters as best she could. She poked her tongue out the side of her mouth as she'd seen Jack do. Seemed to help him concentrate when he wrote. Oddly, the gesture was calming.

Twenty minutes later, fingers cramped from holding the pencil so long, a rarity for her, she tucked the folded note and Jack's journal into her satchel. It was done. Chicken scratching or not, the letter would have to do.

As she pulled on her bonnet, the clock struck the half-hour. Twelve-thirty. There was no time to waste. Satchel in hand, she hurried out the door, down the stairs, and into the lobby. Blue eyes lit up as she approached the front desk.

"Good morning, ma'am," the clerk greeted.

"What can I do for you this fine afternoon? Interested in finding another place to eat?"

"Not today. Thank you." She eyed the registration book. "Are there any rooms available?"

"Yes, ma'am. Had two guests leave just this morn."

She fished in her pocket and withdrew a coin. "I'd like to reserve one of them, please. For my brother, Lance Carleton." Whatever the outcome of her visit to the prison, she wanted to have options.

He took the coin and scribbled a notation in his ledger. "Anything else?"

"I need to know how to get to the prison."

"Camp Rathbun?"

Rathbun? What the devil kind of name was that?

Her confusion must've shown as he added, "The prison where the Rebel prisoners are being taken?"

She nodded. "That's the one."

He scratched his stubbly chin and regarded her over the rims of his spectacles. "Not exactly an ideal place for a woman to go visiting alone."

Lordy, what was it with over-protective men? "I'm meeting my husband."

"Oh, well, that's more tolerable."

She clamped down on a curt reply and merely broadened her smile. *More flies with honey...*

"It's down on Water Street beside the Chemung River," he said. "A short hack ride from here, or longer if you're inclined to a walk."

Hack ride. Not a convenience her meager funds would allow, nor could she afford to wait for one to be sent for. "It's such a nice day. I believe I'll take that walk instead. See a bit of your lovely city on the way."

"Fine afternoon for a stroll, indeed." He flicked a hand at the open doorway. "Outside the door, turn right and continue down Railroad Street until you reach Water Street. Make another right and go about seven blocks to Walnut. You'll see the prison encampment on your left. Can't miss it."

"Thank you, sir. There's one other thing." She pulled the folded note from her satchel along with another coin. Though precious, the payment was a necessary evil. It may very well save all their lives. "I need this delivered to Senator Morgan. I'm not sure where he's staying, but I'm sure a clever man like yourself could find out."

He took the note but left the money. "I'd be more than happy to see this gets to the senator, ma'am."

"Thank you again, sir. I'm mighty beholden to you." She pocketed the coin. *More than you'll ever know.*

She left the hotel, feeling a tad more comfortable with her plan. It was still risky, but she had no other choice. Lance and now possibly Jack depended on her reaching Senator Morgan at the prison.

Hazy shimmers rose from the dirt-packed roadway, carrying with it the rank odors of manure and garbage. Across from her, the farmer and his Negro helper were just loading the last of the melons into the wagon bed. At least the man had sense enough to stop his ranting and help before his produce spoiled.

She glanced down one end of the sidewalk and then the other. *Turn right outside the door*, the clerk had said. Drat. Right and left always got her fiddle-fuddled. Those no-account words ought to be stricken from the English language. She pretended to hold a pencil. She wrote right-handed, so she was told. Therefore...she turned in the direction of her writing hand. *This must be right.* She hoped.

She hurried past the pretty display of dishes and another of ladies bonnets. As much as she enjoyed window gawking, there was no time today for her favorite pastime. The acrid odor of coal smoke drifting across the street from the railroad depot coiled around her. Passengers swarmed on the platform like bees around a hive. With any luck, she and Lance would soon be joining them, heading south, heading home.

Her trek brought her to a junction with another street. Just beyond the intersection, sunlight glistened on the surface of a churning river. Hallelujah. Right had been right, after all.

Smaller than the James, the Chemung still had that same powerful scent, a wet, earthy odor that clung to a person long after a stolen dip. It was a reminder of Spivey Point and the heartache she'd brought her family. Soon, very soon, she'd put things back to right.

She quickened her step, eager to reach her destination. Before long, the massive stockade walls rose into view. Just as at Point Lookout, armed guards patrolled a walkway that stretched along the top edge. As she drew closer, three carriages and a wagon pulled up to the curb. Black-garbed women swarmed from the coaches and gathered in front of the prison.

The Women's League. She'd made it in time.

She crossed the street and searched the chattering flock for the friendly Mrs. Gardner. She found the woman supervising the distribution of baskets from the back of the wagon.

"Miss Carleton, how good to see you." Mrs. Gardner held out a linen-covered basket. "Here. Take this basket of muffins. We'll be going inside soon."

Inside. A familiar jangle played through her. Lance was close. Real close. She could feel his presence straight down to her marrow.

"You can wait over there with the others if you'd like," Mrs. Gardner added.

Louisa joined the other basket-toting ladies

waiting near the entrance. Armed soldiers stood before the massive gate, the last barricade between her and Lance. Off to one side, a tall, arresting Yankee watched over the proceedings, his hawk-like gaze taking in everything around him.

"Major Beale!" a man called out to the officer.

The basket handle bit into her clenched palm. She doubted the major would recognize her as he'd only visited Spivey Point a handful of times. But the toadish man waddling toward him would. Henry Lawrence had practically lived at the plantation after the death of his older brother.

He wore a top hat, fancy suit, and carried a gold-handled cane. Still as dandified as ever. Though there seemed to be more of him. Too much time spent at the slop trough, most likely.

He turned toward the group of women, and she ducked to hide her face. She couldn't let him spot her and spoil her plan. But oh, how she ached to pull the knife from her boot and thrust it into his fat, twisted heart.

Out of the corner of her eye, she caught sight of a thick-chested soldier moving toward them. "Good afternoon, Ladies," he greeted, his voice syrupy sweet and grating on her already splintered nerves. He strutted around them like a rooster in yard full of hens. "Hope you had a pleasant ride through town."

There were a few soft-spoken replies and a faint giggle or two. Reckon Yankee women could also spot a cock for what it was. More crow, than meat.

The burly soldier stopped a few feet away from her and buried his nose in a basket. "Smells mighty fine, Mrs. Johnson." His beady gaze shifted to another woman. "And what about you, Miss Lacey? What goodies have you brought our lucky prisoners?" He angled closer to the blonde, and unfortunately closer to her.

Louisa took a step to the side, putting a broad-hipped woman between her and the nosey bluebelly. Sweat dribbled from beneath the rim of her bonnet and dampened her brow. With both hands occupied holding basket and satchel, she wasn't able to get to her handkerchief. Hopefully the soldiers would credit her perspiration to the heat and not to nerves.

A large hand clamped on her basket handle. "I have to inspect your basket, ma'am."

Startled, she glanced up at her challenger. Not the burly soldier, but one just as unnerving. Blue eyes met hers, interest flaring in their pale depths as he studied her face. His lips curved into a more-than-friendly smile, and he dipped his head in greeting.

Great. Just what she needed, an admirer. She mumbled a polite, "Certainly," and handed him the basket.

He lifted the covering and gave the contents a quick inspection. "Very good." He gestured to her satchel. "Now that."

It'd been risky bringing Jack's journal with her. If anyone read the contents before she could get it to the senator, it'd put them all in danger. Maybe catching the soldier's eye wasn't such a bad thing after all.

"Ma'am?"

She fumbled with the latch, her feeble efforts more genuine than pretend. "I'm so sorry, Lieutenant." She supplied him with her most sugary smile. "The catch sometimes sticks."

He shook his head and pointed to the single stripe on his sleeve. "I'm just a private, ma'am. Not an officer."

"Oh my, you look so imposing in that uniform. I just assumed..."

His chest puffed ever so slightly, and she stuffed down a grin. *Easier than taking candy from a baby.* She yanked on the latch, and it popped open.

"Nothing much in here. Just a few personal items. My diary..." She batted her eyelashes to draw his attention away from the satchel contents.

Her efforts paid off. His gaze barely skimmed the satchel before returning to her face. "Did you just join? The Women's League, I mean. I don't recall seeing you before."

"I'm new in town. Mrs. Gardner invited me to come and see some of the charitable events the League conducts for the city."

He handed her the basket. "It's admirable what you ladies are doing for the prisoners, but you never know what an ornery Reb might do." He leaned closer, his eyes near devouring her. "Pretty thing like you will draw them like bees to clover. You just call out if they bother you. I'll be right there to help."

She bowed her head, feigning coyness while bile rode up her throat. Ornery Rebs, her fanny. "Thank you, Private. I feel much safer knowing you'll be nearby." *Hmmph. Safe as a rabbit in a fox den.*

He gave her one last appreciative look, then moved on to continue his inspections. After a few minutes, he called out an, "All clear."

The signal was repeated down the line until the screech of hinges rang out. A widening arc of daylight bloomed ahead, and the women surged forward. She moved with them, her blood singing, her heart dancing a jig.

They passed through the open gate and into a huge compound. Freshly-hewn plank buildings lined the enclosure. Men knelt on the rooftops, the tap-tap of their hammers echoing against the stockade walls. In the distance, white canvas tents dotted the horizon like clouds in formation. Was Lance in one of them? The thought had her fairly skipping over the ground.

The strutting Sergeant led them into a long, rectangular building where a row of tables had been arranged. "Line up on the other side of these tables," he instructed. "The prisoners will arrive shortly. And remember, ladies, no talking. Just hand out your items."

She joined the other women behind the tables, setting her satchel at her feet and the basket of muffins on the tabletop. Before long, the thud of footsteps sounded, and the prisoners began shuffling inside, one-by-one, eyes down-cast, their bony faces framed by long scraggly hair. Tattered clothing hung on bodies that had no more meat to them than a scarecrow.

As they filed past, some dipped into her basket for a golden muffin while others opted for fruit or a blanket from another. She studied each dirt-smudged face, hope fading as none held the features she'd hoped to find.

Her gaze drifted to the entrance. The major stood by the door, silent and erect as a pine tree, while his piggish partner simpered and fawned over a well-dressed newcomer. Senator Morgan, most likely, considering the herd of newspapermen hovering nearby, pencils busy as they observed the procession. None wore a black eye-patch.

She swiped sweat from her palms and tucked trembling hands into the folds of her skirt. Jack's absence might not mean a thing. No sense getting all worked up. Besides, the last thing she needed was to draw attention to herself.

Pale green eyes staring out from a thin face caught her notice. A quiver started deep inside her, and thoughts of Jack waned as she gave the approaching prisoner a closer look.

Matted locks brushed his shoulders, the color hidden beneath a thick coat of filth. A scruffy beard concealed his chin and jaw. Yet when he brushed a hand through his hair in a familiar gesture, the breath lodged in her throat.

Lance!

Only two buttons held his ragged shirt closed. Weather-worn trousers hung low on his hips, lashed in place by a thin rope. He hobbled forward, favoring one leg. He was alive, but clearly not unharmed.

Tears swam in her eyes. She wanted to reach out and touch him—to see for herself he was real. But such a gesture would put them both at risk. She'd just have to wait until the Lawrences had been dealt with. Then she'd give him the biggest, longest hug ever.

Green eyes met hers and went wide with recognition. His shuffling gait faltered. He started to lift his hand, then dropped it back to his side. He too knew the danger of acknowledging one another.

A shadow fell across the table. Lance gave a slight jerk of his head. Someone was behind her. She nodded in response.

"Is anything amiss, ma'am?"

Drat. It was her admirer. She turned, forcing a smile. "Everything's perfectly fine, Private."

"Frank."

"Pardon?"

"Name's Frank. Frank Schofield." He bent closer and lowered his voice. "If you're interested, I'd like to meet you after my shift. We can talk some. Get to know each other better."

"I don't think that'd be a good idea."

"You sure?" He brushed a finger along her upper arm, then cupped her elbow. "Seemed like you were interested earlier."

She shrank away from his touch. "Please don't."

A blood-curdling yell froze them both. Out of the corner of her eye, she saw a rag-clad figure leap across the table and slam into Private Schofield.

Chapter Eighteen

"Throw Corporal Carleton into the pit with the other one."

Though Lance stood motionless between two rifle-toting guards, his shoulders stiffened at Major Beale's order. Lips smeared with blood pulled tight. Clearly *the pit* was not a good thing.

"Please, Major." She swallowed her pride with a hard gulp. She'd beg 'til the cows came home if it saved Lance. "Don't blame the Corporal. It wasn't his fault. I was the one who broke the rules."

"You'll have your say soon enough, Miss Carleton." He motioned to the row of tables, empty now of the Women's League and their baskets. "Go wait over there. I'll be with you shortly." His tone, though firm, was composed and gave no hint as to his mood.

"But—"

"Let's not cause any more trouble, miss, shall we?"

Trouble. That was her middle name. Yet again, Lance had landed himself in a kettle trying to defend her. Why did she always find herself in situations that provoked his brotherly sense of duty?

Lance looked up, and the love and understanding in his green eyes wrapped around her like a hug. A sob hung in her throat, and she mouthed the words, *I'm sorry*. He gave a tiny shake of his head. He was so forgiving, so caring. She'd get him out of this horrid place, or die trying.

One of the guards shoved him with the butt of a

rifle. Lance stumbled and a pained grimace shot across his face. He righted himself, then shuffled forward, mouth clamped tight, skin pale as the white-washed walls.

She bit down on her bottom lip to keep from crying foul. Hard as it was to watch Lance suffer, taking the major to task would only make matters worse. If she'd learned anything these past few weeks, it was how to hold her tongue. Beale would get his just desserts soon enough.

As Lance exited through one doorway, Mrs. Gardner appeared in the other, her face strained and lined with concern. Probably regretting her decision to let a Rebel Southerner join their outing.

"Major Beale," the League leader called out. "I'd like to have a word with you."

"I'll be with you in a minute, ma'am."

"You have no call to hold Miss Carleton," the woman persisted. "She did nothing wrong."

Louisa straightened. Didn't that beat all? A Yankee was actually defending her.

"I'll be the judge of that, ma'am. We have rules here for a reason."

"I understand, but—"

"Then you'll understand why I must insist you go back outside with the others." Only a slight tightening of Beale's jaw muscle betrayed his annoyance. "Miss Carleton will be dealt with appropriately."

How appropriately? With a knife? A bullet? No runaway carriages around that she could see. But then dead was dead.

The burly soldier from earlier, Sergeant Wilson she overheard someone call him, entered the room and stopped before the major. One eyelid puffed and was going purple. Dried blood clumped in the corner of his mouth. Lance had gotten in a few good licks before being subdued. If she wasn't so worried about what they were going to do to him, she might've cheered.

"Prisoners are all back on their wards, sir," the sergeant reported. "With no further incidents."

"Good." Beale gestured to the doorway. "Escort Mrs. Gardner outside with the other ladies, then see them all to their carriages. This one's staying a while longer."

"Yes, sir."

"Once the League is gone, take care of that situation in the pit. There'll be two of them."

"Yes, sir. Right away, sir." The sergeant pivoted in a squelch of boot leather and headed for the door. He motioned for the two soldiers guarding the entrance to join him, and then guided a protesting Mrs. Gardner through the doorway.

That left her alone—with one of the rattlesnakes that had ordered Papa to be killed and planned God-knew-what for Lance. The other viper had slithered to safety during the ruckus. Lawrence would soon be crawling out from under his rock. Time to leave before she got snake bit.

She took a step forward, only to be rudely jerked to a stop.

"Just where do you think you're going, Missy?"

Henry Lawrence. He'd used that tone with her right after Bart died. He sounded just as venomous now as he had back then, and it made her skin crawl.

She turned and faced him, chin thrust up. A year ago, she had cowered before his vicious taunts, too distraught over Bart's attack and Lance's flight to do much else. Not now. Not since Jack's love had shown her just how valuable she was.

"Take your hands off me," she ground through clenched teeth.

His face turned a mottled red, eyelids narrowing to slits. "Don't go giving me orders, you little strumpet." He tightened his grip, fingers digging like fangs into her skin. "You're the reason my nephew's dead. If you hadn't led him on with your female trickery, he'd still be alive."

Female trickery! Fury bolted inside her like a runaway horse. "Why you overblown, bigoted toad. The only ones to blame for Bart's death are you and your no-account family." She poked a finger at him. "Y'all spoiled that boy. Gave him anything he wanted. He never had to do an honest day's work in his life; thought everything was his for the taking—including me."

He bent toward her, snarling. "Raised by a Negress. Slaves for companions. What would the likes of *you* know about a real family?"

"I know plenty. Family is all about love and forgiveness. Not power and possessions." She curled her upper lip at him. "You're nothing but a pack of vultures making an easy meal off poor folks who can't fight back."

"Shut your mouth." He lifted a hand as if to strike her. "Or I'll shut it for you."

"Easy, Henry," Beale warned. "Not here."

"Where then? Morgan is preparing to leave. He won't be a problem."

So, the senator wasn't part of their wickedness. That made her decision all the easier.

"We'll take her somewhere more private."

As Beale picked up her satchel, the latch slipped free and bared the contents. A gasp skated from her throat before she could stop it. The major regarded her for a moment with those hawk-like eyes, then fished inside.

She held her breath. *Please don't let him—*

He pulled out Jack's journal.

No. No. No. If he read those notes, that letter she left with the desk clerk would become her last line of defense. And it might come too late to save any of them.

Though she itched to grab the journal, she stood still as a statue. Reacting would only show him just how important the ledger was. Better to appear unconcerned and hope his interest moved on to something else.

Her effort was wasted. Beale flipped open the journal and began reading. After a few seconds, he looked up, gaze narrowed. "Where did you get this?"

She remained mute beneath his stare, sifting through the options in her head. Lies, truth, or a shade in between? They all sounded risky. *Drat.* Why couldn't she think as fast on her feet as Jack did?

"Did you steal it?"

"Steal? I don't steal from folks."

"Then how did it come to be in your possession? It sure as hell isn't yours."

Double drat. She chose the only sensible option. "I found it."

"Where?"

"Outside my hotel. I was just walking along, and there it was. Thought it might come in handy." His lips thinned, and she added an off-hand, "For lighting fires and such. With the paper."

"Did you read it?"

"Me? Read?" She gave an unladylike sniff and eyeballed Lawrence. "You know I can't read a lick."

The toad nodded. "She's right. Fannie bemoaned her inability to read and write. Said she made the worst lady's maid she'd ever employed."

Ain't that a shame. For once, her poor reading skills were a cause for rejoicing.

Beale frowned, then burrowed back into the ledger. A few pages later, he snapped the book shut and wagged it under her nose. "If you found this as you claim, how do you explain the notations about you and Corporal Carleton?"

She shrugged, feigning an indifference she was far from feeling. "I have no idea why anyone would want to write about us."

"How do you know Porter?"

Porter? How did he know the journal was Jack's? Her stomach did a nasty summersault. Unless he'd already found Jack out. That would explain why he hadn't been with the other newspapermen. Her love was in danger - terrible danger.

She shook her head, praying the major couldn't see the fear and pretense that must surely be showing on her face. "Never heard of anyone named Porter."

Beale slammed the ledger onto the table, then pushed Lawrence aside and took hold of her arm, his grip steely as the pair of slave manacles she and Lance had once tinkered with. "Don't play games, Miss Carleton. We want to know what you're doing with Porter's journal. Is that why you snuck in here? To help with Porter's scheme?"

She held his stare, refusing to be cowed. "I don't know what you're talking about."

"If you're trying to protect him, you're wasting your breath."

Alarm shot through her, and she couldn't stop from stiffening.

Beale smiled. "Ah, so you do know him."

"He'll be taken care of," Lawrence cut in with a sneer. "Along with that murdering brother of yours."

Will be. They weren't dead—yet. "You can't just kill them. There are laws."

"Not inside this prison, there aren't, Missy."

She ignored Lawrence and gave Beale a pointed look. He was the bigger toad in the puddle. "You could probably get away with killing Lance. But how will you explain Porter's death? People are sure to miss a well-known newspaperman."

He shrugged. "Accidents happen all the time. A

stray bullet meant for a disorderly prisoner. Sharp objects where they shouldn't be..."

"A runaway carriage, perhaps?"

He looked confused for a second, then shook his head. "Don't know what you're babbling about."

Of course he didn't. Papa's death was as piddling to him as swatting a fly.

"It doesn't matter what she's babbling about." Lawrence leaned over her, trying to look all scary and mean and not succeeding. "Justice will be served. Justice for *everyone.*"

It was time to play out her hand, before blood played out of her. She spit out a mocking laugh. "Doing away with me won't solve your problems. It'll only make them worse."

Beale's grip tightened on her arm. "Why is that?"

"I have what you might call *insurance.* A letter to be delivered to Senator Morgan if I don't return this evening." She let that sink in before continuing. "I don't think the good senator will cotton to people embezzling government money." She rather liked using high-falutin words. But the twin expressions of terror on the two men's faces were much more enjoyable.

Beale recovered first and eyed her with snake-like coldness. "You're lying."

"You want to take that chance? If I were you," she said. "And thank God I'm not, I'd make sure Corporal Carleton and Jack Porter remain alive and well. Stealing money is one thing, murder quite another altogether."

Lawrence snorted. "It's too late for that."

Too late. Wilson. The pit. There'll be two of them. The loves of her life were about to be executed. She rammed steel into her backbone. Not while she drew a breath.

She bent and clamped her teeth around Beale's

fingers, biting for all she was worth. He howled and released her. She snatched up the journal and sprinted for the door.

"Dammit, get her," Beale yelled.

Footfalls pounded behind her. She raced through the open doorway and into the bright sunlight, not daring to stop and wait for her vision to adjust. On the other side of the yard, she could just make out a clump of suits—grays and browns. No blues.

She angled toward them, praying her hunch was right. "Senator," she called out. "Senator Morgan!"

The well-dressed gentleman she'd seen earlier turned to face her. He was still here. Thank God. She waved the journal in the air. "I have something I think you should see."

****

As the darkness ebbed, pain surged. Hot and red. Stabbing into his skull like a poker. The smell of old sweat, stale urine, and excrement swirled together in a gut-churning stew. Jack groaned and rubbed at his throbbing temple.

"Landed a good one, did they?"

He opened his eye. Enough sunlight dribbled through the cracks in the plank walls to illuminate the man sitting across from him, back against the wall, one knee drawn to his chest. Like all the other the prisoners he'd met, a tattered Reb uniform barely covered his thin frame. His hair and beard were matted with dirt and grime. What looked like blood crusted one corner of his mouth. He'd recently met the blunt end of something hard.

Jack rolled upright. The room spun for a moment, then settled into place.

"You've been out of it since I was thrown in here with you," the soldier said.

He worked his jaw back and forth, making sure the damn thing still functioned. "Ought to be a law against fists like that."

"Probably Sergeant Wilson."

"Didn't catch his name. Big barrel-chested brute."

"Yep, that's him." The Reb's voice crawled with contempt. "Plenty of prisoners'd like to greet that one with the business end of a shotgun."

"Sounds like you might be one of them."

"That's one mean, toad-eating cuss. Likes to make his ward trot to and from the cookhouse. Ever try to run on weedy legs, toting a hot tin of soup?" He shook his head. "Those who can't keep up or fall are treated to a boot to the backside."

"Guess it wouldn't do any good to complain."

"Are you kiddin'? Protesting only eggs him on. Better to keep quiet than risk an uglier thrashing." He reached up and tapped the bridge of his nose. "Ladies back home won't cotton to a man with a lopsided face and a gaping smile."

He knew all about the fussiness of ladies. Lucky for him, he found a rare jewel. And he intended to return to her—in one piece. He levered to his feet. Fireworks exploded behind his eye, and the floor shifted beneath him like a pile of sand. He put out a hand to brace against the dizziness and grasped at empty air.

"Give yourself a minute. Jus' hold still and take a deep breath."

Open-mouthed, he inhaled, tasting the dust and mold and heaven knew what else. The cell slowly stopped wobbling around him, and he shuffled to the door. With both hands pressed against the rough wood, he gave a push. Damn thing didn't budge. Pulling didn't work either. He hadn't really thought it would, but he had to try.

The other man gave a long stretch and relaxed back into the dirt. "You're wasting your time, friend."

He shook his head. "Can't...can't just..." Methodically he moved around the perimeter, digging in his fingers wherever he found a crack wide enough between the planks. Foot planted against the wall he jiggled and pulled.

"Like I said, you're wasting time and energy," his cellmate drawled. "'Course, we got plenty of time. There's no escaping from the Hellmira pit."

"Fitting name for it." With no windows and the door shut tighter than a virgin's thighs, the six-by-six, woodshed of a cell sweltered like Satan's caldron.

"Might as well make yourself comfortable. You aren't going anywhere until they come for you."

His ears rang with a high-pitched buzz. It was a whole different kettle of fish *being* a prisoner rather than observing them. The loss of freedom. The knowing that someone has complete control over you—to hurt or slaughter as they saw fit.

Beale had been waiting at the main gate to escort him to Senator Morgan. They never made it to the congressman. A trip between two buildings had resulted in a cracked skull and a search of his person for the stolen requisition.

From what conversation he could piece together through the pained fog in his head, Beale had discovered the document missing from his desk and put two and two together. He had no doubt the major or one of his henchmen would come to finish what they'd started. For now, as his cellmate had so succinctly put it, there wasn't anything he could do but wait.

"You're that newspaperman, aren't you? From yesterday. You were questioning some of the prisoners."

He lowered himself onto the lumpy dirt and extended a hand. "Yes, that was me. Jackson Porter, with *The New York Herald*."

Something furry darted across the floor and disappeared into a corner. The Reb banged a fist against the wall, sending dust drizzling down from the ceiling. "Damn varmints." He gave the wall another whack. "Hate those filthy things. Creeping around, gnawing on your fingers and toes while you're sleeping. Some fellas eat 'em. Not me. I'd rather starve."

A spasm swept through him. Waking from nightmares with the tremors was bad enough. He couldn't imagine waking to something chewing on his flesh.

The Reb scooted closer, hand outstretched. "Sorry 'bout that. Corporal Lance Carleton, twenty-forth Virginia."

Gripes, either *The Man* upstairs had a sense of humor, or this was intentional. His gut screamed it was the latter. He grasped Carleton's hand in a firm handshake. "Good to meet you, Corporal."

"So, what'd you do to earn a stint in this hell-hole?"

"Guess I poked at a hornet's nest."

"Not a healthy thing to do."

"No, but it had to be done." Had to be done for the two things he treasured most in life.

"For your newspaper job?"

"That's one reason." He brushed at the dirt soiling his trousers. Thank God the Provost knew nothing about Kitty's involvement. She'd go mad as a March hare if they confined her in a crypt like this.

"You're gonna wear a hole in them pants if you keep going at 'em like that."

He stilled his brushing. Observant little cuss, this one.

"Only one thing can worry at a man like that," Carleton added. "Sweetheart or a wife?"

Shrewd, too. "Wife, if I manage to get out of this rat-hole and into a chapel."

"Good luck with that." Lance stretched out his bent leg, then grimaced and rubbed his knee.

"New injury or old?"

"Old. Mini-ball skipped off it at Gettysburg. Ain't never had anything hurt so bad." His scowl flipped into a grin. "But then having a bevy of pretty nurses to look after me in the Fredericksburg hospital helped."

Thoughts surfaced of Kitty holding his hand in the steamer cabin, helping to push back the nightmares. "Nothing like a beautiful lady to take your mind off your troubles."

"Your gal waiting for you back home?"

Don't I wish. "No. She came with me to Elmira. Well, more like I came with her. No force on earth could stop her from finding her brother. Her tenacity is one of the things I love most about her." Time to let the corporal in on his secret. "That and her flaming red hair. Got a temper to match it, too."

Green eyes narrowed. "What the hell? You aren't talking about my Lou are ya?"

"I think Kitty suits her better, but yes, my wife to be is your sister."

Carleton shook his head. "Don't that beat all. Never expected her to catch herself a newspaperman. She isn't much for words and such."

"You'd be surprised at what she's accomplished since you left. She's one determined lady."

"She's dogged, that's for sure. I sure hope nothing bad has happened to her."

"She should be fine. No one knows she's here or what she's up to."

Carleton laughed, but without any humor. "Neither do you, it appears."

An instant passed, no more than that, as the comment echoed in his head. Then the plank walls, the noxious smells, the dirt, and the pain faded away. The world squeezed down to the gist of

Carleton's words. "What do you mean?"

"She came in with the Women's League this afternoon. Surprised the hell out of me to find her in the eating hall handing out foodstuff with a bunch of Yankee do-gooders."

His blood heated. "Damn her hide. I should've known she wouldn't stay put."

"That's my Lou. Gets herself into more pickles." He swiped the crusted blood from the corner of his mouth. "I got this trying to keep some damn bluebelly from pawing her."

His gut lunged. "Did the bastard hurt her?"

"Didn't appear to. But the ruckus exposed her ruse. Last I saw, Lawrence and Major Beale had separated her from the other ladies. Gives me the shakes thinking about what they'll do to her. They've been trying to get at us ever since—" He snapped off the rest with a click of his teeth.

Loyal and astute. Lance was definitely Kitty's twin. "No need to worry. I know all about Bart and the Lawrence vendetta."

"She told you?"

"Everything."

"Dang. You must really mean something special to her."

"She's special to me, too. Real special." *If anything were to happen to her*...He pushed stiff fingers through his tangled hair.

"Lou usually lands on her feet. Just like a kitty. You give her that nickname?"

He nodded, the only response he could give at the moment without his voice cracking.

"Where'd you two meet?"

That was a story for his and Kitty's children. To be told around the hearth on a cold winter's night while sipping mulled cider, like his parents had done with him. He pulled himself together and gave a simple, "On the way to Point Lookout Prison."

"Point Lookout? She's been trailing me that long?"

"Her and her friend Jeb."

Carleton's head and shoulders came up. "Jeb's here, too?"

"No. Unfortunately, he took a bullet in the back while running from a Yankee patrol just north of Point Lookout."

"Oh, hell no. Did he make it?"

"Far as I know. He's recuperating in the prison hospital. Once he's strong enough, I arranged for him to be sent to my grandfather's home in Baltimore. Kitty wouldn't leave Maryland until she knew he was safe."

Carleton nodded. "Jeb means a lot to Lou and me. Thank you for seeing to him."

"Glad I could help."

"Well, future brother-in-law." Lance clapped him on the shoulder. "Welcome to the Carleton clan. Though the only thing that's gonna get you is an early grave."

The bolt scraped back, and the door screeched open. A stab of sunlight silhouetted the burly frame of Beale's henchman. The wait was apparently over.

"On yer feet, you two," Wilson growled.

Jack groped in the dirt and palmed a rock-hard lump of clay. If an opportunity presented itself, he wanted to be prepared to take advantage of it.

He squinted against the glare of light. "Where are we going, Sergeant?"

"Shut yer trap, Porter, and just do as I say."

Lance rolled to his feet and offered a hand. "Come on. Let's see what they want with us. At least we'll be out of this sweat box."

And into what? He seized the boy's hand and found a dirt clod being shoved into his palm. *Great minds think alike.* He rose, pretended to steady himself, and pulled out of Lance's grasp. "Thanks.

I'm good."

Carleton nodded and hobbled toward the door. Boy had more grit than Kitty gave him credit for.

Jack paused in the doorway as his vision adjusted to the abrupt change in light. The blinding brightness set his skull back to thumping, and he pressed the heel of his hand against his temple. He needed a clear head for what lay ahead. Something told him it was going to be bad.

The sergeant jabbed his spine with the rifle butt. "Move along, Porter."

He clenched his teeth around a nasty retort. It'd only egg the brute on as Carleton had said. And his sore head couldn't take another wallop.

Wilson herded them down the now deserted street. Jack glanced skyward. The sun sat two hand-widths from the horizon. Three o'clock or close to it. Mealtime. That meant the prisoners and guards would be at the eating hall and almost guaranteed there would be no witnesses.

They weaved around frame buildings and crossed over a stagnant creek. Firm ground gave way to soggy sod. A muddied stench rode the breeze. They were getting close to the river. Ice coated his insides. Would water turn out to be his final resting place after all?

"Turn left at the next building." Wilson punctuated the order with another poke of his rifle.

The shadows behind the structure weren't deep enough to disguise two distinctly shaped boxes. The coffins, lids off, sat placidly in the cool of the shade, waiting to be filled.

Chapter Nineteen

"It's empty, Senator Morgan, sir."

Empty? She pushed past the guard. The opening to the pit gaped like a wolf's maw, ready to snatch her into its gullet. She fisted her hands and stepped into the doorway. Bart Lawrence and his dastardly deed no longer held sway over her. She was whole again. Thanks to one man.

She peered into the gloominess. The cell was barren. And rancid. The smell swirled around her, burning her nostrils. Her stomach churned at the thought of her brother and Jack trapped in such a skunk hole. She whirled and stalked toward Major Beale. "Where are they?"

He gave a careless shrug, at odds with the tightness rimming his eyes. "I have no idea. I ordered them put in here."

"And you also ordered Sergeant Wilson to 'take care of the situation in the pit.' What did you mean by that?"

He remained mute, his expression unreadable. Unlike his fat partner. Lawrence twitched and fidgeted, gnawing on his fingernail like it was a chicken bone. Worried, was he? If Jack and Lance were found dead, a noose would soon be worrying his neck.

"I ask again," she said through clenched teeth. "Where are my brother and—"

A gunshot cut into her question. Another shot followed right on its heels.

"It came from that way," shouted one of the

guards. "Near the river."

Senator Morgan pointed to the soldier. "Lock the Major and Mr. Lawrence in that cell until I can sort this out. The rest of you come with me."

Louisa hiked up her skirt and joined the senator and his posse in a footrace for the river. She tossed a prayer skyward that those shots didn't mean what she thought they meant. Lance and Jack were fine. They had to be. She didn't want to consider the alternative.

The path ahead curved around a row of frame buildings. As they made the turn, a figure dashed from the shadows, his tattered shirttails billowing behind him like sails on a ship. It took only a second to recognize the ragged hair and shuffling gait. *Lance!*

Before she could call out, one of the guards took a bead on him. "Halt or I'll shoot!"

Lance paused, glanced over his shoulder, then hunkered down, arms upraised. "Don't shoot. I'm unarmed."

Sergeant Wilson emerged from the side of the building, rifle pointed at Lance. "Gotcha now, you damn—" He stopped in his tracks, eyes going wide as he caught sight of the other soldiers with their guns trained on him.

"Drop your weapon, Sergeant," the Senator ordered.

Wilson eyed them for a second, then finding a smidgen of smarts somewhere in that empty skull of his, dropped his rifle and raised his hands.

"Take the sergeant into custody."

As the soldiers rushed to carry out the senator's orders, Louisa sprinted to her brother and launched into his arms. "Oh, Lance, thank God." Tears of relief and joy burned her eyes.

"My sweet, sweet Lou." He gave her a fierce hug and kissed the top of her head.

"When I heard those shots..." She shuddered and tightened her hold. "I thought you were dead."

"Nah, honey. I'm fine. Wilson shoots worse than he smells. And that's pretty dang bad." He pried her away from him. "Here now, you're gonna get all dirty."

"I don't care. I'm just happy you're alive."

"I am alive, thanks to your husband-to-be."

Husband-to-be. Maybe. Maybe not. Jack Porter had a lot of explaining to do before she jumped the broom with him. She turned in a circle, scouring the area. "Where is he? Wasn't he with you?"

Lance glanced over his shoulder. "He was, 'til we took off in opposite directions."

She went cold as if suddenly doused by a bucket of icy water. "Was he shot?"

"I don't know. Like I said, we ran in opposite directions."

"Then I have to find him." She whirled and raced for the spot where Lance and Wilson had appeared. A salty, metallic taste flooded her mouth. Better a bitten lip than a shredded heart.

"Wait! Lou!"

She kept going. Jack was out there, possibly hurt—or worse.

A sprint between buildings brought her to a barren plot that stretched to a low berm. Footprints tracked through the red clay, some climbing the embankment, others heading back the way she'd come. He wasn't that way, so...

She scrambled up the hill, slipping and sliding in the loose soil until she reached the top. "Jack!" She cupped her hands to her mouth, calling in one direction and then the other. "Jack Porter!"

Nothing. The footprints disappeared into the mush at the edge of the river. Her stomach sank. Surely he hadn't tried to swim to freedom. He was terrified of deep-running water.

She scrabbled along the spine, listening to the tumbling water and the breeze playing tag through the tufts of grass. She strained to hear other sounds.

A faint noise rose over the rush of the river.

She froze and cocked an ear. The sound came again, louder this time.

She followed the noise, hands outstretched to keep her balance on the ridge. Just beyond a rocky outcrop, a patch of white shimmered in the mud. Heart thudding, she plunged down to the river bank. Her boots sank in the soggy loam. She fought the pull of the sucking mud and rounded the outcrop.

Only the upper half of his body was visible. The rest disappeared into a mire at the river's edge. He turned his head, his dark gaze latching onto her.

She slumped against the rock. He was alive! Stuck faster than a fly in molasses, but still alive.

"Kitty. Thank God. Help me out."

She angled closer to the hillside where the ground was firmer and extended a hand. When his fingers closed around her wrist, she dug in her heels and tugged.

He twisted back and forth, trying to free himself. "Harder, Kitty. Pull harder."

She clenched her teeth and pulled with all her might. A loud sucking noise sounded, then he sprawled at her feet, gasping for breath. She sank to her knees beside him, working to fill her own lungs.

After a few seconds, he rolled to a sitting position, heels pressed into the soft mud. "We have to go. Wilson—"

"Is under arrest. Along with Major Beale and Henry Lawrence."

"How?"

"Your journal. I showed it to Senator Morgan, and he agreed something smelled awful fishy. He made Beale take us to the pit, and when we discovered you and Lance missing and then heard those gunshots, he had them locked up until everything could be sorted out." She swept at the mud clinging to his sleeve. He hated being untidy. "Reckon they'll get a taste of what you and Lance had to put up with in that nasty cell."

"Gripes, Kitty. Do you know how dangerous coming to the prison was?"

"I knew. I waited long past the time you said you'd be back. Then I had to see if you needed help." She pushed upright and brushed dirt from her palms. "Good thing I did. You and Lance were in a right pickle."

A shout carried over the hillock. "Lou? Lou, where are you?"

"Over here, Lance. Everything's fine."

Jack rose beside her, shucking mud from his hands and arms as he stood. "Your brother's unhurt then?"

"Yes."

"I'm glad. We got on well while locked in that cell. Had a nice long talk."

More fodder for your article, no doubt. She braced her legs, then eyed him from head to toe, checking for bullet holes and blood. "You sure you're not hurt? No gunshot wounds? No broken bones?"

"I'm fine. Just covered in this damn mud."

"Good." She swung her hand in a sweeping arc and landed a stinging slap along his cheek.

A second passed. Then another. He blinked, mouth sagging like a dumbfounded oaf. "What did you do that for?"

She gathered her skirts and started up the hill. That wounded tone wasn't going to make her feel guilty. She was the wronged one.

"For being a rotten, lying polecat."

****

"Now that we're all cleaned up, it's time we talked."

He'd bathed in the chamber down the hall. His hair was still damp and mussed from toweling. One unruly lock dangled rakishly over his forehead. She wanted to smooth it into place. She shoved her hairbrush into her satchel instead.

"You haven't said two words since we left the prison, Kitty. What has you so upset?"

A light breeze ruffled the curtains and lifted fine strands of hair across the top of his head. Confusion and hurt showed in his face. With effort, she pulled her gaze away. How easy it'd be to give in, looking at his sorrowful, hound dog expression. She was tired of giving in. Tired of backing down. If she'd learned anything from this whole mess, it was her own ability to stand her ground.

She picked up her satchel and walked to the wardrobe. It wasn't that far, really, but enough to give her some breathing room.

"Was it something I did?" he pleaded. "Something I said?"

She yanked open the wardrobe door and continued to stew in silence. Belle always said, "if you can't say anything nice, don't say nothing a'tall". There wasn't anything nice she wanted to say.

She pulled out the farmwoman's drab sack-dress and smoothed a wrinkle with her finger. She should've tossed out the ugly garment when they bought its replacement at the sutler's store. Back then, it'd been a matter of squirreling away the spare dress in case she needed it. Now, it was a reminder of the start of their journey and how much her life had changed since meeting Jack Porter—for the better.

"What are you doing, Kitty?"

"Packing."

"I can see that. Why? I thought you'd want to wait for your brother to be released."

She folded the dress into a neat square and

gently tucked it into her bag. "I *am* going to wait for him, but not here with you."

"Where will you stay?"

"I reserved a room in Lance's name. It's all taken care of."

He wagged his head. "You can't stay alone, Kitty. It's not safe."

"I'm perfectly capable of taking care of myself." Though if she were honest with herself, she'd come to like having him look after her. Made her feel special.

"Yes, you're entirely capable of caring for yourself. I've never seen a more determined woman in all my life."

His admiration swirled around her like heady perfume. She snagged her satchel and crossed to the dresser. She wouldn't be swayed by sweet-smelling words. Not this time.

He stepped in front of her, blocking her path. "What's wrong? I don't understand. I thought you'd be happy. Lance is going to be released soon. The Lawrences are locked up." Lines furrowed his brow. "So there has to be something else."

"You bet there's something else. You lied to me."

"Why do you think I lied to you?"

"I don't think you did." She stepped around him. "I know you did."

"Lied about what, for God's sake?"

She plucked his journal off the bureau. The spine bit into her clenched palm. "This."

"What about it?"

"I read your notes, Jack. You wrote about me, my family, our affairs. Things that are personal and private." Her chest filled with pain. She thrust the journal at him. "For a damned newspaper article."

"You read my journal?"

"Maybe I shouldn't have been going through your things—"

"And maybe I should be angry with *you*." His tone softened. "But it's more important to me that you were able to read."

That caught her off-guard. She folded her arms over her chest, holding onto an anger that was fast fading. "Would you have told me about your plans if I hadn't read it?"

"Yes, I would have."

"When?"

"Soon. I meant to. Started to back in Baltimore, but then all that mess happened with Calhoun. You don't think I was sneaking around..?" He rifled a hand through his hair. "Lord, you do."

"You should've asked my permission to write any of it, Jack."

"Maybe I wanted the work to be pure. An objective portrayal of the events, and not colored with your perception of things. But as I got to know you, fell in love with you, it became harder to stay objective." He grimaced and shook his head. "Worst thing that can happen to a journalist...getting too close to his subject."

"Subject? That's all I am to you? I should've known. Tarnation, I'm so gullible." She bent and jerked on the dresser drawer. It came out crooked and stuck. Dratted drawer. She yanked harder. It didn't budge.

"Let me help you."

She swatted away his hand. "I can do it myself."

His fingers fisted into a ball. "Gripes, you're one stubborn female."

"Hmmph. This stubborn female will soon be out of your life. Then you can do whatever you please with your precious writings."

He slammed his palm on the top of the bureau, startling her. "So, you're leaving because of a damned article?"

"To you, it's an article. To me, it's my family, my

life. You had no right putting that to paper." Hands trembling, she pushed the drawer closed, then pulled it out slowly. Miracle of miracles, the thing opened straight. She scooped up a handful of underclothing. "I suppose you're still planning to send it to your editor."

"It's a grand story, Kitty."

"I'm sure they'll pay you well for it."

"It's not about the money. Not entirely." He reached out and cupped her hands still full of clothes. "Don't you realize how wonderful it is? The trials your family has endured. How you've persevered and overcome them. Other people could derive so much strength from reading about you and Lance."

"You think other people will admire us for that?" She wiggled out of his grasp and stuffed her things into the bag. "You've been out in the sun too long, Jack. We'll be looked down on even more than we were at Spivey Point."

"Why would anyone look down on you? Because you've had hard times? You're not the only ones who have suffered. This War has torn the country apart. But you're one of the people who have triumphed, in your own way, in spite of it." His expression softened. "That's to be admired. And I do admire you—a great deal."

Her heart trilled at his words. "Jack—"

"No, let me finish. You're right. I probably should've discussed it with you. At least mentioned I was thinking about using your plight as the subject of my article. Heck, I was even thinking it could make a book."

"A book?" She shook her head. "I don't want the whole world reading about my family's private affairs."

"I didn't realize it would upset you like this."

"Well, it does." She snapped her satchel closed

and straightened. "And no amount of pretty words will change my mind."

His mouth tightened. "Is that all that's between us, Kitty? Does it mean so little that a damned article is all it takes to make you walk out on me?"

"If you kept that from me, what else might you lie about? It appears my leaving will save you from committing yet another sin. You can return to Baltimore without dishonoring your promise."

"You're wrong, on both accounts. This..." He shook the journal at her. "...is a good article. Hell, it's great. Probably one of the best things I've ever written. Probably because the subject is so damn important to me. You might let it stand between us. I sure as hell won't." He wheeled around and stomped to the fireplace where he knelt and jerked open the ledger.

Hogs rooted in her belly. He was madder than she'd ever seen him before. Even at his granddaddy's house. "What are you doing, Jack?"

"Doesn't matter. Finish your packing." He began ripping out the pages and tossing them onto the grate.

Her pulse tripped. He was destroying the work he'd poured his heart and soul into. She dropped her satchel and crossed to the hearth, standing behind him, fingers aching to knead the tautness from his shoulders.

"Someday, Louisa dear..." He didn't look up, merely continued shredding his journal. "...You're going to have to trust somebody. Apparently it's not going to be me."

Louisa, not Kitty. The shush of ripping paper mirrored the tearing of her heart. Was she about to lose a love she might never find again? He reached for a match, and she stiffened. "You'd burn your notes? For me?"

"That's what you want, isn't it?"

"No. I don't."

"Your story is personal and private. You're madder than blazes because I've committed it to paper, and now that I'm willing to destroy it, you say no." He shook his head. "When you snuck into my tent that night, I knew you were crazy. Should've held with my instincts and tossed you out on your sweet little backside. Saved myself a pack of trouble."

Sandalwood and soap filled her nostrils. The scent of clean. Just as he'd washed the mud from his body, his goodness had washed the taint from hers. She should be thanking her lucky stars he *hadn't* tossed her out on her backside.

She dropped to her knees and rested a hand on his arm. "This article is important to you. You say it's your best work. You can't...I can't ask you to destroy it."

"You're not asking me. I'm making a choice."

"But your career...and your debt. How will you pay back your granddaddy?"

"I love you, Kitty. I want you to be my wife." He struck the match head to the bricks. "There'll be other articles. Other stories. Other ways to make money. There's only one you."

Her heart soared. He loved her. More than any words on a page. She snuffed out the flame with a quick puff. "I won't let you do this, Jack. I care about you and everything that's part of you. And I don't want to lose any of it. It's unfair of me to expect you to give up something important just to save my pride."

"You mean that?"

"With all my heart. Where's the closest church?"

"As much as I want to marry you, our nuptials will have to wait. I have to settle my debt in Baltimore and convince a stubborn mule he's wrong."

273

Epilogue

The mouth-watering aroma of baking chicken filled the parlor. Rosemary and thyme, Nanny Belle's favorite herbs for spicing yard bird. Sally had, no doubt, added her two cents worth. Both women knew their way around a cookstove and seemed to be getting along like old friends. Their combined efforts in the kitchen would soon have everyone's bones fleshed out.

A movement in the doorway caught her eye. Mr. Porter wandered in toting a bolt of cloth under each arm. His health was much improved. His face had fleshed out, the skin pink and shiny. He had a lively, almost boyish hitch to his gait.

"Miriam Goldstein sent these over to you, my dear."

She crossed the room and relieved him of his burden. "I wasn't expecting them until next week. Thank you for bringing them to me."

"You're welcome." He gave her a nod and turned for the door. "I know you're eager to get started, so I'll leave you to your decorating."

"Won't you stay and help decide which looks best? It is your house after all."

He swiveled back around and shook his head. "It's your house, too. Besides, I trust your judgment."

"Like you trusted me with Jack's heart? That was a rotten trick you and Sally pulled on us."

He chuckled. "It worked didn't it? When you arrived from Point Lookout, neither of you were anywhere near to making a commitment, much as we wanted to see your sham of a marriage made real. We knew if we pushed, you'd rebel. Pardon the pun. So we figured we'd turn Jackson's propensity for doing the opposite of what I wanted against him."

She laughed with him. He certainly knew his grandson. "And here we are, preparing for a wedding."

"I had my concerns when you went missing. But luckily an acquaintance sent word that he'd seen you staying with Jonas and Mary Sloan. The Sloans are good people. I knew you were safe, and that Jackson would soon find you. So we just let nature take its course."

"You are a wily one. It's no wonder you beat me at checkers."

Smile lines creased the skin around his eyes and mouth. "You hold your own pretty well. In all respects. I'm proud to call you Granddaughter."

Her heart swelled. "Thank you, Mister Porter. That means more to me than you'll ever know."

"Grandfather. You must call me Grandfather now."

"I'd be happy to...Granddaddy."

A twinkle lit his eyes. "Jackson will have his hands full keeping up with his Rebel wife, pun intended this time. I couldn't have selected a more fitting bride for him if I tried."

He turned and headed for the doorway, his laugher trailing after him until he disappeared from view. Louisa smiled. Her life was complete. She had a new home filled with people she loved. The only gray cloud—Calhoun's whereabouts and the unsolved murder of the Yankee courier. But she wouldn't think about that now. She wanted to enjoy this undertaking she'd only dreamed of doing.

As she unrolled one of the bolts, a familiar auburn-topped head poked around the door jamb. "We're off now, Sis."

"Oh, Lance. Good. Is Jeb with you?"

Lance stepped into the doorway. "He is. Do you need something?"

"Yes. Could you help me with these fabrics before you go?"

"Sure." He moved into the room, followed by Jeb. Both men walked gingerly, but not near as badly as when they arrived several weeks ago. Their wounds were healing nicely, thanks to Sally's superb doctoring.

"What you gonna do with 'em, Miz Lou?" Jeb asked.

"I'm going to make curtains. But I can't decide which of them would look best."

"They mighty pretty. Hard choice to make."

"Yes, it is." She handed one bolt to Jeb and the other to Lance. "Unfurl the cloth, then stand on either side of the window and hold your piece as high as you can."

She moved between them and eyed the fabrics. The dark green velvet picked up the earthy colors in the furniture coverings, yet the red made the white walls gleam. Decisions. Decisions. She smiled. She wouldn't have it any other way.

The creak of the front door sounded, then came Jack's, "Anyone home?"

"In the parlor, sweetheart," she called out.

Boot heels clicked in the hallway, then he entered the room. "What have we here?"

"She's trying to decide which of these to use for curtains." Lance grinned impishly. "Which do you prefer, the garnet or the emerald?"

"I prefer the jewel in the middle."

"Wise choice, soon to be brother-in-law." Lance tossed the fabric onto the chair, then gave her a peck on the cheek. "We have to skedaddle, Sis. See you at dinner."

"Good-bye. And good luck with your sale. I'm

sure Mr. Randolph will love your sketches."

"I hope you're right. I could sure use his endorsement."

As Lance and Jeb left the parlor, Jack crossed to her side, his loving smile, as always, making her pulse thrum. "Speaking of jewels, I have something for you."

"You do? What?"

He reached inside his jacket and pulled out a tiny black box. "This."

"What is it?"

"Open it and see."

She lifted the lid and gasped at the huge ruby nested inside. "Oh, Jack, it's lovely."

"A precious, fiery engagement ring. Just like my gem of a wife."

He always said the sweetest things. Was full up with them. And she loved every bit of it. She slid the ring on her finger and tilted her hand to and fro, making light spark off the facets. "I've never had anything so beautiful. Or expensive. Are you sure you can afford it?"

"Mr. Abell gave me a generous bonus for returning to *The Sun*. I even have my own office now."

"How wonderful. Though any newspaperman as gifted as you should have his own office. Your article in *The Herald* was incomparable."

"Incomparable, huh. Who's using high-falutin words now?"

"I'm just saying how good it was." She bent and picked up the green velvet cloth. "The way you described the conditions at the prisons. Made my heart bleed."

He snagged the other end of the bolt. "It was good, wasn't it? Even without the Carleton saga."

Grinning, she walked toward him, folding the bolt end over end until she pressed herself and the folded fabric against him. "And I didn't even have to hold you at knifepoint."

He kissed the tip of her nose. "Those flashing green eyes of yours are more lethal than any blade."

"Hmmph. Don't tell that to the bluebellies. They already think I'm dangerous enough."

"You don't have to worry about the soldiers any more. I learned today they located the man who killed that courier at Point Lookout."

"Well that's comforting. Now I won't have to go around looking over my shoulder all the time." She placed the folded fabric on the end table and picked up the red. "Who was it? Anybody you know?"

"Remember that fellow Smith who crossed the Potomac with you?"

"I saw him get arrested at the train station. The soldiers said he was a spy. Was it him?"

"No. But after a bit of persuasion, he gave up the name of the killer. It was Calhoun."

The red fabric slipped from her fingers and pooled in the floor. "Calhoun!"

"It appears Calhoun and Smith were working together. The lieutenant would pass information to Smith, who then sent it to the Confederates."

A double agent. He was a slimy skunk, but she never would've guessed that of the Texan. He had covered his tracks well. In more ways than one. She sank on to the chair behind her. "So that's how Calhoun knew so much about me. Smith must have told him."

Jack retrieved the fallen cloth and draped it over the back of the settee. "I convinced the guards to allow me to speak with Smith privately, on the pretense of conducting an interview before his execution. I wanted to find out what he knew about you and Calhoun."

If anyone could dig out the truth, Jack could. "What did you learn?"

"He said he's the one who helped Calhoun get away after the statue fell on him. Apparently the lieutenant never intended to turn you over to the provost. When you recognized Smith at the docks, he got scared, talked Calhoun into helping him head-off trouble. Smith had a carriage waiting at the edge of the property to spirit you away after Calhoun abducted you. But their plan misfired."

Thank the Lord and Saint Francis it had. "So, if Smith saved Calhoun, that means he might still be alive. What if he comes after us?"

"He won't. He somehow survived his head injury. But not a posse's bullet. He was shot while trying to escape after Smith gave up his whereabouts."

The air went out of her. As she slumped back in the chair, a thought took hold. "What about my locket? Did they find it on Calhoun?"

"Smith didn't know about any locket. It was most likely lost or buried along with the lieutenant." He patted her shoulder. "I'm sorry, sweetheart."

"No. I'm much happier having Lance with me than the locket. It's probably a good thing it wasn't found anyway. It might have raised too many questions." The image of Calhoun twirling the locket chain around his finger rose in her mind. He was so young. So misguided. Like her. Before Jack.

"I'm sorry about the lieutenant's death," she added. "But, I have to admit, it's a relief not having that cloud of worry hanging over me any longer."

"Unfortunately, there's one other cloud to be cleared up." He knelt beside her and cupped her hand in his. "It's about your father."

Her heart lurched at his serious tone. "Papa? What about him?"

"I heard from my contact in Richmond. Seems the Lawrences had no hand in your father's death."

"How can that be?"

"Your father was helping escaped slaves flee north. The wrong people found out and well...they weren't happy about his involvement in the Underground Railroad."

"The Underground Railroad? That sounds like something he'd do." Tears stung her eyes. "Oh, Papa..."

Ever the loving husband, Jack scooped her up, then sat in the chair with her cradled in his lap. "You've been through so much, sweetheart. How would you like to get away for a few weeks?"

"What do you mean?"

"Grandfather purchased us passage to Paris as a wedding gift. We can visit *The Louvre*. See all those statues you so admire."

"But what about your fear of water? The nightmares?"

"I'll be fine, as long as I have you by my side."

Her heart radiated with sunshine. "I can read to you this time."

He nuzzled her neck. "I'm thinking of something a lot more distracting than words."

A word about the author...

Donna Dalton lives in Central Virginia with her husband, two sons, and a pitbull mix named Gizmo. An avid reader of historical romances, Donna used the rich history of the "Old Dominion State" to craft this action-packed story set during the American Civil War.

Visit her at her website www.donnadalton.net or on Facebook at DonnaDaltonbooks.